Just for Clicks

KARA McDOWELL

AMBERJACK
PUBLISHING

Idaho

Amberjack Publishing
1472 E. Iron Eagle Drive
Eagle, ID 83616
amberjackpublishing.com

10 9 8 7 6 5 4 3 2

Library of Congress Cataloging-in-Publication Data

Names: McDowell, Kara J., author.
Title: Just for clicks / Kara J. McDowell.
Description: Idaho : Amberjack Publishing, [2019] | Summary: "Twin sisters Claire and Poppy are accidental social media stars thanks to Mom going viral when they were babies. But what happens when, as teens, they're expected to contribute by building their own brand?"-- Provided by publisher. Identifiers: LCCN 2018037088 (print) | LCCN 2018043149 (ebook) | ISBN 9781948705233 (ebook) | ISBN 9781948705196 (pbk. : alk. paper)
Subjects: | CYAC: Social media--Fiction. | Celebrities--Fiction. | Sisters--Fiction. | Twins--Fiction. | Mothers and daughters--Fiction. | Dating (Social customs)--Fiction.
Classification: LCC PZ7.1.M43452 (ebook) | LCC PZ7.1.M43452 Jus 2019 (print) | DDC [Fic]--dc23
LC record available at https://lccn.loc.gov/2018037088

To Scott
The boy who inspired the first book I ever wrote

Chapter 1

I need a balcony. Maybe a trellis, ivy-covered or otherwise. A sturdy drainpipe positioned just outside my window would work too. Or a single-story home. Unfortunately for me, I haven't been blessed with any of those things. Despite what people say online, I'm obviously *not* "Teenage Goals."

I gently nudge open my bedroom door, flip-flops in hand, and hold my breath. I'm listening for any sound other than my neighbor's yapping beagle. A shaft of early morning sunlight spills across the hall, illuminating my escape route. It's not ideal. Why couldn't my existential crisis and accompanying need to flee happen under the cover of darkness?

The dog mercifully stops barking, and a stillness settles over the house, interrupted only by dust motes dancing in the light. I gingerly step out of my room and tiptoe toward the stairs. As I place my foot on the top step, the silence is disrupted by the muffled sound of a shower turning on. My heart sputters in response before realizing it's a good sign. At least one person in this house is otherwise occupied.

Sneaking out was not on today's agenda. At least not on the one Mom sent before I went to bed last night, which had 6:30–7:30 reserved for "outfit photos." It's repetitive but not excruciating work, and it's usually easier to comply than complain. But my grimace-and-bear-it attitude has resulted in *a lot* of outfit photos.

To be more specific, some troll is claiming there are more pictures of me online than works of art on display in the Louvre.

Just when I thought I'd read every insane comment the internet had to offer, DixonDummies16 claims my image is pervasive enough to fill the world's largest art museum. It's the craziest thing I've ever read about myself, which is saying something. Apparently, I had a boob job last fall (sure . . . if puberty is another term for boob job), my calves flow directly into my feet in a situation that can only be described as "cankles," and there's a small but devoted faction of people who believe my twin sister and I aren't really related.

I sneak down the staircase as quickly and quietly as the marble flooring will allow, only to get smacked in the face by the large portrait umbrella that my mother uses to light the room during photoshoots. The warm, metallic taste of blood floods my mouth. I hold my fingers to my lip to stop the bleeding and wind my way through a maze of portable garment racks, stepping over piles of boots, wedges, and stilettos on my way to the front door. When I reach it, I allow myself a silent victory dance, which is interrupted by the sound of my stomach growling.

Traitor.

My fingers pause briefly on the door handle as I weigh the pros and cons of skipping breakfast. Pro—I'll definitely get out of the house unnoticed and will have an extra hour at the library to research colleges. Con—if I don't eat something now, I'll be hangry by first period. It's not even a choice, I realize with a sigh, and tiptoe back through the haute couture obstacle course and into the kitchen. I slip into the pantry for a granola bar and am enjoying a peanut buttery bite when the silence is pierced by the all too familiar sound of a garment bag unzipping.

"Claire!" Mom's usual morning cheer is laced with intensity. I shove the rest of the granola bar in my mouth and brace myself for whatever I'm about to see. When I turn around, Mom is holding a ten-thousand-dollar evening gown.

"Look what came!" She brandishes the blush-pink dress with a flourish. I point to my full mouth, making slow, exaggerated chewing motions in order to buy myself time.

"Let's get it on you!" She drapes the gown across my arms and steers me toward the bathroom.

I choke down the granola bar and try to shove the gown back into her arms. "Poppy should wear this one."

"It's your size!" She refuses to take it back.

"Perfect! That means it's Poppy's size too!" Mom made sure of that, after a humiliating experience at New York Fashion Week three years ago.

"It's too short for Poppy. Wait! What happened to your lip?" She furrows her brow in concern. "Never mind, it doesn't matter. We're just doing test shots today." She gives me a final push across the bathroom threshold and shuts the door firmly behind me.

"Thanks for your concern," I mumble as I shimmy out of my jeans and T-shirt.

"It's a reimagined version of the one you wore on your first birthday." Her voice is loud, even though the door.

"I know."

"I should show you the pictures. You girls looked like princesses!"

"I've seen the pictures." If I had a dollar for every time I'd seen the pictures, I could buy this gown—and burn it.

The dress has long sleeves and a high neck, with rosette appliqués on the bodice. I open the door and turn, lifting my hair off my neck so Mom can do up the buttons in the back. The final one tightens around my neck like a noose. When she's done, I turn around to face her.

"Oh, Claire." Instant tears.

"I'm out." Desperate for breathing room, I stick my finger between the collar and my neck and lunge for the bathroom door.

"No! I need to see what it looks like on camera." She directs me to the base of the large staircase and fiddles with the lighting.

Eleven months. I repeat the words to myself as Mom twirls me around the room like a prop, looking for the most flattering angle. *Eleven more months of this, and my term is up. I've survived this long, I can do eleven more months.*

Eventually I'm able to make a break for the kitchen and throw together a smoothie for second breakfast. Back in the front room, I drape a towel across my lap to protect Allegra

Esposito's hand-stitching from green smoothie stains and watch my employer in action.

Mom is standing behind the light umbrellas, scrolling through images on her camera with pursed lips. It's a classic Ashley Dixon pose. Her deep auburn hair falls into her eyes and across the bridge of her nose, where she has a small sprinkling of freckles. She doesn't have as many freckles as I do, but then again, no one does.

"Alexa, how many works of art are on display in the Louvre?" I direct my question at the smart speaker sitting on a side table across the room.

"The Musée de Louvre displays thirty-five thousand works over eight curatorial departments." The cool, female voice sounds almost smug, as if she's proud of herself for finding the answer. Her tone displays none of the horror the response deserves.

Thirty-five thousand. If there are that many pictures of me, there are at least that many of my twin sister, Poppy. Despite the obvious discrepancy in comments and likes, Mom has always been really careful to keep our numbers even. She says it's because she loves us equally, but I think it's to keep the fans happy. It wouldn't be good for business if people thought she preferred one of her daughters over the other.

The fans are the only ones allowed to pick favorites.

"Are we done here?" I ask, desperate for a distraction. My brain keeps trying to divide thirty-five-thousand by my seventeen years of age to figure out how many pictures that averages per year. I don't have to do the math to know the number is Stephen King–level horrifying.

Mom checks the time on her watch and nods. "How are you and Poppy doing on your latest vlog?"

As if she's been summoned, a loud shriek pierces the air. My twin sister bounds down the stairs, phone in hand. "You will never believe what just happened!" Her victory dance looks a lot like mine did only an hour ago, only louder. She thrusts her phone at Mom, who glances at the screen and matches Poppy's squeal with an even louder one.

"Is someone going to tell me what's going on?"

Poppy tosses the phone into my lap. "We just reached one million subscribers!"

"Wait, really?" I look at her phone, which is open to our online video channel. Below our latest video (Five Totally Cute Outfits That Are as Comfortable as Pajamas) is a little box that says SUBSCRIBERS: 1 million. Poppy has been waiting for this moment for a long time, but my stomach lurches uncomfortably.

"This is amazing!" Poppy's fingers are already flying over her phone, probably sending excited texts to her friends. Mom is also eager to share the news and leaves the room in a hurry.

I pick up my smoothie and take a slow sip.

Poppy watches me for several long seconds. "Aren't you happy?"

"Yeah, sure," I lie. When Poppy and I branched out from Mom's blog and started our own brand, we both wanted the same thing. Followers, fame, fortune. *Influence*, as Poppy always calls it. We were on the same train hurtling toward our future, but somewhere along the way I jumped off, and

Poppy hasn't realized it yet. And I haven't worked up the nerve to tell her.

Mom sticks her head around the corner. "Claire didn't answer me. How's the vlog going?"

"I mean . . ." Poppy flicks her eyes in my direction. "Not great."

Mom sighs and walks into the room. "What's the problem?"

"I'm sick of doing hair tutorials," I say.

"That's because you're not as 'hair goals' as I am," Poppy says, referencing the many "goals" comments that populate our YouTube channel. When we have good hair, we're "hair goals." When we take a cute picture together, we're "sister goals." Travel goals, mom goals, life goals. You name it, someone will find a way to envy us for it.

"We have the same hair, genius," I say, even though it's not totally true. We're fraternal twins, which means we look no more alike than any other sisters. We both have thick hair that falls past our shoulder blades; hers is a warm brown, mine is almost black. But still, Poppy's right about the viewers' comments, and it stings. No matter what I do, mine doesn't shine quite like hers, nor does it achieve the magical state between undone and trying-too-hard.

"I don't want to do another tutorial because I lose an IQ point every time I'm forced to braid my hair on camera." I turn to Mom for backup, though a lifetime of experience has taught me she's an unlikely ally. "Can we *please* do something else this time?"

"How about a Q&A session with your fans, as a thank-you for reaching one million."

Well, my plan backfired. I was hoping to buy us an extension, not swap out the tutorial for an extended interaction with people I don't know.

Poppy quickly agrees. *Damn people pleaser*. Mom disappears into the next room and I turn to my sister. "Some creep on the internet claims there are more pictures of us online than works of art on display in the Louvre."

She smiles, clearly amused. "I thought you quit reading the comments?"

"I did." It's a lie, but not a big one.

"Sure you did."

"Seriously though. Doesn't that make you think?"

The smile on her face blossoms into a wicked grin. "Yeah. It makes me think the Mona Lisa has nothing on us."

I roll my eyes and take another drink of my smoothie. "As soon as I go to college, you and Mona can duke it out over who's more famous."

"It's not about fame, it's about influence."

There it is again. Poppy's buzz word. "Of course."

Her face falls. "Are you really ready to give all this up?" She gestures to my over-the-top gown, and then spreads her arms to include the entire room, which is overflowing with free clothes and camera equipment.

My answer is delayed by a beep. I flinch, an old reflex from when my phone used to notify me about vlog comments. I turned off that feature months ago, but sometimes the sound still catches me off guard.

"I've been ready for a long time."

Email from Mom

From: ashdixon@dixondaily.com
To: poppyandclaire@dixondaily.com
Subject: Tomorrow's Agenda

6:30-7:30—Outfit photos (test shots with your new Esposito gowns)

8:00-3:00—School

3:00-4:30—Swim practice (Poppy), Respond to vlog comments (Claire)

5:30—Family dinner

7:00-8:00—Finish filming and editing hair tutorial

P.S. There's a problem with my site! Photos are taking way too long to load. Claire, I need you to look at it ASAP.

Chapter 2

Twenty minutes later, I pull into the school parking lot behind Poppy. As usual, we're cutting it close on time. We find two empty spots near the back of the lot between a rusty pickup whose bed is filled with empty Slurpee cups, and a first-generation Prius. Before I quit the swim team, we drove together, but driving by myself isn't so bad. Perk one of quitting the team: controlling the music. Perk two: no longer hanging out with people who secretly hate me.

It's bright and clear outside, and the sun is doing its job a little too well for a September morning. Instinctively, I hold my breath, but the still air means the smell of the dairy farm hasn't reached this far north.

When we reach the front door of Highland High School, I hold it open for Poppy. Instead of walking through, she sticks her hand in her pocket and comes up empty. "Do you have Chapstick?"

"I think so." I prop the door open against my back and begin to rummage inside my bag. One by one, I pull out things that aren't Chapstick: lip gloss, calculator, my phone, water bottle, a book.

"One day, you're going to need to find something quickly in there, and you'll hear my voice telling you not to be such a slob."

I ignore her and keep looking. By this time my left hand is completely full of, well, junk, and I still can't find my Chapstick. I sigh and try to shift everything from my left hand to my right. As I bend forward, I let go of the door a little bit and it slams against my back. Everything goes flying out of my hands. Lip gloss and calculator land at my feet. A bookmark falls out of my copy of *Know Your Onions —Graphic Design*. My water bottle rolls down the cement steps and my phone goes clunking after it.

My phone! Poppy and I race toward it, but Poppy gets there first. She gasps as she picks it up and that's when I know it's gone.

"Uh-oh." She hands it to me, her face full of sympathy. "That really sucks."

It *really* does. "Now I'll have no way of knowing when we hit one-million-and-one." The sarcasm is thick in my voice as I chuck the device with its shattered screen into the depths of my purse.

"I'll let you know." She helps me gather the rest of my belongings as the first bell rings.

The morning passes slowly. In between classes my hand reaches into my bag no less than half a dozen times before I remember my phone is dead and gone, six feet under a pile of crap. It's not a huge problem until I'm sitting alone at my usual lunch table, waiting for Poppy and Olivia. When they don't show up after a couple of minutes, self-consciousness spreads across my skin like a virus. There are worse things than eating alone, but with no one to talk to, my hands get restless. I pull my phone out of my bag yet again, and stare at the screen, pretending to read something riveting. It doesn't help. Now I feel dumber than before, and I'm positive someone is going to notice the broken glass spiderwebbing itself across my screen. I drop it back into my bag with a sigh.

The general sounds of laughter and talking and scraping chairs are pierced by a familiar high-pitched cackle. Emily and Erica sweep past me, but now that we aren't on the swim team together, they don't so much as glance in my direction. Paranoia creeps into my brain, and I remind myself that just because they're laughing does not mean they're laughing at *me*. I reach into my bag again, and pull out my book.

Someone loudly clanks into the seat across from me.

"Finally." I look up into the dark eyes of a boy who is definitely not my sister.

"My thoughts exactly." He smiles, plucks a tortilla chip off my plate, and pops it into his mouth. He has light brown skin and dark brown hair that's styled in an undercut; shaved on the sides and long on top, it sticks up in every direction. It's a haphazard and supposedly effortless look that is never an accident, just like the messy buns that take me ten minutes to get right.

The book slips from my fingers and clunks against the table. I snatch it against my chest as I stare at his flawless hair, wondering why I haven't seen him before.

"So, what's wrong with you?"

"Excuse me?"

"Where's your screen? Your device? Your fancy, newfangled technology?"

"What are you talking about?" A smile tugs at the corner of my lips, but I chase it away with a drink of water.

"You're the only person in this room not staring at a screen right now."

"That's not true," I say, but a quick glance around the room tells me he's right. Even the kids who are not technically staring at a screen at this exact moment are clutching their phones in their hands or spinning them on top of the table while talking to friends.

He watches me watch the room and flashes a satisfied smirk. "I told you."

I lean toward him on my elbows. "Why are you sitting with me?" Poppy's voice fills my head, warning me not to act like a jerk to strangers. Instead of looking offended, however, he steals another chip before I have the chance to stop him. It is not abnormal for someone I don't know to touch me or my stuff, but it is strange for me to let him.

"That's what I was trying to tell you. Everyone else is busy."

"I'm busy." I hold up my book as proof.

"*Know Your Onions—Graphic Design: How to Think Like a Creative, Act like a Businessman and Design Like a God.* Sounds . . . fascinating." The amusement in his voice is unmistakable.

"Gender-specific terminology aside, it is, actually. So, if you'll leave me to it." I do my best impression of a Person

Interested in the Book They're Reading. My vision closes in on the black lines without comprehension as my pulse works overtime. I simply don't have the bandwidth to converse with cute strangers. *When is he going to take the hint?*

He doesn't say anything, but he doesn't leave either. I sneak a glance over the top of my book. He folds his arms across his chest and smiles. "Are you a genius or something?"

My head snaps up as heat rushes to my cheeks. "No!" It's been a long time since anyone's been impressed by my hobby.

"Are you one of those Girls Who Code?"

I shake my head and let the book fall closed. "No. I mean, I'm a girl." His smile widens at this. I cringe but forge ahead anyway. "And I code, but I still have a lot to learn. I've taught myself CSS and HTML, and I'm working on JavaScript, which is essential for front-end develop—" My mouth snaps shut as I'm struck by the realization that I don't know this guy *at all* and I should really stop talking. "Why are you smiling like that?"

"CSS? HTML? Ironic T-shirts I don't understand?"

I look down at my T-shirt, which says ALL ROADS LEAD TO 127.0.0.1.

"It's a loopback IP address that always takes you back to your home computer."

"Sounds like genius speak to me."

"Really, really not." Anyone can learn basic web design if they're interested enough. Not everyone teaches themselves at age thirteen, but then again, not everyone was raised on the internet, either. The way I see it, web design is basically my birthright.

"How'd you get into this stuff?" He gestures to my book.

I don't feel like talking about my mom, so I ignore the question. "What's your name?"

"Rafael Alejandro Luna." He extends his hand with a broad grin. I shake it, because apparently, we're doing this.

"What can I call you?"

I raise my eyebrows, caught off guard by his question. At the risk of sounding like the most conceited person in the history of the world, I'd assumed he knew who I was.

Poppy and I basically have two categories of fans. First, are the middle-aged women who got hooked on my mom's famous fashion blog way back when. Her fans got invested in her pregnancy, so after we were born, she wrote a post about us every week called Twin Tuesday. She chronicled our first steps, dance recitals, lost teeth, and everything in between.

People ate it up. They loved seeing pictures of us. As we outgrew the cute baby phase and social media changed, Mom moved most of her fashion posts to Instagram and started an online video channel for Poppy and me. Enter stage two of people who know who we are—teenagers who watch our videos for hair, makeup, and fashion tips. It seems like that should be the end of it, but for reasons I don't understand, Mom refuses to let the "Mommy Blog" part of her brand die. She still does a Twin Tuesday post every week, resulting in the occasional stranger who wants to talk to us about when we were potty trained.

The internet is so bizarre.

Gilbert, Arizona, is a fishbowl, magnifying our fame far beyond what it would be anywhere else offline. It's rare to be recognized when we travel, especially out of the country, but school is a different story. Our videos are big enough that people know us, even if they don't watch. But Rafael must be new, so it's entirely possible he has no idea who I am, or what Mom does for a living. Then again, he still has a goofy grin plastered across his face, so maybe he's messing with me.

"You can call me the same thing everyone else calls me."

"Which is . . .?" He gestures for me to continue.

"Claire."

"Just Claire?"

I sit up straighter in my chair. "I'm not *just* anyone."

His eyes spark with amusement. "Do tell."

I'm tempted to rattle off our stats: subscribers and downloads and likes and follows. But those things don't mean anything, really. If he's not teasing me, if he really doesn't have a clue who I am, I can be "just Claire," normal girl in a normal town. And maybe that's a good thing. Lately, I've been craving freedom and anonymity more than ever.

"You asked my name, I told you." I shrug. "Claire is all you're going to get."

"Fair enough. But if you ever change your mind, I'm here." He eats another chip, completely unflustered by this completely flustering conversation. For the first time since he sat down, I wish Poppy were here. She'd be able to tell me if he's flirting with me. I honestly can't tell. Believe it or not, being the child star of a Fashion/Mommy Blog hybrid doesn't exactly make the boys come running.

"We'll get back to the name later. For now, tell me something else about yourself." He brushes chip dust from his fingers and leans forward. I get the distinct impression I'm about to be buried under a deluge of questions. "What movies do you like, Just Claire? What books do you read when you're not studying web design?"

A smile forces its way onto my lips. Under the table, my legs jump like a startled cricket. I tuck the right one behind the left to calm the fidgeting. "I'm not that interesting. I promise."

"I don't believe you. At least tell me what you do for fun."

Once again, the question surprises me; it's been so long since anyone asked. Strangers stop me in the aisles of Target to ask for fashion advice or critique my outfit. No one ever asks what I like to do, because everyone who cares thinks they already know.

But not Rafael. He doesn't know who I am, and the thrill is intoxicating. I open my mouth to respond but no words come out.

On Mom's blog, I'm Claire Dixon: Poppy's twin. Ashley's daughter. A decent swimmer, but slower than my sister. The short one. The one with freckles and cankles and big teeth. On my vlog, I'm the one who prefers messy buns to mermaid braids, "natural makeup" to Poppy's evening looks. If I'm not that, then who am I?

That's when I realize I can tell him whatever I want and he will believe me.

"Um . . . you've been quiet for like, a minute and a half. Sorry I stumped you with such a tough question, *Just Claire*."

I roll my eyes. "You didn't. I was just trying to decide if I want to tell you what I like to do for fun."

Rafael leans back in his chair and folds his arms. "No pressure. Take your time. It's a very serious question." His voice is cool and mocking, and I'm overcome by the urge to say something completely unexpected.

"I rock climb!"

"You do?" Surprise is etched across every inch of his face, and I revel in the satisfaction of putting it there.

"All the time. Every weekend, in fact. I use a harness and those . . . those things you shove in the rocks . . ." I flail about for *any* rock climbing term and come up short. "You know what, it's not important." We lock eyes and my stomach falters.

"Where do you climb? Who do you climb with? What's your favorite mountain?" He places his elbow on the table and rests his chin on his palm without breaking eye contact.

"And I play chess, constantly. I'm a chess master, in fact. One of the youngest in the country."

Rafael raises his eyebrows. "A rock climbing chess master. Really? You don't look—"

"Rethink that sentence."

His hands go up in a gesture of surrender. "My bad."

"It's not cool to judge people based on their looks." It's basically the story of my entire life, but he doesn't know that. "How would you like it if I looked at you and assumed . . ." My eyes search his faux-messy hair, big grin, and dark eyes, for something to say, but I come up blank.

"Assume away! Or better yet, ask me a question and I'll answer it. No assumptions necessary."

"Okay, here's one, how long does it take to make your hair look like that?"

"Six minutes. Usually four, but today I was nervous. New kid, new school, and all that. So that's what you assume when you look at me? That I spend an obnoxious amount of time on my hair?" He shrugs off the implied insult like it's no big deal. Like these are the kinds of conversations he has every day of his life.

I don't know what to say, so I do the next best thing. "I should go."

Rafael reaches out his hand and touches me on the arm. "Hey! Don't go anywhere; I'm sorry I offended you. It was supposed to be a compliment about how pretty you are, but it was a dumb thing to imply pretty girls aren't smart enough to play chess or tough enough to climb."

If I'm a spinning top, his compliment nudges me just enough to disrupt my balance. I stare at his hand on my skin, and he quickly pulls it away. His eyebrows are drawn, and for the first time since I've met him, there isn't a smile in sight. His face looks wrong without it.

"Right. Well, thanks, I guess. . ." I stammer, looking around the room for something to say.

"Don't worry about it. We're officially changing the subject, starting now."

"Okay."

I look at him. He looks at me. After five seconds, this becomes so unbearable that I tear my gaze away and focus on the ceiling. When he doesn't say anything for several more seconds, I look back down at him, exasperated. "Well?"

"Well, what?"

"I thought you were going to change the subject."

A short burst of laughter escapes him. Eyes shining, he gestures across the table to the space between us. "What I actually said was *we* were going to change the subject. But I figured I would let you have the honors, considering how well things went when I was asking questions."

I'm relieved to see him smiling again, but I still can't keep the eye contact he's so insistent on maintaining. My fingers itch for my phone. I need something, anything, to distract myself from his dark brown eyes, which haven't left my face once since he sat down.

"Stop doing that!" I poke my bean and cheese burrito with a fork, just to give my fingers something to do.

He glances around the cafeteria with a frown. "Doing what?"

"Looking at me like that."

"Like what?"

"Like . . . I don't know. Like, right at me."

He scratches his cheek, looking baffled. "We're having a conversation. Where else would I look?"

I gesture to the room around us, which is full of teen-agers who have their heads bent over screens. "Ask one of them."

"I don't have a cell phone." His tone is matter-of-fact, as if he just said Arizona is hot, or Poppy loves the camera. It does *not* sound like he just casually admitted the one thing that makes him different from every other person in our class.

"Why not?" The shock in my voice causes Rafael's lips to twitch.

"I've been living in India for the past fourteen months."

Who is this guy? Every time he opens his mouth, he surprises me. I didn't realize how predictable all the other guys at school are until this exact moment. "What were you doing in India?" I scoot my chair closer to the table, grateful I'd decided to stay.

"My dad's with Doctors Without Borders. We move around a lot. Sometimes I get a phone, but mostly the places we live are rural villages with no reception, so I don't bother." He shrugs.

"Wow. That's . . . amazing." And to think, my mom takes pictures of her own clothes for a living. For the millionth time today, I hope he doesn't ask about her. "What'd you do with your time?" Surviving without a phone for one morning has been tough. I can't imagine living that way for more than a year.

"Normal stuff. I did schoolwork with a tutor and played cricket with kids in the village. Of course, my schedule was pretty busy, what with all the time I spent styling my hair." He grins, and the heat creeps up my face.

"What are you doing in Arizona?"

"Living with my abuela. My abuelo died a few months ago, and my dad didn't want her to live alone, so we moved back."

"Oh. I, uh, I'm sorry," I stammer awkwardly, wondering why he shared that personal bit of information with a total stranger.

"Thanks. I didn't know him well, but it's still hard."

"Right. Well . . ." I cast about for something to talk about other than his dead grandpa. "Are you going to get one?"

He quirks and eyebrow, clearly puzzled by my clumsy segue. "A phone? Probably. Eventually. I'm not too worried about it." He runs his hand through his hair with a shrug.

I look at him for as long as I can stand it without breaking eye contact. "You're officially unlike every other person I've ever met."

He laughs. "Who do I need to call, anyway? I just moved here. I don't have any friends. Yet." His final word sounds like a promise.

I shake my head. If he thinks phones are about making calls, maybe he doesn't need one after all.

He rests his arms on the table and leans toward me. "You never answered my first question."

"Which was?"

"Why weren't you staring at a screen when I first saw you?" He gets straight to the point, and it sounds like the answer is important to him.

I crumble a chip between my fingers. The obvious thing to do is tell him the truth, but I don't want him to know how desperately I was wishing for my phone before he sat down. I use my legs as a napkin for the chip dust on my fingers and say "I prefer books." After all, what's one more lie on top of the pile of ones I've already told him?

Out of the corner of my eye I see Poppy charge toward our table. "You won't believe what happened." She collapses into the chair next to me with a heavy sigh. "Torres gave Olivia and me lunch detention. He only let me out now because it's, like, against the law to deprive children of food." She shakes her head and sighs again.

"What happened?" I ask.

"He thinks we were cheating on our exam. Olivia sent a text during the test so I was looking at my phone, and of course he thought I was sneaking answers. As if I need to cheat on his dumb exam." Poppy may be a phone addict, but she's not stupid enough to cheat. Plus, she's smart enough she doesn't need to. She's never gotten less than an A in her life.

"Sorry, Pop. That's harsh."

"Tell me about it. Olivia and I both have lunch detention tomorrow, too."

"Where is she now?"

"Calling her dad. She wanted to tell him before Torres had the chance. Anyway, sorry I left you alone. I sent you a text, but then I remembered your phone is broken."

Busted.

Rafael smirks at me from across the table.

"That's okay. I wasn't alone." I nod in Rafael's direction.

"I kept her company. Tough job, but someone had to do it."

Poppy plasters on her camera smile. "Hi. I'm Poppy Dixon!"

He matches her smile. "Rafael Alejandro Luna." They shake hands, and he shoots me a smug glance that seems to say "That's how a proper introduction is made." But whatever. Even hearing our last name and seeing the two of us together, his expression displays no hint of recognition.

He really, truly, has no idea who I am. This fact makes me absurdly happy.

"Rafael Luna . . . your name sounds familiar." Poppy purses her lips and drums her fingers against her chin. It's a rehearsed gesture, designed to make her most rabid fans believe she recognizes them from their social media profiles. As if she can distinguish their *OMG SO CUTE!* comments from the hundreds of others. *No wonder she's the favorite.* I shake my head. She was born for this. And any second now, she's going to give me away.

I grab her arm. "I need you to quiz me on my Spanish vocab."

"I can help," Rafael offers. Which, come on! *Stop being so nice!* I would love to stay and keep talking to him, but I'm not ready for him to discover the truth about me.

Not yet.

It's nice to have a secret. For once, I get to decide what story to tell and when to tell it. Even if that story requires a few lies along the way.

Incoming Text Messages (currently lost in cyberspace)

Mom
9:04 AM

Page views are way down today. Please look at the site when you have a chance!

9:44 AM

Call me on your lunch break! We need to fix this.

9:54 AM

Claire? This is important!

9:55 AM

Okay, focus on school. Talk when you get home.

Poppy
11:38 AM

Won't be at lunch today because teachers are morons.

11:39 AM

Sit with E & E. They're not the people you think they are.

Oops, forgot your phone broke.

Ha. Did it again.

Dairy Queen
1:10 PM

Buy one blizzard, get one free! Today only!
Text STOP to unsubscribe.

Poppy
1:14 PM

Want me to stop for ice cream after practice?

Ugh. Your dumb phone.

Chapter 3

"Poppy's in the bathroom." Olivia's fingers are flying over her phone when I get to the second story drinking fountain.

"Oh." I can't think of anything else to add. Olivia and I are only friends through Poppy, and when my sister isn't around, we don't have much to say to each other. Not that Olivia is talkative around Poppy either. Her phone habits make Poppy look like an amateur.

I lean against the balcony rail overlooking the main hall on the first floor. Hundreds of students jostle around each other as they break off into groups. From up here, it seems like a lot of work for a few short minutes gossiping with friends. When the thirty second warning bell rings, it will be chaos once again as everyone scrambles to get to class on time. Without fully realizing it, I scan the crowd for messy brown hair. Instead, my eyes land on a group of swim team girls in a tight circle.

"I hear you got busted by Torres." I turn my back to the main hall. "That sucks."

Olivia shakes her head and sighs. "Don't get me started." Her loose blonde curls swing around her shoulders.

I bite back a smile, wondering what it would take for her to put down her phone and "get started." Several seconds pass, and when I'm confident I can leave without seeming like I ditched her, I say, "If you see Poppy, tell her I went to class."

"Don't leave me alone!" She widens her eyes in disbelief and looks up at me for the first time. "We still have two minutes."

I sigh and lean against the balcony rail again. We don't say anything else until the warning bell rings and Olivia slides her phone in her bag. "I heard you ate lunch with the new boy today."

"Um, yeah, I guess so." I start down the hall toward my next class.

"Poppy said he's cute." She raises her voice to be heard over the crowd.

"I have to go! We'll talk later!"

"I'll text you!" she calls before she disappears behind a crowd. I sprint down a long hall to get to class on time. The bell rings as I walk in the room, where Poppy is already in her seat. She looks up at me and says something, but I don't register the words because sitting next to her, in my usual seat, is Rafael.

I should have expected he'd be placed in College Prep. It's the biggest joke class in the school and one of the only electives with open seats. I originally registered for Computer Programming, but not enough students signed up for the class. Shuffled into the only open elective that fit my schedule, I get to spend the semester learning how to write a resume and answer interview questions. I was hoping it would be an easy A, but Ms. Grant is stricter than any elective teacher has the right to be.

Rafael smiles at me and pats the empty desk in front of him. "We meet again, Just Claire!"

I want to say something, but Ms. Grant is clearing her throat and waiting for me to sit down. When I do, I swear I can feel his eyes on the back of my neck. It takes all of my self-control not to turn around and look at him.

Fifty-five of the world's longest minutes later, class ends. I briefly consider hanging back to talk to Rafael, but I don't want to be obvious. Instead, I wave goodbye to Poppy and am the first one out the door. A few steps later, a voice calls my name. "Hey! Just Claire!" Rafael jogs toward me, dodging people left and right.

"So. Hi. How are you, Just Claire?" He falls into step next to me as we descend the stairs in the main hall.

"That's not actually my name, you know?" The words sounded flirty in my head, but they come out annoyed.

"Do tell."

Crap. If I tell him my last name, he'll realize Poppy and I are sisters, and he might make the connection between Just Claire from the cafeteria and Claire Dixon of social media fame.

"Never mind. Just Claire is fine."

"Where are you going?"

"To my car."

"Can I walk with you?"

"It appears you already are."

He pushes the exit door open and waits for me to walk though. "True. But I'm nothing if not a gentleman."

I glance sideways at him. Now that he's not sitting across from me, or behind me, I can look at him for more than a few seconds at a time. His gait is longer than mine, but he's slowed down to keep pace with me. His messy hair looks like it's been through a wind tunnel since lunch, and somehow more perfect for it.

But the thing that stands out the most about him is how relaxed he looks. His arms swing easily by his sides, his eyes straight ahead, not darting around to see who might be lurking behind the nearby trio of minivans. He's been at this school all of one day, and he already looks more comfortable than I feel after three years.

"Where are the lockers?" he asks suddenly.

"We don't have lockers."

He adopts a scandalized expression. "But they're a staple of all the teen dramas on Netflix."

"Let me guess, you were hoping to decorate it with pictures of your girlfriend?" I didn't plan on saying that, but I don't take it back, either.

He raises an eyebrow but otherwise ignores my implied question. "Actually, I wanted to put up a mirror, to check my hair."

A bead of sweat trickles into my eye as I laugh. "Is it as hot in India as it is here?"

"Nope. It didn't get much above thirty degrees."

"Celsius?" We fall into rhythm next to each other as we weave through the parking lot. A few cars are already lining up to leave, but most people aren't in a hurry. They're leaning against car doors and chatting with their friends, relieved to be done with another day. For the first time all year, I feel like one of them, just a girl hanging out with her friend instead of sprinting toward my car with my head down.

"Yeah, sorry. That's in the upper eighties, Fahrenheit."

All I really know about India is that it is hot, but apparently, it's not as hot there as it is here. I smile, strangely proud of my state. "Arizona wins."

"It's a contest?"

"Oh yeah."

Rafael uses his hand to shade his eyes against the sun. "Do you like the heat?"

"Not even a little bit."

"Doesn't that mean you lose?" He steps to the side to avoid being hit by a girl who is dribbling a soccer ball through the parking lot.

"I guess it does." I laugh and come to a stop in front of my car.

Rafael stops short, lips parted in obvious surprise.

"Something wrong?"

"Not a lot of kids drive a Mercedes where I'm from, that's all."

I shrug, unsure of what to say. Mine and Poppy's luxury vehicles are rare in our high school's parking lot, but everyone knows how we can afford them. It's another thing I've never needed to explain before now.

Fortunately, Rafael doesn't ask for an explanation. He simply nods goodbye and doubles back to his car.

"**D**id you look at the website?" Mom asks when I walk in the door ten minutes later. She's sitting on the couch, her feet propped up on the ottoman. Next to her is a diet soda and a bowl of popcorn. On her lap is her computer, where she's editing a batch of outfit photos. Behold, my mother in her natural habitat.

I sit next to her on the couch and grab a handful of popcorn from the bowl. "Not yet."

She transfers her computer to me and I navigate to the front-end of her blog. It takes about two minutes to find and fix the bug that is causing her photos to have trouble loading.

"Done."

"Thanks. And to think, if you'd answered my texts, that could've been solved hours ago."

"I didn't get them. My phone broke." I pull my purse onto my lap and fish out my phone.

She tries to turn it on. When that doesn't work, she turns it over and takes the battery out.

"Don't bother. It's toast."

She frowns at the useless hunk of metal. "At least you're off the hook for ignoring my texts."

"Forever?"

"Nice try." She opens the internet browser on her computer. "I'll order you a new one. Same one as before?" She pulls up a picture of my current phone, which is the newest model on the market.

"Please and thank you!"

She nods her head and puts it in her virtual cart. "Oh, shoot! This one is on backorder. It won't be here until next week."

I'm about to tell her to get something else when I hear Rafael's voice in my head. *A phone? Probably. Eventually. I'm not too worried about it.* And then I think about all the kids in the cafeteria bent over their screens, and how I may have never gotten to look into Rafael's eyes if my phone had been working.

"I can wait."

She raises one eyebrow at me. "What are you going to do until then?"

"I'm not too worried about it." I toss some popcorn into my mouth and try to mimic her expression, but I know from experience that my right eyebrow stubbornly refuses to move while my left eye twitches uncontrollably. Poppy can do it just like Mom, but I've yet to master the skill.

"Well, I'm worried about it. What if I need to contact you while you're at school, like I did today?"

"Text Poppy."

"What about while she's swimming?"

"I'm at home then."

Mom purses her lips and looks as if she's about to disagree with me. Then she changes her mind and clicks the checkout button. "Done. It will be here next week."

"Thanks." I pick up my laptop from the end table, put a pillow on my outstretched legs, and balance the computer on top. I pull up my latest coding project, a 15-puzzle created from a picture of Poppy mid-sneeze.

Mom peers over my shoulder with a frown. "Shouldn't you be doing something else?"

"Homework?" I ask hopefully, knowing full well she has something else in mind. Thanks to the agenda, I always know what I "should" be doing.

"What homework?" She eyes me suspiciously.

"Online quiz for my Spanish class."

"After that, you need to spend some time engaging with your community, responding to comments. When you quit the swim team, you promised you'd spend more time working."

I *did* say that.

Why did I say that?

"It's the reason I let you quit."

Oh yeah.

"You never hang out with your friends anymore—"

"They weren't really my friends." A fact she would know if she ever listened.

". . . and your work is slacking." She tilts her head to the side, awaiting an explanation for the reason I'm spending less time online. You know, just your average teenage rebellion and debauchery.

I thread my fingers together and avoid her eyes. "The vicious comments are still happening. And the emails."

Mom takes my hands in hers and squeezes. "Don't give away a single second of your happiness for people who don't care about you."

No, just give it all to you.

"If you're going to make it in this business, you need to build a thicker skin."

Maybe I don't want to make it.

"A thick skin can't protect me from everything," I mumble.

"I know. That's what Poppy and I are for." She releases my hands and returns to her computer, signaling the end of our conversation. I gather my laptop and my bag and reluctantly pull myself off the couch. If I try *really* hard, I can make my Spanish quiz last twenty minutes. Twenty-five, if I pretend to be super dumb. The more time I spend on homework, the less time I have to spend reading vlog comments.

"Dinner at 5:30," Mom says as I leave the room.

I stick my head around the corner so I can see her. "Dinner-dinner, or work-dinner?" I narrow my eyes. You never know with her.

"We'll go downtown and celebrate one million subscribers! You deserve a night off."

My shoulders relax and tension flows from my body. *A night off.* It has a nice ring to it. And just like that, my bad mood evaporates, and I take the rest of the steps two at a time.

---

noraborealis

I quit. I quit I quit I quit I quit I quit. I've been stuck on a runway in Iceland for F I V E hours. The brat behind me has kicked my seat a grand freaking total of 667 times. When he gets to 1000, I'm going to cut off his feet. Too bad I can't light up on the plane. Please, someone, somewhere, make it stop. You're up @HOMESTEADHELL

 homesteadhell

I share a room with F I V E of my brothers. My entire life is an airplane runway in Iceland. Try again,
@NORABOREALIS

P.S. You're not quitting.

 noraborealis

At least you have your own bed to sleep in. I haven't slept in my bed in 27 days. And you can't use SHARE A ROOM WITH FIVE BROTHERS every single time. Give us something good,
@SIGNOFTHETIMES

P.S. I'm quitting and you should too. It'll be an uprising.

A loud crash comes from inside my closet, and I look up from my laptop. "Need help in there?"

"Um, yeah. That's why I asked for help," Poppy growls, stepping over a mountain of shoes into my bedroom. Her arms are piled high with various articles of my clothing.

"Sorry. I didn't hear you."

"Shocker. What are you looking at?"

"BITES."

"Anything good?" Poppy asks.

"Nora is tossing around the word 'uprising' again."

"What else is new?" She rolls her eyes as she drops the clothes on the corner of my bed and sits next to me, leaning over my shoulder to look at my screen.

Because They Said So, or BITES, is my baby. My pride and joy. The heart that beats outside my body. Okay, really, it's just a website I created, but unlike the vlog, this is all mine. The whole thing started a couple of years ago when Poppy and I attended a "Voices of the Next Generation" party thrown by some teen magazine. Basically, if you were the offspring of someone with an impressive online following, you were invited. It was amazing. For the first time in my life, I was in a room full of people who grew up like I did. Despite the fact that our lives look different from the outside, we instantly connected over our shared experiences (i.e., inexplicable fame and utter lack of privacy).

After the party, some of us kept in touch through group text messages and emails. This lasted for a few months until I got tired of being woken up in the middle of the night by texts from the European kids, so I created a place for us to go online. It's not fancy, just a private message board with a direct chat feature, but it's mine. And it's theirs. It's a place we can go to vent about our parents. It's also the only online platform where I'm not constantly compared to my sister.

"Nora needs to get over herself. No one wants to hear complaints from Iceland." Poppy stands up to sort through the clothes on the bed.

Nora, or NORABOREALIS, as she's known on BITES, is the daughter of travel bloggers. She spends her entire life vacationing across the globe, and she never stops complaining about it. All she wants is to settle down in some boring suburban town and go to high school like Poppy and I. Which just goes to show you some people are insane. HOMESTEADHELL, on the other hand, has a legitimate right to complain. Gideon has fifteen brothers and sisters and lives on a farm in the middle of nowhere. His parents homeschool him and his siblings and make a fat paycheck writing about it. Whenever we start playing the one-up game, he always brings up the fact that he shares a bedroom with five of his brothers. From where I stand, he wins every time.

"Help me!" Poppy insists, pulling my thoughts from BITES and back onto her.

"What about your new yellow dress?"

"I wore that last weekend," she whines.

"So?"

"People will notice."

"We're just going to dinner. Not a photo shoot." I say the words, but I don't believe them.

"What about this?" She reenters the closet, pulls a flowy floral tank top off a hanger and tosses it onto the bed.

"I don't care." I have been ready to go for forty-five minutes because, as Mom so thoughtfully pointed out this afternoon, I have no life beyond my computer screen.

Poppy comes out of the closet and pulls the shirt on. She turns left and then right in front of the mirror. "This looks fine, right?"

"Yes."

Her eyes glare at me from the mirror. "You're extra chatty tonight."

For the first time, I sit up and look at her in my top. "It looks good. Besides, people love it when you wear florals. Poppy wearing poppies! They eat that crap up."

Now Poppy is smiling at her reflection. "You're right. It's perfect. Let's go."

Mom parks the SUV in a dirt lot that functions as overflow parking, and I jump out, ready to celebrate. She loves downtown because there's no shortage of good photo backdrops, and I love it because it bleeds charm. Whenever I see the historic water tower with our town name painted on it or the old railroad tracks that cut through the main road, I can't help but smile. Mom grabs three garment bags from the back of the SUV and unzips them, handing us each an army green trench coat.

So much for a night off.

Poppy looks at me with one raised eyebrow. Even she has her limit, and I have a feeling we've reached it.

"Mom, no. Seriously. Just no," she says.

"What are you talking about?" Mom looks at us with a frown. "You agreed to wear them last month."

"This is supposed to be a celebration, and a night off! Besides, it's 110 degrees outside," Poppy insists. "No way." Her eyes widen, pleading with me for help. Part of me wants to stay quiet and let her be the problem child for once, but I can't leave her hanging. Wearing a coat in the scorching heat isn't going to garner much sympathy on BITES, but it's still absurd. And not happening.

"Heat stroke. It's a real thing," I say.

"The sponsor wants us to do a post featuring these coats this week. It's non-negotiable."

"Why are we being sponsored by these people? It's never cold enough to wear these," Poppy points out.

"Not everyone lives in Arizona. Coats on."

We don't move.

"I'll snap a few pictures now and you can take them off during dinner. Final offer."

This is obviously the best deal we're going to get, so we pull on the coats despite the heat. I catch my reflection in the car window as we pass. The coat is cute, but I don't have to admit that to Mom when sweat is already pooling under my arms.

While we wait for a table to become available, Poppy and I take turns in front of the camera. First, we pose separately, then together. After Mom is satisfied, she hands the camera off to me and I get a couple of "candid" shots of her and Poppy sitting together on a bench in front of an old brick wall. I keep taking photos even after I'm confident that I have the shot. I would much rather be behind the camera than in front of it.

When I get bored taking fashion shots, I turn my camera on the people milling about downtown Gilbert. Don't let the word "downtown" fool you. This isn't the place for skyscrapers or bustling nightlife. You'd have to go into Phoenix to find that. This stretch of road is reserved for trendy restaurants, farmers markets, and food trucks, which have all popped up in the last few years. I love to see the new venues integrated into the old backdrop.

Eventually, we get a table inside and Mom lets us take off the coats after we order dinner. She leaves hers on, despite the beads of sweat dripping down her neck. She's trying to prove a point, but I have no idea how she stands it. Sweat is pouring down the small of my back and my coat is damp as I peel it off. I pull a hair tie out of my purse and twist my hair up into a bun on top of my head. The server brings me a glass of ice water, and we're thankfully positioned under a vent. By the time the chips and salsa arrive, we have all cooled off considerably.

"Have people sent questions for the Q&A vlog yet?" Mom asks. Poppy put out a call for questions on her Instagram this morning, and the messages have been rolling in.

"Yeah. Some of them are kind of invasive," I say.

"Like what?"

"Someone asked what kind of underwear we wear," Poppy says. She was not nearly as horrified as I was to find that gem waiting in our inbox.

Mom waves her hand dismissively. "I've gotten that question once a week since I started blogging. Ignore the weird ones and answer whatever you feel comfortable with."

"What if I don't feel comfortable answering any of them?" I ask. Mom and Poppy exchange amused looks. *Silly Claire. Always reluctant to pay the price of fame.* I let it go. There's no use arguing when it's two against one, and the numbers are always against me.

While we're waiting for the check after our meal, Mom goes to the bathroom. As soon as she's out of earshot, Poppy turns to face me. "Who's the guy? Tell me everything."

"You mean Rafael?" I ask, even though I know that Rafael is the only guy she could possibly be talking about.

She rolls her eyes. "Duh."

"Not much to tell. He's new in school, obviously. He's been in India for the last year because his dad is some kind of Good Samaritan doctor."

"He's cute." She takes a sip of her soda.

"He's okay." I don't know why I'm bothering to play it cool with Poppy, who can always see through my evasions.

"Don't tell me you're still hung up on Jackson." She shakes her head in disbelief.

My cheeks burn with shame at the mention of his name. "I'm not."

"Good. I know you and Mom thought he was going to be the love of your life or whatever, but he's ridiculous. You shouldn't waste your senior year pining over him."

As much as I hate to admit it, Poppy's right. I had the most obsessive crush on Jackson Hunt all through junior high and high school. Our moms are best friends, he was the boy next door (or close enough—he lived down the street), and he spent every day of every summer swimming in our pool. It's the kind of stuff romantic comedies are made of. When he asked me to senior prom last spring, Mom and I both believed it was fate. We bought half a dozen prom dresses and let our fans vote on the one I should wear. They even chose Jackson's matching tux. I assume Mom wrote about it on the blog too, but I don't bother to check anymore.

The followers went bonkers for those vlogs. It was the Jackson Effect. Everyone loved the idea of the two of us dating and falling in love after growing up together. We made it look like a real-life fairy tale.

It wasn't.

Prom was our first and only date, and when Jackson dropped me off on my doorstep that night, he gave me a high five.

A high five.

I almost died of embarrassment. But since that piece of horrifying news never made the vlog, some fans still speculate that we're dating long distance while I finish high school and he attends college at the University of San Diego. In reality, he hasn't exactly been chatty since he moved to California in June. We used to text all the time. Now he can't even be bothered to answer me.

"He gave me a high five." I remind Poppy.

"I remember. I'm just making sure that you do too."

"Trust me. It's not an easy thing to forget."

Poppy tilts her head and frowns. *Pity face.* "Don't worry. You'll get kissed eventually."

She knows how much I want to be kissed, but I hate it when she feels sorry for me. "You don't worry either, your boyfriend will kiss you eventually."

The look of pity morphs into one of disdain. "He's not my boyfriend."

"I should hope not, considering the fact that you've never met him."

She rolls her eyes. "I wouldn't expect you to understand."

Poppy is completely in love with this guy she met online over the summer. Brayden lives in Chicago and is semi-famous for playing cover songs on his guitar and posting them online. When he realized that Poppy was a fan of his videos, he dedicated a song to her, and they have been obsessed with each other ever since. It's sort of weird, but I'm also sort of jealous because it's not like any boys are serenading me with love songs.

I push my chair back from the table and stand up. "All I'm saying is that I'm not in love with Jackson anymore." This is not the first time I've said those words, but it's the first time I start to believe them.

Mom and I cross paths as I walk to the bathroom, and she winks at me. I know that coming here tonight was her way of apologizing for our argument after school. She could have chosen anywhere for dinner tonight, but she must have picked downtown because I love it. Just before I push open the bathroom door, a group of women about Mom's age point to me from across the restaurant. I smile at them and then to myself, knowing that my family would be proud of me for trying to engage.

The bathroom door bangs open while I'm washing my hands, still aglow in the memory of my small personal victory. A woman walks in. She stands at the sink next to me and brushes her bangs out of her eyes. "I could not believe it when I saw you! I've lived in Gilbert for fifteen years, and I've never seen you or your mother or sister in real life. But here you are! At *Barrio Queen*!" She turns the faucet on and scrubs her hands under the water.

One of the weirdest things about being internet-famous is that it leads people to believe they really know you, even if you've never met. Poppy has always been better than me about talking to strangers. After all this time, it still gives me a queasy feeling in my stomach, like I'm strangling my intestines with a too-small belt. She's constantly reminding me that if we're not nice to someone, they may show up in the comments section of our vlog and tell everyone we're bitches in real life.

Now I recognize her as one of the women who saw me walk into the bathroom, and I freeze. For the first time in years, I give an unsolicited smile to a stranger, and now I'm stuck making awkward small talk in the bathroom. "Ni-nice to meet you. I love your necklace." It's a throwaway compliment, but I've learned from watching Poppy that Mom's fans love it when we compliment their sense of style. As a rule, they're very into fashion. That's why they follow her, after all.

"I can't believe how grown up you are! It seems like just yesterday you and Poppy were in matching pigtails."

Perfect. One of those nut jobs.

I dry my hands on my jeans and make a move to leave.

"I've been a fan of your Mom for years, and I still love reading about you girls!" She beams at me. I cringe in response, thinking about the things she knows about me, the pictures she's seen. I don't even know her name, but she knows my whole history. It's hard to believe people still care about us after all this time.

I duck around her and make a mental note to beg Mom to stop writing about me. *Again.*

"Wait! Don't go! I need a picture!" She steps in front of the door, blocking my path.

"In here?"

"Why not? Unless we could get Poppy too! Ooh, I'd love to meet her. There's something about her, you know? Her personality shines through in every picture!" She sees my horrified expression and apparently decides it's better to settle for a picture of the less shiny twin than risk getting nothing. She pulls a tube of lipstick from her purse and swipes it on before holding her cell phone at arm's length for a picture of us together. Her fingers wrap around my forearm. I recoil at the contact, but her grip is tight as she pulls me close, pressing her cheek against mine. I swallow the painful lump in my throat and fight to keep my breathing normal. She snaps a picture and reviews it, clucking her tongue, obviously unhappy with my frown and panicked eyes. "One more."

Half a dozen pictures later, we still haven't gotten a shot that satisfies her. "I really have to go." I wrench my arm out of her grasp and see faint nail marks on my skin. I instinctively shudder away from her and push away the memory of another woman, another clenched hand, my sister's screams.

"Perfect! We'll find Ashley and Poppy and get that group picture! That'll be better anyway." Her smile looks genuine, but my chest tightens. I learned a long time ago that bad people can have nice smiles.

The door swings open and Poppy looks in, her eyebrows drawn. As soon as she sees us, her frown deepens.

"Poppy! There you are! Come here, sweetie, your sister and I are taking a selfie."

My sister looks at me for confirmation. I don't make a single move, but my fear must be written all over my face.

"Sorry. Not tonight." She holds the door open and gestures for the woman to leave.

"Just one? Please?" The woman smiles hopefully, looking from Poppy to me and back again. I expect Poppy to acquiesce, but she shakes her head without hesitation. The woman frowns but leaves without a fuss.

"Are you okay?" Poppy leans against the door to prevent anyone else from entering.

I nod, afraid if I say anything I'll start to cry.

"I'm so sorry." She wraps me in a hug and in this moment, I'm overflowing with gratitude that she's my sister.

"How'd you know I needed you?" I pull back and wipe my eyes before my mascara runs all the way down my cheeks.

"I saw them watching us through dinner. I should have said something before you left, but I didn't want to scare you. When she followed you in here, I promised myself I'd come in after you if you were gone too long."

"Thanks for saving me."

She takes my hand and squeezes it. "Consider it payback for the time you saved me."

Super chill, not-at-all-desperate texts to Jackson

JUNE

Me

Good luck in California! You're going to kill it!

Jackson

Thanks. Miss you!

Me

I miss you too!

JULY

Me

Sick of Cali yet? Ready to come home?

Jackson

Never

SEPTEMBER

Me

So how's college life??? Tell me everything!

Jackson

It's cool. Studying a lot.

OCTOBER

Me

Whatcha up to??

Chapter 4

"**P**artner up for an activity. Today we're conducting mock job interviews, because many college students need to work to afford tuition, text books, and room and board." Ms. Grant gathers a stack of papers and waits for us to follow instructions.

I turn immediately to Poppy. First, because she's always my partner for class projects. And second, because I don't need Rafael asking me any probing questions about myself. I looked up a few rock climbing terms (those things you shove in the rocks are apparently called cams) but I can only lie about it for so long.

Poppy becomes fascinated by something on the bottom of her shoe and refuses to look at me. I roll my eyes at the back of her head as Rafael leans forward and clears his throat loudly. "Partner?"

"Partner," I agree.

Ms. Grant hands out the papers of sample interview questions. It's basic stuff: What experience do you have?

What are your strengths and weaknesses? Why do you want this job?

I breathe a small sigh of relief. There's nothing incriminating about these. For the first time in years, I've met someone who doesn't see me as Claire Dixon: Internet Famous, and I'm determined to keep it that way. If last year taught me anything, it's that some my classmates view me through a constant "goals" filter, regardless of how unglamorous my life really is. Or they straight up hate me. It's exhausting. As long as I keep the truth about my online life from Rafael, I won't have to worry about that with him.

"Do you want to be the interviewer or the interviewee?" Rafael asks he scans the paper.

"Interviewer." There's nothing too revealing about the interview questions, but I don't want to take any chances.

"Fire away." He sets down his paper and sits up straighter in his chair.

"Tell me about your previous job experience." My "professional" voice ends up sounding like a voiceover from a dramatic nature documentary. Rafael's lips twitch but he clears his throat and doesn't laugh.

"I've never had a paying job—"

"Strike one!"

"But that doesn't mean I don't have any experience," he says, as if I never interrupted him. "I just returned from a fourteen-month stay in India. While there, I spent a lot of time doing volunteer work."

"Points for composure," I say, breaking character again. And then I return to my faux-professional voice. "That sounds interesting. Tell me more about that." The voice is fake but my interest in his answer is real.

"I sometimes helped clean the clinics, but mostly I talked."

"Shocking."

He grins and continues undeterred. "Not all of the patients had visitors, so I'd sit with them and talk, play card games and stuff."

"Stop!" Ms. Grant calls from behind her desk. "This is pathetic. Hardly anyone is making eye contact. Abigail is staring at her hands, Ethan is doodling on his paper, and Parker is texting because he thinks I can't see him."

Parker Evans tears his eyes away from his lap. He doesn't even have the decency to look guilty.

"Body language is a huge part of the interview process. The right body language conveys confidence and preparedness. The wrong body language can send the message that you're nervous and unqualified." She points to Rafael. "Do you see the way Rafael is straight up in his chair, feet on the ground? That's how you should be sitting."

At least half the class shifts positions in their chairs. "And above all else—you must make eye contact. Eye contact shows that you're listening and engaged in the process. It shows you care whether or not you get the job." She's in lecture mode, pacing the room as she speaks.

"New assignment. Forget the interview for a moment. For the next five minutes, you must make eye contact with the person across from you. Talk about whatever you want, but you can't look away. No cell phones, no tablets— no screens of any kind. You have to learn how to have a conversation without distractions. Starting now." She sits at her desk and the room falls silent. "Start talking or we do ten minutes," she warns.

I turn to face Rafael. He's leaning forward, arms crossed on his desk. "So what do you want to talk about?" I ask in a voice that sounds calmer than I really feel.

"Did you know that eye contact can make two strangers fall in love?"

I swallow, and it feels like downing a fistful of sand. *Is he messing with me on purpose?* "I have no idea how to respond to that."

"A group of psychologists did an experiment a few decades ago. They took two strangers off the street and brought them into a lab. The strangers answered a bunch of questions about themselves and then stared into each other's eyes for a few minutes. Six months later, they got married."

I narrow my eyes. "You're lying."

He mimics my expression before breaking into a smile. "I swear I'm not."

"How do you know that?"

"I read an article online. This was when I was in Mexico City, where I did have a phone for about six months while my dad helped with earthquake aftermath. Have you ever been?"

"Not to the capital city, but my family went to Mexico a few years ago."

"I want to go back soon and see the place where my grandparents were born. It's an amazing country."

I nod in agreement, hoping I don't have to confess that the only place I've been is Cancún, and only because the white sand beaches look gorgeous in pictures. "My mom loves it there."

"I don't know my mom. My parents met in Greece, when they were both young and new to the Doctors Without Borders program. She didn't want a kid, but my dad did, so after I was born she signed away all her parental rights to me. I haven't seen or heard from her since."

Whoa. Here I am, trying to hide my last name, and he just told me his entire origin story. The sheer level of candor makes me so uncomfortable I'm compelled to break eye contact in favor of looking at the wall behind him.

"Hey! No cheating."

I tear my eyes off an inspirational cat poster and look at him again.

Silence.

Self-consciousness overwhelms me. To release some of my restlessness, I stretch my legs while scratching a nonexistent itch on my nose.

But I keep looking into his eyes.

"We have to start over, you know." He rubs the back of his neck with his hand while maintaining laser focus on me.

"We do not." If this lasts much longer, I'll combust from the tension.

"I'll tell Ms. Grant." Based on his smile, it's an empty threat.

"I wonder if eye-contact love works through video chat." I think about Poppy and Brayden, and seize an opportunity to change the subject.

Rafael sits back in his chair and considers my words. "I doubt it. You have to really know someone to fall in love with them. I don't believe in falling in love through the internet."

"I'm pretty sure there are millions of people in happy relationships that would have a different opinion on the matter."

"Don't get me wrong. I'm not knocking internet dating. There's nothing wrong with meeting someone online. But it can't stop there. You have to get to know the other person in real life. You have to do this kind of stuff." He gestures between us.

Blood rushes to my cheeks, and it takes me several seconds to get out a few strangled words. "This kind of stuff? You mean class assignments, or . . ."

Rafael laughs. "Eye contact. Sitting in the same room. Kissing. The physical stuff. It's important."

I nearly slip sideways out of my chair. I grip the hard edge of the desk to keep my composure and remind myself that Rafael finds amusement in knocking me off kilter. This is not about wanting to do physical stuff *with me*, it's about saying something surprising and watching me squirm. But that doesn't mean I have to.

I flash him a cool smile. "I don't think there's anything wrong with internet dating or long-distance relationships or anything. If you find someone you like, and they like you, isn't that all that matters?"

Ms. Grant cuts him off before he can respond. "Time's up! Most of you did a fine job, although I doubt any of you were able to go the whole five minutes without breaking eye contact. It's not an easy thing to do, but it's an important skill to learn. Tonight. Go home. Practice. Have a conversation with someone. Look at them, not a screen." The bell rings. "Have a good day."

Rafael waits for me at the door. It's nice, having someone to walk with again. I spent the last few months convincing myself I was fine without the swim team. Without my old friends. But as Rafael holds the door open for me and we fall into stride next to each other, I realize it was one of those lies you tell yourself when the truth is too painful to handle. Rafael is a rainy day at the end of an unbearable drought. Unexpected, refreshing, and enchanting.

Just like yesterday, he is completely at ease in his new surroundings, nodding to people he's barely known twenty-four hours. If I wasn't so baffled, I might be annoyed at how seamlessly he's slipped into the part of Highland High School senior. He's like Poppy, with the exception that his smile seems sincere.

"How do you do that?" I ask after he greets some guy whose name I can't even begin to guess. "You've been here, what, a day? And you're already best friends with everyone." It's half compliment, half accusation. It's possible the enchantment is slipping.

"It's a learned habit. When you move countries every twelve months, give or take, you get pretty good at meeting new people. I wasn't always like this. I used to waste the first six months in a new place being shy, then spend three months slowly making small talk. Then another three months actually making friends. And then it was time to leave again. I eventually realized if I want real friends, I have to cut through those first nine months and get to the good stuff faster. It's like that experiment I was telling you about."

"So, you'll just tell random strangers everything about your life?" Like the information about his grandpa, or the fact that his mom abandoned him.

He shoots me a sideways glance. "Not 'random strangers.' I talk to people who seem cool. People I want to be friends with."

Right. He has more in common with Poppy than I thought. Both of them willing to talk to anyone, about anything. He's the exact opposite of me, basically. And he's probably done this same shtick with different girls across the globe. A new one every year.

"But that's the general idea," he continues. "I'll honestly answer any question about myself. It's the only way to let people know me. Since I'm always the new kid, I'm at the serious disadvantage when it comes to breaking into existing friend groups."

"Any question?" My mind races with possibilities. I could ask him about those other girls, or his most embarrassing moment, or his biggest fear, and he'd tell me? Here in the school parking lot? Gratuitous oversharing is not uncommon among my generation (or my mother's, let's be honest), but the distance provided by our screens keep us from being truly vulnerable. Rafael is the only person I know who is willing to look me in the eye while he spills his deep, dark secrets. Hypothetically, of course.

"Any question." He stops abruptly at the door of an old Honda Accord and waits a beat, maybe to see if I'm going to take him up on his offer. He watches me with dark eyes, and it startles me how much I'm dying to know about this globe-trotting boy with no secrets. But if I start asking questions, he'll probably do the same, and it's a game I could never play. A few clicks online, and he'd have the ultimate advantage.

He breaks several long seconds of silence. "See you tomorrow."

"Oh. I . . . uh . . . won't be here." My mind frantically searches for a believable excuse for my absence.

He rests his arm on top of his open door. "Why not?"

I'm taking a red-eye flight to New York Fashion Week to hang out backstage at Allegra Esposito's show. I smile to myself, realizing any excuse will sound more believable than the truth.

"It's Take Your Daughter to Work Day."

Email from Allegra Esposito's Assistant

From: ruby@aedesigns.com
To: poppyandclaire@dixondaily.com
Subject: NYFW

Dear Poppy and Claire,
Ms. Esposito would once again like to extend an invitation to her runway show at New York Fashion Week in September. Please RSVP as soon as possible so we can reserve your seats in the tent. As per previous conversations with your mother, understand that this invitation is directed at both of you, and respond accordingly. If one of you is unable to attend, we will be unable to accommodate the other.

Allegra will not have time to dress you in the tent this year. Your outfits will be shipped closer to the date of the show. If you find issues with the fit, alert me ASAP.

Ruby Costa
Personal Assistant to Allegra Esposito

Chapter 5

New York Fashion Week.

For some people, it's a lifelong dream. For me, it's kind of an accident.

No, that's not the right word. It's more like an inevitability. Like this was always the plan, but no one stopped to ask if it was what I wanted. Until recently, I didn't even bother to ask myself.

Poppy and I were fourteen the first year we were invited. Our YouTube channel was gaining hundreds of new followers every day, and people talked about us as actual, independent humans, separate from our fashion-blogging mom. We were no longer "Ashley Dixon's twin daughters." We were "Poppy and Claire. YouTube Famous." Now, it doesn't seem like such a distinction. At the time, it was everything.

We squealed over the invitation to Allegra Esposito's runway show, where we would sit in the front row in custom dresses. She had us fill out a fashion profile with our measurements. But I was too lazy to double-check mine, copying the numbers on Poppy's profile instead. We had been the same everything for so long, I didn't think about it twice.

Until Allegra's assistant tried to zip me into a dress that didn't fit.

"Suck in your stomach." Her Italian accent lengthened every vowel and consonant in the word 'stomach,' drawing attention from all eyes in the crowded room.

My stomach and hips and boobs were already sucked in a far as they would go, but I closed my eyes and willed myself to shrink as she tugged on the zipper. It didn't budge. My armpits began to sweat all over Allegra's custom gown.

At the time, all I could think was this was it. This was officially the most mortifying moment of my whole, over-exposed life. *This* was how I would ruin the *brand*. By being too "fat" and too sweaty for high fashion, which I never cared all that much about anyway. I liked creating funny videos with Poppy and feeling like people valued my opinions. And I especially loved the way Mom smiled proudly as our numbers grew, but I was not on board with humiliating myself for the sake of one stupid dress.

Every inch of my skin burned with embarrassment as a flock of people gathered in a circle, discussing our options. In a last-ditch effort before scrapping the dress completely, a seamstress was able to let out the seams of the dress enough to zip it. By the end of the show, I was dizzy with lack of oxygen and desperate to get back into leggings and Converse. But first, Allegra's social media intern insisted on pictures.

When we checked Allegra's Instagram an hour later, a solo picture of Poppy graced her profile. My heart sank. Sure, I didn't love the dress, or the experience of wearing it. But to come in second place to Poppy, in such a deliberate and public way, confirmed all my hidden fears. If I kept going down this path with her, I would never be good enough.

Poppy grasped her phone with both hands as she scanned the comments and likes. I could hear her thoughts as if she spoke them out loud. More exposure plus more engagement equaled more followers for us. *For her.* Her face fell as she continued to scroll. I peeked over her arm, trying to catch of glimpse of whatever nasty comment made her look so unhappy.

"Where's your picture?" she demanded.

Well, Poppy, obviously Allegra didn't think I was a good representation of her brand. Obviously, you looked better. Obviously, they like you more than me. I shrugged, hoping she wouldn't make me say the words.

She stomped to the social media intern on the other side of the fashion tent and shoved the phone in her face. "Where's Claire?"

"That was the best picture," the too-tall intern said in a bored voice. She was at least a foot taller and five years older than either of us. But Poppy was undeterred.

"Allegra invited both of us. That's our brand. If she doesn't understand that, our entire family will find someone else to work with."

They stared each other down for a full five seconds, but Poppy refused to flinch.

"Fine," the intern sighed and clicked her long nails against the screen of her phone. Poppy returned and together we looked at the newly posted photo of me. My face was a little grimace-y, but it wasn't terrible.

"Nice work," a cameraman nodded at Poppy as he walked by. "You've got influence."

"Influence." Poppy repeated the word. Her small smile grew as she considered the concept. "That's a synonym for power, right?"

I nodded.

"Good."

Poppy's photo raked in more likes than mine did. A lot more. But back in Arizona, away from the judgmental eyes of assistants and interns and photographers and seamstresses, it didn't feel like such a big deal. It was easier to pretend we were still in this thing together, both of us pulling equal weight as we strived to climb the ranks of online influencers. Sometimes I regret not quitting that day in New York, when I had the chance. Before everything spiraled so far out of my control.

"You're welcome." Poppy flops into the seat next to me and flips the *SkyMall* magazine open to the first page.

I pull my gaze from the twinkly yellow grid outside my small airplane window, my thoughts returning to the present. "For what?"

"I knew if I ignored you for long enough in College Prep, you'd have to team up with Rafael. It's not like you have any other friends. No offense."

I adjust the air conditioning vent without looking at her. "Offense taken. Why'd you want me to partner with Rafael?"

"Because he's hot and you're lonely." She says this as if it's the most obvious thing in the world.

"I'm not lonely."

"You're lonely and in denial. Lovely." She pauses to examine something in the magazine and then holds it up for me to see. It's a bra that can be filled with wine, complete with a nozzle for easy drinking access. "For Mom?"

"Filled with Diet Coke."

"Of course." She returns to perusing the magazine.

"Do you think that's why Rafael teamed up with me?" The thought of him partnering with me because I'm the pathetic girl who has no friends is beyond depressing. Then again, is it any worse than randomly choosing me to be his new best friend like drawing a piece of paper from a hat?

"Please. No. I saw the way he was looking at you during that ridiculous 'The-Eyes-Are-The-Window-To-The-Soul' assignment. You're lucky I love you. I had to partner with Parker Evans." She shudders.

"How was he looking at me?" Unless the expression is *friend zone*, it's not one I'm familiar with.

"Parker? He wasn't. He kept throwing spit wads at his friends and laughing like a six year old."

"Not Parker! How was Rafael looking at me?"

"Oh." She smiles. "I was right. You're into him."

"I'm not. And you still didn't answer my question." I'll never understand how Poppy gets good grades. Getting her to focus on one topic is like trying to get a puppy to sit still for a picture.

She rolls her eyes and smacks on her gum. "He was looking at you, like, you know."

"I *don't* know. That's why I'm asking."

"He was looking at you like he *wished* he was looking at you with no clothes on."

My faces flushes as Poppy cackles. A woman across the aisle shoots us a dirty look.

"I sometimes wonder how we're even related."

"You and me both."

I turn back to the window as she gets absorbed in the magazine. "Like I said, I'm not interested in him."

"Mm-hmm. Okay."

"I'm serious! He's too . . . friendly."

She bolts upright in her seat with a murderous expression. "Did he do something to you? Did he make you feel uncomfortable?"

"No!" I realize immediately how I've made him sound, and that's not at all what I meant. I search for the right way to explain what I'm feeling. When Rafael and I are talking, he has a way of making me feel like I'm the only one in the room. But that doesn't mean anything other than the fact that he has a master plan for making people like him and no cell phone to divide his attention. "He's just *so nice* to everyone he meets, all the time."

She stares at me blankly. "And?"

"And . . . I don't know, it's weird."

"You'd rather him be one of those conceited, hot guys that's a jerk to everyone but nice to you? Or do you want him to be a jerk to you, also?"

I sigh. Of course, she wouldn't understand, because she and Rafael are too similar. So I change the subject. Sort of. "I haven't told him about the vlog yet. Or about Mom."

"He doesn't know?" Her mouth gapes open.

"Not everyone knows about us, Poppy. We're not that famous."

She shakes her head. "He's going to find out eventually. Wouldn't it be better if you told him yourself?"

"Probably."

"Then why don't you?"

"I don't know . . . Don't you ever get tired of having your life on display?"

"No. It's an important step in our plan."

I groan and let my head drop against the window. *I hate "the plan."*

"Step one, conquer the internet. Step two, earn a butt-load of money. Step three, and this is the important part, do whatever the hell we want. Literally. It'll be so much easier to be a Girl Boss with your own computer company, or whatever, when you have the power and money needed to get there. And if we get to wear free shoes on our climb to the top, all the better."

"It's not all free shoes."

"I know. It's also free dresses and bags and makeup. I don't know why you always act like this life is such a burden. You didn't seem *burdened* two summers ago when we visited Europe. In fact, you said it was the best summer of your life. Where do you think Mom got the money to pay for that trip?"

"She could get another job." So could we, for that matter.

"Not making the kind of money she is now. That trip was a tax write-off because of the outfit photos we took. That's how the business works."

"There's bad stuff too. You always pretend like there's not."

"I know. We all remember the time some jerk at school found the pictures of you online with your braces and your acne and your stuffed bra. The way you go on about that, I swear. Mom deleted the pictures after you freaked out. You have to give her a break." Poppy jams the magazine back in its pocket and redirects the air conditioning back at me.

"Just because she deleted it doesn't mean it stopped existing. Parker Evans took screenshots and kept them on his phone for the entire semester. But that's not what I'm talking about and you know it."

Poppy doesn't respond.

"You can't pretend like it never happened," I say.

"Actually, I can." She claps her headphones over her ears and turns to face the aisle.

By the time a taxi spits us out in the heart of Lincoln Center the next morning, all is forgiven. Thrilled to be here at last, Poppy grabs my hand and pulls me onto the curb. We wind our way through massive crowds of people as we head straight for the tents of New York Fashion Week. Agoraphobia grips my chest as we get closer to the heart of the action and people jostle around us. I squeeze Poppy's hand, and remind myself to take slow, deep breaths.

Mom, who left the hotel bright and early this morning, flags us down outside one of the biggest tents in the middle of the chaos. She beams at us as, but her face falters as we get closer.

"What are you wearing?" It's clear from the shocked look on her face that she's talking to me.

My gray T-shirt says KEEP CALM AND CODE ON. Only the whole thing is written in HTML, so it actually looks like this:

```
<center>
<img src=crown.jpg>
<br>
<font color=white>
KEEP<br>
CALM<br>
<small>AND</small>
<br>
CODE<br>
ON</font>
</center>
```

I think it's hilarious, but it's been brought to my attention that I'm the only one who does.

"I told her to change," Poppy says.

Mom shakes her head. "You cannot be seen on camera like that. Did you at least bring the clothes Allegra sent you?"

"I brought them for her." Poppy opens her bag to reveal the free clothes that were sent by the designer, who often cites our family as her "muse." Allegra even warmed up to me eventually after the dress debacle, though not until Mom put me on a diet and Poppy and I once again had similar measurements.

"I don't want to change."

Mom shakes her head. "Why do you have to turn everything into a fight?"

The truth is, I have no idea. Life would be so much easier if I was like Poppy. I should just shut my mouth and nod and smile and wear my free clothes, but it's getting harder and harder to do. Maybe I would feel differently if I was given a choice, but this life was picked for me before I was born. Some days, I want to quit the internet entirely. But most days, it feels like my family *is* the internet, and I can't quit one without quitting the other.

Mom and Poppy stare me down, leaving me with no choice but to give in. I sigh as we enter the tent. About half of the seats are filled, and photographers are setting up equipment on both sides of the runway. The show is scheduled to begin in five minutes, but that means we have another half an hour, at least. I duck into an empty corner and change into the Esposito originals while Poppy hides me from view. When I'm done, we find our way to our assigned seats and wait.

I check my notifications on Poppy's phone and see that I've been tagged by SIGNOFTHETIMES. Serge always tags me in his posts, and I assume it's because he likes me, or doesn't like me, or maybe because he feels a weird kinship with me because his mom is also a fashion blogger, albeit one who lives in France. I'll probably never know why he actually tags me, because his posts consist entirely of emojis that are frustratingly hard to decipher.

I log into BITES to see his newest offering.

signofthetimes

@GIRLCODE

As usual, I have no idea what he's trying to say, but I have a hunch I'm not going to one-up him by telling a sob story about my mom flying me to Fashion Week and demanding I wear designer clothes. I decide to wait to post until something more interesting happens. It always does.

The show is a blur of loud music and sparkly sequins. Mom, Poppy, and the rest of the crowd are in heaven. It's fun to look at, but I can't get excited about it the way they do. When the show ends, Mom hisses instructions at us as we make our way backstage to greet Allegra.

"Thank her for the gowns. Tell her how much you love them. Compliment the show." I'm trying to remember a specific piece to talk about when I run smack into a short woman in a seriously over-sized sweater and tottering on six-inch stilettos. A travel coffee mug flies out of her hand onto the ground.

"I'm sorry!" she gasps. We bend over at the same time to pick it up.

"Here you go." I hand her the mug. When she looks at me she gasps again.

"Claire? Claire Dixon? I can't believe it!" She throws her arms around me and squeezes. She looks so fragile, I can't help but feel like she would break in half if I returned the gesture, so I do what comes naturally in these situations. I grimace under her arms and pray for release.

"I love your family!" She gathers Mom and Poppy in for hugs and introduces herself as Lena, a reporter for *MyStyle* magazine. "Can I buy you drinks? This is empty anyway." She shakes her travel mug and smiles warmly.

I pull Mom aside. "We don't even know her."

She pats my shoulder in what is supposed to be a sympathetic gesture. "She's wearing a press badge. You don't have to worry."

Ten minutes later, we're seated at a picnic table near a coffee cart and surrounded by trees. The leaves are starting to turn golden, which won't happen back home for another three months. Lena insists that she absolutely must interview us for the Fashion Week issue of *MyStyle*, and before I know it, Poppy and I are answering questions about our vlog and all things social media.

"What's it like growing up in front of the camera?" Lena sets down her paper coffee cup and picks up her tablet.

Poppy and I look at each other. I shrug, telling her she can take this one.

"It took us a long time to understand Mom's job. When we were little, we just thought we were playing dress up and having our picture taken. We didn't even realize she had 'fans' until we were a lot older," Poppy says.

I still remember the first time I realized I was working and not just playing. I was eight years old and Mom took

Poppy and me on a picnic. It seemed so special and fun, and I felt just like Dorothy from *The Wizard of Oz* in my blue gingham dress. Mom took pictures during lunch, but they must not have been turning out the way she wanted, because she was getting impatient. I was bored, grumpy, and eager to play soccer with some nearby kids, but when I tried to leave, Mom snapped at me that I wasn't done yet. I wasn't allowed to get the dress dirty, because then nobody would want to buy it and Mom wouldn't get paid. It was hard to trust any of my memories after that, because I didn't know what was real and what was an advertisement.

Lena finishes typing on her tablet and looks up at us again. "What's the best perk of your online fame?"

I cede the floor to Poppy again, because I'm definitely not the right daughter to talk to about industry "perks."

"The free clothes are amazing, of course. Every day feels like playing dress up. But the best part is meeting our fans."

Ugh. Poppy is so good at this.

"She's right." Mom says. "Our online community is filled with the most amazing people. It's been life changing. After I lost Jason . . ." She hesitates so long that I begin to wonder if she's going to finish her thought. "Well, let's just say I've never felt so alone in my entire life. But people from all over the country rallied around me and picked me back up. Having that support system made all the difference in the world."

Lena shakes her head sympathetically as she types on her tablet. It's weird to think a stranger might remember that time better than I do. Poppy and I were only six years old when our dad died in a car accident on his way to work. I don't remember anything about that day, but I've read about it on the blog. A few weeks after he died, Mom wrote about the accident and explained that she was going to keep blogging to support her family.

The response was insane. People from all over the world sent donations and flowers. Our house was filled with bouquets for months. I remember thinking there was no way my dad could have known that many people. But they knew him.

Lena's fingers slow down and she turns to my mom again. "There must be hard things about having such a large online presence. People can be really critical."

Mom nods. "On the internet, I've learned that people are quicker to judge, slower to forgive, and ten times more vocal than they would otherwise be."

"What do you mean?"

"If someone disagrees with me or doesn't like me, it's easy to write an anonymous comment voicing their opinion. I've been called ugly, fat, stupid, a bad parent—you name it. Most people don't have the stomach for that degree of cruelty in real life, but there's something about the internet that blurs that line."

"How do you deal with it?"

"It was harder when the girls were younger. I felt like every parenting decision I made was judged, and my words were constantly taken out of context and used against me. But now I try not to focus on negative things."

"What about you girls? How do you deal with the constant criticism?"

"I used to read the mean things people write about me online, but I stopped when I realized no good can come from it," Poppy says.

I think about telling Lena that Poppy was reading a critical online forum about the two of us *in the taxi on the way here,* but I don't.

"It sounds like you're a smart girl," Lena says and Poppy basks in the praise. "Let's move on to happier subjects. How did you girls get into vlogging?"

I've been silent this whole interview, and everyone turns to me. "Um . . . Mom made us a video channel and said 'start vlogging.'" It's the stone-cold truth, and I'm hoping to get a laugh. Instead, Mom's jaw drops as an awkward silence settles over us.

Poppy sits up straighter and smiles. "I think what she meant to say——"

"What I meant to say is that we were always bugging Mom, trying to help her pick outfits or take pictures. I think she finally directed us toward vlogging just to get us out of her hair!" I force a laugh this time, hoping it's enough to get Mom off my back.

She throws a warning glance in my direction. I've salvaged the interview, but she's still pissed.

"On our walk over here, I sent a tweet to my followers with the hashtag 'PoppyandClaire,' telling them to send questions they want me to ask you. Let's see what they sent." Her fingers swipe across the screen as she scrolls through her Twitter feed.

"A lot of people are asking about Jackson. Are you two still together?"

I roll my eyes. "No comment." That'll play with our audience a lot better than explaining that we never were together.

"Here's a good one. How do you pick your vlog topics?"

"We like to choose things that interest us, whether that's tips and tricks for simplifying our morning routine or finding the best hairstyle to beat the summer heat."

I tune out Poppy's voice, painfully aware that my contributions are not welcome in this conversation. I'd much rather be at school bantering with Rafael than sitting through this interview. It's the first time in recent memory that I've wanted to be in Gilbert as opposed to, well, anywhere else.

Lena scrolls through more questions with a chuckle. "There are some doozies here."

"If it's the perv asking about our underwear, just ignore it."

"Feel free to ask *anything*," Mom says. "There's nothing we haven't heard." She takes a sip of her soda.

"Okay. This one says, 'Ask them about the time they were kidnapped.' She laughs again. "I told you, the trolls are out in full force today."

Poppy stiffens beside me. It's a busy New York day in the middle of Fashion Week, but I swear I can hear her breath turn shallow and ragged. Or maybe that's mine.

"Who said that?" I ask, genuinely curious. As far I knew, Mom had this secret on lockdown. She never even talks about it with Poppy or me, let alone anyone else.

Lena's eyes widen in shock. She looks down at the tablet again. "He says his father was the police officer on the case. It's true? You were kidnapped?" She leans forward, the amusement on her face replaced with something hungrier. She smells a story.

Poppy grabs my hand and pulls me to my feet. "Let's get out of here." The message is clear. Lena won't get any information from us.

I wrench my hand from Poppy's. "What else does it say?" I know I should follow Poppy, but curiosity keeps me rooted to the spot.

"Claire." Mom's tone warns me against saying another word. Panic flashes in her eyes. It's the same expression she has any time plans go awry. But just as quickly as it came, the look is replaced with one of derision. "There's no story." She sounds so convincing even *I* almost believe her.

Lena turns to me. "Claire, is there anything you want to tell me?" Her voice is soft and sugary, as if she's speaking to a little child. The implication is insulting. She obviously thinks I'm the weak link, the one who will give up our family secret. Poppy grabs my elbow from behind, another warning.

Pressure builds inside my chest, pulling me in two directions. I want to tell Lena to go to hell and get out of here as quickly as possible. But I also want to tell my family to back off. Everyone is making decisions about something that happened *to me,* and I'm not allowed to say anything?

"You must be under a lot of pressure," Lena's spun-sugar voice is full of sympathy. "The pressure to have perfect hair and a revolving door of new outfits and a thigh gap—which, let's be honest, is a ridiculous, dangerous, unattainable goal. Not to mention the pressure to crank out content and engage with fans and ignore the trolls. It can't be easy."

"It's not." The words tumble from my mouth without permission.

"And the pressure to keep a secret like this? It must be eating away at you."

"It is," I whisper as I thread my fingers anxiously together. "I get panicky and nervous all the time. I don't trust anyone."

Poppy's fingers dig harder into my elbow.

"It might be a relief to finally tell the story," Lena says.

Is she right? All I know for sure is that nine years of holding this information in has shredded my nerves in a serious way. I'm so badly damaged, and so deeply screwed up, that I can't have a normal conversation with a cute boy without lying about myself. I take a deep breath, and nod my head. It's time to talk about it.

LENA'S TWITTER FEED

Lena Bristow @mystylelena
About to sit down with teen fashion YouTubers
Poppy & Claire Dixon. Send questions my way using
#poppyandclaire

Alex Cox @alexcox03
How much money do they make? #poppyandclaire

Heidi @heidiho16
Do #poppyandclaire get all their makeup for free?

Carli @fashionismylife
#poppyandclaire have any tips for new fashion vloggers?

Chad @chadslife
What color is your underwear? #poppyandclaire

Alyssa @ababy14
What's your favorite trend for fall? #poppyandclaire

Darcy Girl @darcygirl2002
I'm a YouTuber! Follow me and I'll follow back!
#poppyandclaire

Blaine Butler @blainebutler
Poppy will you go to prom with me? (If she says no, ask
Claire.) #poppyandclaire

Chad @chadddddddd
Ask them about the time they were kidnapped

Chapter 6

"It's not a big deal," Mom insists. "They were *almost* kidnapped, which means you *almost* have a story."

Lena frowns. "Sure, some of your fans will feel that way. I bet others will wonder why you didn't shield Poppy and Claire from the public eye. They'll assume you put yourself and your blog above the safety of your daughters."

Mom takes a deep breath, and I'm genuinely curious what she's going to say. If she denies the story now, she'll make me look like a liar. But if she finally admits the truth, well . . . I think Lena just gave us a pretty clear picture of what that would look like.

"Fine," she snaps. "I'll give you the story, which we all know is worth more than wild speculation, but you can't spin it."

"Give me something interesting to write and I won't have to."

"Okay." Mom closes her eyes and sighs. I'm still frozen next to Poppy, scared, confused, and a little excited for what will come next. Mom sits on a bench and motions for Poppy and me to sit next to her. "Where do I start?" This time, her words aren't an act. This is not a story she's used to telling.

"Nine years ago, I almost lost my girls. An unstable woman tried to take them while they were walking home from school. She parked on the side of the road, rolled down her window, and called their names. Poppy, my trusting and caring little girl, walked up to the van. The woman said she had lost her dog and needed help finding it. She opened the back door and asked them to get in."

Lena types furiously while Mom talks. Poppy has tears running down her face. I feel hollow inside, like a pumpkin ready for carving. I thought talking about this would help, but I should have known that Mom would never actually let *me* talk about it. I'm furious with myself for saying anything. I consider tattooing the words "Keep Your Mouth Shut" on the back of my hand so I'll never forget.

"Poppy was about to climb into the van, but Claire ran up to her and pulled her away. She pushed her toward home and told her to run and yell for help. When Poppy took off, the woman picked up Claire and was trying to force her into the van, but Claire was fighting and kicking and screaming for help." She looks at me with an unreadable expression. "Claire has always been my fighter. A car stopped, and a man got out to help. That's when the woman dropped Claire on the sidewalk and took off."

Lena looks stunned. I can't tell if she's shocked by the story or by the fact that she gets to be the one to tell the story to the world. "What happened after that?"

"The man took down the van's plates and called the police. They picked the woman up later that night. She was an addict and a stalker who was obsessed with the blog and my girls. The police say she was trying to live my life. She went to prison."

Silence is thick in the air as Lena finishes her notes. When she's done, she looks my mom straight in the eye. "Why didn't you shut down the blog?"

And there it is.

We never talk about the kidnapping. Poppy and I were both sent to a few counseling sessions right after it happened, but when those ended it felt like Mom wanted to pretend the whole thing never happened. Other than installing a state-of-the-art security system in our home, she continued on with life and work and the website as if nothing ever happened.

So when Lena asks The Question, the one I have wondered about for so long, I sit up a little straighter because I need to know the answer.

"I did shut it down for about a week," Mom says.

Poppy inhales sharply, as surprised by this revelation as I am.

"I was so scared and so sick by the thought that I could have lost them because of the blog. I blamed myself. But then I realized that quitting the blog was like giving in."

"What do you mean?" Lena asks.

Mom chews on her lip. "Even though the woman was arrested and sent to prison . . . if I let her stop me from blogging then it felt like she was winning, somehow. Up until that moment, the blog had brought so many opportunities and so many good things into our lives. To give that all up because of the actions of one woman didn't seem right or fair. I also realized that I could not let fear rule my life. I had to keep living it in the way that was best for my family."

"And that includes blogging," Lena clarifies.

"Yes," Mom answers. "I did make some changes though. From that moment on I became extremely careful about what details I posted online. The safety of my girls is always my number one priority. Soon after the incident, the blog took a back seat while I built my Instagram brand."

"Not everyone is going to believe that you made the right choice, given the circumstances," Lena says. "What would you say to the people who would question your decision?"

Mom shrugs. "What else is new? I can't get dressed in the morning without people questioning my decisions."

Lena chuckles. "Fair point. Anything else you'd like to add?"

"I would also ask that people respect my daughters' privacy. Even if you don't agree with me." Mom grabs my hand and squeezes it. "This is a really personal and difficult thing that our family experienced. The girls have been through enough without having to relive it, and they shouldn't have to talk about it with anyone."

I roll my eyes and pull my hand out of Mom's grasp. She never even asked if we wanted to talk about it. For all she knows, I want to shout it from the rooftops.

"Thanks, Ashley. The reaction probably won't be as bad as you're expecting," Lena says as she turns off her tablet.

"Girls, hail a taxi while I finish up here."

Poppy and I stand up without a word and walk to the curb.

"I can't believe Mom did that," I say, while we wait for a taxi to stop.

"Are you serious? You're actually mad at Mom?"

"Did you see what she did? She took something from our childhood and twisted it into her own sob story. We weren't allowed to say a thing!"

Poppy turns to face me. Her eyes are filled with angry tears and her face is bright red. "It *is* her story. Her daughters were almost kidnapped. You think that doesn't have anything to do with her?"

I've never really thought about it that way. I'm not sure how I feel about Poppy's question, so I ignore it. "You were such a hypocrite during that interview. 'Oh, I never read online comments about myself!'" I try to imitate her but my eyes are swimming with tears, and the words come out as strangled sobs.

"I'm a hypocrite?!" Poppy raises her voice. "*You're* the hypocrite. You say that you don't want everyone to know our business, and then you go and confirm Lena's story, even though you know it's the *one* thing I don't like to talk about. I know you're pissed at Mom or whatever, but did you stop to think how I would feel about it?"

My stomach twists uncomfortably. "I wasn't trying to confirm Lena's story. I wasn't thinking!"

She narrows her eyes at me. "That's my point. You should have been thinking about us! Everything you do has the potential to affect our business. You know that."

Poppy's right. I've known for a long time that my actions are always a reflection of the business, the brand, and of my family. And that's the whole problem.

My tears are building, ready to spill over my cheeks. I look up at the cloudless blue sky and try to blink them away while taking slow, steady breaths. Something warm and sticky splats on my face, part of it sliding into my open mouth. I scream in horror and swipe my fingers against my cheek. I don't even have to look at them. The disgust on Poppy's face tells me everything I need to know.

A bird just pooped in my mouth.

Email from Anonymous

From: youareawasteofspace@gmail.com
To: poppyandclaire@dixondaily.com
Subject: kill yourselves

whoring yourselves out at fashion week again? don't you have anything better to do? oh wait you don't. instead of brains you have selfie sticks.

Block this email address
Future messages from youareawasteofspace@gmail.com will be marked as Spam.

Chapter 7

FASHION BLOGGER EATS SHIT AT NYFW!

The video shows a profile shot of Poppy and me, standing on the curb and yelling at each other. I look up at the sky, and SPLAT! Bird poop all over my face. Then it flies back into the air as the clip rewinds and plays again. And again, and again, and again. It's a five second clip stuck in a time warp, set to the tune of an electronica song.

I sink as low as possible in my seat and bury my face in my hands.

"How many views does it have now? No, don't tell me." I cringe as Poppy checks her phone. "Yes, tell me." I have to know how quickly this is spreading. The cell phone video was uploaded before our cab ride was over. It didn't take long before someone tagged us in the comments. I was mortified but could not tear my eyes away. The second we were on board the plane I made Poppy buy the in-flight Wi-Fi so I could continue to torture myself.

"Five thousand." Poppy says. "But at least one hundred of those were you, so it's not as bad as it seems!" Her voice is light, trying to play this off as no big deal.

I groan and pull my legs up to my chin, willing this video to magically disappear from existence.

"Maybe no one from school will even see it." Mom's voice cuts through the tragic silence from the front seat, on our ride home from the airport. The only good thing to come out of this video is that she feels so bad for me she's not angry about what happened at the interview. Not right at this moment, anyway.

Poppy's phone beeps. "That's someone from school, isn't it?" I ask.

"Olivia," she confirms. She types a quick reply. "Do you think Rafael will see it?"

A fresh wave of misery washes over me. I grab my stomach and double over, resting my forehead on my knees. "I can't believe I forgot about Rafael."

"Do I know Rafael?" Mom asks from the front seat.

"No," Poppy and I say.

"Maybe he won't see it. Isn't he technophobic, or something?" Poppy says.

"You're friends with a boy who's afraid of computers?" Mom looks in the rearview mirror, trying to figure out what's going on.

"No. Maybe. It's unclear."

Mom pulls the car into the driveway. We climb out of the car, and I see a box with my new cell phone sitting on the porch.

"I thought it wasn't in stock until next week." The last thing I want right now is a way to communicate with the outside world. What I need is a way to pretend the outside world doesn't exist.

"I found it on a different website and had it sent overnight." Mom gives me a sympathetic smile and follows Poppy inside, leaving me on the porch.

"I told you, you didn't have to do that," I mumble as I sit with my back against the door. The heat leeches through my clothes uncomfortably, but instead of moving, I lean my head back and close my eyes.

The video is bad enough, but it's only one item on a long list of things that have gone wrong today. Pretty soon Rafael will know exactly who I am, and he'll know I lied to him. And to top it off, Lena is going to write that terrible story about my family.

I should have known better than to confirm the allegations, but I was so tired of not talking about it. It sounds weird, but *not* talking about how I was almost kidnapped is a lot of work. I'm probably the only person in the world who gets exhausted by not doing something. When I want to say something but can't, it takes all of my effort to keep my mouth shut. And I've been choking down this secret for nine years.

But pretty soon it won't be a secret anymore, and I'll be free to talk about it as much as I want. So . . . what will I say? And who will I say it to? No one will understand except Poppy, and she's made her feelings perfectly clear.

The brown cardboard box is heavy in my hands. I can't ignore it forever, I guess. Up in my room with a locked door, I plug in the new phone and connect to our Wi-Fi. Within seconds, the buzzing starts. Text messages, emails, and notifications from every social media site available come rushing in. I ignore the backlog of texts from the last few days and concentrate on the recent ones, most of which contain a link to the video. A couple of people from school ask how I'm doing, but mostly it seems everyone just wants to make sure I've seen it.

I ignore them and log into the BITES message board. The one-up game has thrived in my absence. I scroll through several familiar comments from the regulars. Nora is complaining about her latest red-eye, one of Gideon's brothers did something unforgiveable to the keyboard of his laptop, and Serge evidently got into it with a clown, if I'm understanding his use of emoji. I crack my knuckles and type out my contribution.

girlcode

At an interview with a fashion magazine, I accidentally told the reporter my mom's DEEP DARK SECRET, and now my family thinks the reporter is going to use that secret to destroy our family's brand. Also, a bird pooped in my mouth, someone recorded it on their phone, and the video is going viral.

I didn't tag anyone in my post, but Nora's response is instantaneous.

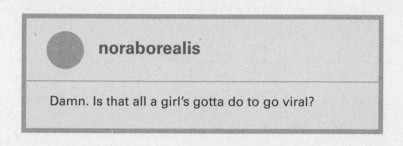

noraborealis

Damn. Is that all a girl's gotta do to go viral?

I can't help but laugh. Of course Nora wishes she could switch places with me. I don't know why, but she always acts like she wants her parents to give up travel blogging for the less transient gig my mom has, while I'd be happy to take the next flight to Iceland or Thailand or Greece. Especially right now.

Another text comes in. My heart skips a beat, wondering if it's Rafael, before I remember that he doesn't have a phone. Or my number. Or a reason to contact me.

Olivia

That video is insane! Maybe it'll make you more famous?

I roll my eyes.

Olivia

I met Rafael. Super cute.

I'm tempted to open my window and throw my phone into oncoming traffic, but I know it would be pointless. A new one would just show up on my doorstep tomorrow. I flop down on my bed, close my eyes, and let my mind wander to Rafael. The first thing I noticed about him was his dark eyes, followed by his unruly hair. But it's the smile that I can't shake from my mind, and the way his grin dominates every feature on his face, demanding attention. And most intriguing of all is the way he has nothing to hide. He offered to tell me anything, and I asked for nothing. It's not a mistake I'll make twice.

Resentment floods my stomach as I picture him eating lunch with Olivia. She would shake her curls, obviously. It's her go-to move, and it mesmerizes the boys every time. Rafael would smile, and they'd take turns asking and answering questions about their childhoods and their favorite foods and pet peeves. And Olivia would answer honestly, because she's got nothing to hide. Instant connection, just like he described. I hate how much this warped fantasy bothers me.

Jealousy is new territory, because even though Jackson never had feelings for me, I always knew he liked me best. Of all the girls at Highland, I was his favorite. The thought of competing with Olivia for Rafael's attention is as uncomfortable as it is unfamiliar. The only person I've ever competed with is Poppy, and it's pretty clear how that's turned out. She wins everything, every time.

I go to YouTube and find the video of me. There are now twenty thousand views. Fan-freaking-tastic. I scroll down to the comments, even though my gut is screaming that I shouldn't. Poppy and I don't even moderate the comments on our own videos, because it takes too much time and energy. It's also depressing as hell.

It's mostly people laughing, at me, which doesn't feel good, but there's meaner stuff too.

Princess Claire got exactly what she deserved.

These girls are dumb and ugly I don't understand why they're famous!!!!!

Bird shit is a better look than most of the crap she wears.

Come to my house and I'll show you what you can eat.

If I have to see one more picture of these skanks modeling clothes, I'm going to lose it. NO ONE CARES ABOUT YOUR DAMN OUTFIT OF THE DAY.

I roll my eyes at that one. Maybe no one should care, but my entire life is proof they do.

I continue reading the comments.

Did you ever notice that Claire is the obvious misfit of the family? Ashley and Poppy are both tall and gorgeous and Claire's not. I feel bad for her, I really do.

I won't lose sleep over any of today's comments, but what will they say when they find out Poppy and I were almost kidnapped, and Mom kept blogging like nothing had happened? It'll probably be horrible stuff about how Mom doesn't love us and she only uses us to make money.

In other words, nothing that hasn't been said before.

Email from Mint Condition

From: advertising@mintcondition.com
To: poppyandclaire@dixondaily.com
Subject: Sponsorship Opportunity

Hi There!

My name is Caleb Woods, and I work in advertising at Mint Condition Antiseptic Mouthwash. Our team has seen your viral video, and we love it! You girls are young and fun and exactly the right people to help us launch our new Antiseptic Mouthwash for teens! Now is the perfect time to capitalize on all your new viewers with a funny and lighthearted take on the "bird incident," while also helping your viewers get cleaners mouth, stronger teeth, and fresher breath.

Please let us know as soon as possible if you are interested in a collaboration, and we can talk specifics.

Have a great day!
Caleb

Chapter 8

"Hey Claire! Want to come to my party this weekend?" Parker's voice carries across my first period English classroom.

I sit taller in my seat and fix him with a withering stare. "Not on your life."

"But my boy Wyatt is bringing a keg." Wyatt smirks as Parker slaps him on the back. "We're going get shit-faced!"

At least half the class bursts into laughter, but no one is louder than Parker and his buddies.

That's how my morning goes. Views on the video were up to fifty thousand by the time I left for school. I begged Mom to let me stay home, but she sent me out the front door with a smile, a wave, and the unhelpful advice to "shake it off."

When the bell rings for lunch, I make a beeline for the library. I'm not about to face a crowded cafeteria full of people who are openly laughing at me. I weave through the stacks, looking for an empty table where I can wallow in peace, when a voice stops me in my tracks.

"What're you doing here?" Rafael clears away a pile of books to make room for me to sit. My stomach catapults into my throat and my hands start to sweat for reasons that have nothing do with the temperature in the room. I hesitate, torn between competing desires to sit down and run away.

"What're *you* doing here?"

He holds up his physics textbook in response. "How was your weekend?"

I narrow my eyes, unable to believe he hasn't seen the video, or at least heard about it. But then again, he's sitting by himself in the library, he's new at school, and he doesn't have a cell phone. Maybe I've lucked out big time. I push aside a handful of flyers for the school blood drive and sit down across from him.

"It was . . . unexpected." Since I'm on the verge of being caught, I may as well keep the lies to a bare minimum.

"Well, I missed you. Parker and I were partners in College Prep. He was even less interested in talking than you."

"That's not fair! I like to talk."

He raises an eyebrow and waits. An invitation to talk, to ask any question. I don't want to start with something too personal, but I want to know more than his favorite color. "What do you miss most about India?"

He runs a hand through his hair with a dreamy look in his eyes. "That's a good one. Probably the festivals. There's always something to celebrate, and I loved that."

I mentally add India to my bucket list, and make a note to ask Nora if she's ever been there.

"What do you miss most?" He asks, catching me off guard.

"About what?"

"Anything. Your choice."

No. *No, no, no.* I did not sign up for this. "Pass."

"Sure thing, Parker." His smile is playful and inviting. Just like him.

I sigh, resigning myself to the question. This is one thing I won't lie about. I'd never do that to my dad. "I miss my dad. He died."

Rafael's face falls, and I'm compelled to keep talking. "I've forgotten a lot of specific details about him, which makes me feel guilty and sad—and also a little relieved. And then I feel guilty that I'm relieved. If it hurts this bad with the few memories I have, I can't imagine how unbearable it would be if I remembered everything. But I still think I'd rather remember, because those memories are all I'll ever have, you know?"

I'm pretty sure that jumbled mess of word vomit made zero sense, but Rafael nods anyway, like he really does know. His eyes lock on mine. In this instant, I feel more seen than I ever have on the internet, despite the thousands of likes and comments and views from strangers.

"See?" I sit back in my chair and attempt to lighten the mood. "I can talk."

He pretends to bow before me in worship. "You put Parker to shame."

"Oh, come on now. I'm sure that Parker is halfway toward falling in love with you after staring into your eyes during class."

His eyebrows shoot up, and I realize way too late that my attempt at a joke makes it sound like *I'm* halfway toward falling in love with Rafael. "Not that looking into your eyes means that someone is going to fall in love with you. I mean, I still don't believe that science experiment you told me about. I just meant that, you know, Parker's a pretty good-looking guy. I wouldn't blame you if you two hit it off."

A girl with a clipboard walks up to our table, putting an effective end to my rambling. *Thank goodness.* Flames of embarrassment are still crawling up my neck.

"Want to sign up for the school blood drive?" She thrusts the clipboard in front of me. I grab it and quickly scrawl my name, before she has a chance to make a crack about bird crap.

"Have you donated before?" Rafael asks as he takes the clipboard from my outstretched hand.

I shake my head. I signed up to do it last semester, but Mom told me not to because she didn't want me to be dizzy for our photo shoot. *Yes, really.* "Have you?"

He nods. "A few times, when Dad's clinics were low in supply."

"Does it hurt?" I don't think I'm scared of needles, but I can't remember the last time I got a shot, so maybe I am. Just like there are probably thousands of people who have never been on an airplane but would be afraid to fly, once they're sitting on the runway with the engine rumbling under their feet.

"No." He shakes his head, then pauses. "Not really, anyway."

I laugh. "Great. That'll help me sleep tonight."

"Don't sweat it. You'll be fine. But . . ." He trails off with a bizarre look on his face.

"What?" Is he trying to tell me I *won't* be fine?

"If you're worried about it, you could give me your phone number. I give great pep talks." He signs his name on the sign-up sheet next to mine, like it's no big deal, like he didn't *just ask me for my phone number!* I break out in a grin as he hands the clipboard back to the girl and she leaves.

"Did you get a cell phone?"

"No. But I've never let that get in my way before," he says with a wicked glint in his eye.

My eyes land on the vein that trails down his forearm and into his hand. I had no idea arms could be such an attractive feature. Eyes? Yes. Teeth? Yes. Hair? Obviously. But arms? I'd never noticed before this exact moment. I tear my eyes away and shake my head, trying to clear it from the bicep-induced fog. "You're serious?"

"Afraid so. Besides, you never know when I'll have a College Prep emergency one of these days and need your help." The teasing glint is still in his eye, and it makes me feel reckless and breathless. I grab a pen from my bag and take his palm in mine. I write my phone number in big, bold numerals, the way girls do in movies.

And that's that. He has my phone number. And I don't have his. *If he even has one?* He must have one. He was obviously teasing me before; there's no reason to ask for my number if he doesn't have a phone.

I promise myself I absolutely, under no circumstances, will sit around clutching my phone in my hands. But every hour after school that passes without hearing from him feels like a very peculiar kind of torment. I wonder if "waiting for a cute guy to text" has ever been employed as an actual torture device. If not, it should be.

I'm in my bedroom avoiding vlog edits when my phone buzzes. I look at the screen, expecting to see a message, but it *keeps* buzzing; it's a phone call from an unknown number. It must be the solar panel salespeople again. I want to ignore it, but if I do, they'll leave a voicemail, and if I ignore that then that tiny icon will haunt my home screen for eternity. Which, ugh. When will they realize that leaving a voice-mail makes me actively hate them?

I pick up the phone just in time. "Stop calling me."

"Claire?" Rafael's voice surprises me so much I almost drop the phone.

"Why are you calling me?"

"Oh, uh . . ." His voice falters. "You gave me your phone number."

"So you could *text* me." No one actually calls each other anymore.

"Contrary to popular belief, not all telephones are equipped to send or receive text messages." I swear I can hear the amused smile on his lips.

"Are you . . . are you at a payphone?" I picture him in a glass box, feeding quarters into the phone. The image makes me question his sanity. But also, it's kind of endearing.

"What? No!" Rafael laughs loud and long, and my cheeks flush. His voice is so close, right in my ear, and I can hear his slow breath. It's strangely intimate. "This is my abuela's landline."

So much for intimate. "Why are you calling?"

"I have a College Prep emergency." His voice is calm and matter-of-fact. It couldn't sound less like an emergency.

"That's not a thing."

"I need help with the homework."

"Is this about your handshake? Ms. Grant was right. It could use some work."

"Damn. You know how to hit a guy where it hurts," he says, which makes me laugh. "But really, my resume needs work. Will you look at it for me?"

"Sure." I give him my email address, and thirty second later my phone beeps, alerting me his resume landed in my inbox. We hang up, and I open the document.

RAFAEL ALEJANDRO LUNA
645 E. Encinas Avenue
The Surface of The Sun, USA

• SUMMARY •

I would really like a job at your company, but you should know that I have no professional job experience and have only been to four days of "College Prep." My teacher thinks I need to work on my handshake but says that I show great potential.

• OBJECTIVES •

To get a job that will give me a lot of money in exchange for a minimal amount of work. Weekends off would be appreciated.

• EDUCATION •

Twelve years of tutoring in various countries. Five days of public school in Gilbert, Arizona. (Don't forget about the College Prep though!)

• EMPLOYMENT HISTORY •

Does volunteering count? What about involuntary volunteering that was mostly mandated by my father? I did a lot of that.

• PROFESSIONAL SKILLS •

I'm a pretty good bowler. But not that thing with pins and an alley. It's a cricket thing. Hard to explain. Also good at: making friends and binge-watching Netflix.

• HOBBIES & INTERESTS •

See above.

By the time I'm finished reading the resume, tears are running down my face from laughing so hard. I open his resume in a word processing program and begin making notes. When I'm finished, it looks like this.

RAFAEL ALEJANDRO LUNA
645 E. Encinas Avenue
The Surface of The Sun, USA
Alternate Address: Hell on Earth

• SUMMARY •

I would really like a job at your company, but you should know that I have no professional job experience and have only been to four days of "College Prep." My teacher thinks I need work on my handshake but says that I show great potential.

Is it okay to lie on your resume? I don't remember Ms. Grant ever praising you for your potential.

• OBJECTIVES •

To get a job that will give me a lot of money in exchange for a minimal amount of work. Weekends off would be appreciated.

Don't forget to ask for holidays off too. If you don't ask now, you'll be stuck working Christmases from now until forever.

• EDUCATION •

Twelve years of tutoring in various countries. Five days of private school in Gilbert, Arizona. (Don't forget about the College Prep though!)

This is a good place to mention your staring contest with Parker Evans. That should really highlight the caliber of education we receive at Highland.

• **EMPLOYMENT HISTORY** •

Does volunteering count? What about involuntary volunteering that was mostly mandated by my father? I did a lot of that.

Pretty sure it doesn't count.

• **PROFESSIONAL SKILLS** •

I'm a pretty good bowler. But not that thing with pins and an alley. It's a cricket thing. Hard to explain. Also good at: making friends and binge-watching Netflix.

I think the employer would appreciate a running list of all the shows you're currently binge watching.

• **HOBBIES & INTERESTS** •

See above.

Nothing says "I put a lot of time and hard work into this resume like the answer 'See above.'"

I email him my updated version of his resume, as well as my resume for him to proofread, and impatiently wait for a reply. Three minutes later, he responds.

I knew I liked you.

I reply with a smiley face emoji. SIGNOFTHETIMES would be so proud.

Email from Sun + Sky Apparel!

From: molly@sunandskyapparel.com
To: poppyandclaire@gmail.com
Subject: Free T-shirts!

Poppy and Claire!

I'm a huge fan! I recently came aboard as the marketing and advertising director for Sun + Sky Apparel! We're a family-owned small business that specializes in graphic T-shirts! Our designs are clean and minimalist and super chic! If you send me your sizes, I would love to get some free T-shirts in the mail for you, no obligations! (That said, you may have noticed that our logo is a bird, and after your recent video, it could be SO GREAT for both of us if we collaborated in some way!)

I hope to hear from you soon! And I hope you love our shirts!

Molly!

Chapter 9

The sweaty and humid atmosphere that usually permeates the school gymnasium is gone. Instead, it's currently cold and smells faintly of a doctor's office. The room has been transformed into a blood donation center and is filled with Red Cross workers and students who are thrilled to have a valid excuse to skip class. A guest lecturer is talking to my class about college admissions right now, but I'm not worried about missing it because I've been obsessively researching colleges for months.

A student council member checks me in and directs me to a tall, thin woman with a nametag that reads "Jada," who has long black cornrows wrapped in a big bun on top of her head. She ushers me into a makeshift cubicle on the left side of the room. The cubicle is small, with only two folding chairs and one computer inside. I take a seat in one of the chairs and wrap my arms around myself.

"Sorry about the temperature. If we keep it too warm, people tend to pass out." Jada pushes a few keys on her computer.

"Should I be worried about passing out?"

"Do you pass out easily?" Her face is expressionless, and it worries me that she took my joke seriously.

"No?"

"Then you should be fine. Just follow the instructions. Now, I'm going to ask you a series of questions. Please answer yes or no." She charges forward before I can dwell on the idea of passing out in front of all my classmates and asks me a long series of questions about my current heath, my medical history, my travels, and my sexual history. Every time I answer, she types a notation on the computer keyboard.

I guess I pass the test because soon she's checking my temperature, blood pressure, and pulse. After those tests, she pulls a needle out of a sealed package and explains that she needs a blood sample to assess my iron levels. She pricks my finger and has it drip into a small vial filled with liquid, explaining as she does so that if it doesn't drop to the bottom quickly enough, I won't be allowed to donate. But I pass this test too, and she prints out sticky labels with my name and a bar code on them, slaps them on a handful of empty vials, and walks me across the room.

A plump older woman with gray hair and rosy cheeks motions for me to sit down in a chair that is part recliner, part hospital bed. She reminds me of a fairy tale grandma. I place both my arms up on the armrests and wait for her to untangle a mess of clear tubes.

"Do you have a preference which arm?" Her friendly and reassuring voice perfectly pairs with her soft face and gray hair.

"I don't think so."

"Are you right handed?"

I nod, and she walks over to my left side. She scrubs my arm with an alcohol swab, tells me I'll feel a small pinch, and before I know it, the needle is in my arm.

"You can breathe now, sweetheart."

"That's it?" I exhale. "That wasn't so bad." She pats my arm and walks away.

I watch the blood drain from my arm, through the tube, into a clear vial. It's flowing way faster than I expected.

"You did it!" I look up to see Rafael standing by my feet, donning a sticker that says, "I tried!"

"You didn't?"

He shakes his head and pulls up an empty chair next to me. "I've spent too much time out of the country."

"Ahh. You failed the test." I try to sit up, but get a head rush and fall back against the chair.

"I suppose so." He cocks his head to the side and examines me with a smirk.

"Are you going back to class?" I ask. *Please say no.*

"I think I can stay long enough for a cookie." He nods toward the front of the room, where a folding table is piled high with bakery boxes and juice pouches. "Did it hurt?"

I shake my head vigorously and am overcome by the need to puke. I close my eyes. "Nope. Not even a little bit. Felt great. I could do this all day."

Metal chair legs scrape against the floor, but I'm afraid if I open my eyes I'll vomit, so I leave them closed. With my luck, someone would film me puking. It's been two weeks since the bird video went viral, and though my inbox is still filling with sponsorship requests, people at school are over it.

Mostly.

Fortunately, Rafael really does live off the grid, and seems to have missed the scandal. I find myself gravitating automatically to him at lunch and in class. Despite my lies, it's easier to be myself around him than the other kids at school.

"I have another question." My eyes are still closed, and the words sound fuzzy in my own ears. We've been asking and answering questions all week, slowly getting to know more about each other, and I've been thinking about this one for a while. I'm finally going to ask him about his exes, about all the other girls he charmed with his hair and his eyes and his premeditated vulnerability.

"Excuse me! Is she okay? She looks . . . not okay." Rafael's voice gets far away and then close again.

"Claire, can you open your eyes for me?" It's the grandma voice, and this time, I do. My head spins. She studies my face closely. "Can you hear me?"

I nod.

"Do you feel okay?"

I nod again, not really registering her question.

"Well, you're done anyway. That was fast." She unhooks the tubes from my arm, pulls out the needle, and wraps my elbow with a neon green bandage.

I try to stand up but she holds out a hand to keep me in the chair. "Stay here for at least fifteen minutes." I slump back, more than happy to oblige.

Rafael brings me a handful of cookies and three different kinds of juice. He looks sheepish as he holds them out to me. "I wasn't sure what to get."

I accept a chocolate chunk cookie and close my eyes while I nibble on it. Before long I'm feeling less dizzy, and I tell Rafael he can go back to class. I don't want him to feel the need to hang with me just because I got sick.

He must not hear me because he sticks around. When the fairy-tale grandma gives me the go-ahead to leave, there are only ten minutes of class left and it seems pointless to attend. Without talking about it, we both turn toward the parking lot. He holds the door open, and I walk through it into the blazing sunshine. Everyone always characterizes Arizona weather as a dry heat, as if that's a good thing. All that means is that when you walk outside it feels like stepping into Satan's oven, even in early October.

"Where were you at lunch today?" I ask as I step off the sidewalk curb into the parking lot. My knee gives a little as I do, and Rafael immediately reaches out and grabs my arm to steady me. My skin heats at his touch. He holds on for a couple of seconds, and I feel myself getting woozy again. Maybe there was something to Jada's claim that the heat makes people pass out. "Did you ditch me for Parker?"

He laughs and releases my arm. "I was working on a project."

"For what class?"

"College Prep."

"Your resume? I think you nailed it on your first try."
I glance at Rafael but he's no longer walking next to me.
He's stopped a few paces behind, opens his backpack, and
pulls out a piece of paper.

"Are you sure you're feeling alright? You look pale
again," he says and catches up to me in two big steps. He
studies the paper in his hands with a frown.

"I feel fine. What is that?" I reach for it, but he pulls it
back.

"I was working on your resume, but I can show it to you
another time." He tries to stuff it in his backpack, but this
time I grab it from him, ripping the corner.

"My resume?" I raise my eyebrows and look down at the
paper in my hand.

CLAIRE DIXON
702 E. San Pedro Avenue
The Sahara Desert, USA

• SUMMARY •

I definitely don't need a job at your company because I'm
super famous, but you probably do want to hire me so I
can take pictures of your business and promote it online.

• OBJECTIVES •

To have a reason to buy fancy new work clothes.

• EDUCATION •

Twelve years of public school in Gilbert, Arizona, plus
one whole month of College Prep!

• EMPLOYMENT HISTORY •

Seventeen years of unpaid modeling.

• PROFESSIONAL SKILLS •

Styling outfits, putting on makeup, and braiding my hair.

• HOBBIES & INTERESTS •

Reading graphic design books. Sometimes I pretend to be into rock climbing and chess, but I'm really not. Will not work with birds.

My nose burns as tears build behind my eyes. I clear my throat as my hand drops to my side. My fingers are tingly and numb. "You *know*?"

"About the bird? Of course I know. It's all anyone's talking about!" He shakes his head with a laugh. It makes me feel even worse.

"Why didn't you say something earlier?" My voice is small, and I hate myself for it.

"I was giving you a chance to tell me yourself."

I cringe. *Why didn't I tell him myself?* It was obvious he was going to find out sooner or later. "I didn't know how to bring it up!" I cross my arms over my chest. "Hi Rafael! My name is Claire and I'm a fashion vlogger with an embarrassing viral video. Want to be friends?" I scuff my toe against the ground so I don't have to look at him.

"Well . . . There's more to it than that."

My head snaps up. "What are you talking about?"

Not the blog. Please not the blog.

Finding my vlog is one thing. It's a little embarrassing, but whatever. I can even handle him knowing about Mom's Instagram. But I don't know what I'll do if he found the Mommy Blog.

"What do you want to know?" he asks.

I cross my arms and stare at him, waiting for the bomb to drop.

"I know that your mom didn't know she was having twins until you were born. I also know Santa brought you a puppy when you were seven years old. Poppy wanted to name him Marshmallow because he was white. You wanted to name him Chocolate because it annoyed Poppy. Your mom eventually called him S'more. What else? How about the time you got mono in seventh grade from a game of spin the bottle?" He pauses, a smile in his eyes, like this is all some big joke.

I turn toward my car, willing myself not to cry. I don't care that he knows those things. Not really. What I'm most upset about is the fact that the illusion is shattered. I don't have a blank slate with him anymore.

"Hey—wait up!" He jogs after me, and when we reach my car I turn to face him.

He smiles wider and takes a step toward me. Instinctively, I step away until my back is pinned against the car and I hold my breath. The irony is not lost on me. Less than ten minutes ago, I would have jumped at the chance to be this close to him, and now, I want nothing more than to get away from him.

I try to fight back the tears, but fail spectacularly. To keep him from seeing them, I squeeze my eyes shut. My legs are shaking, and I brace myself for whatever is coming next. How many things about myself Rafael is going to tell me? When he doesn't say anything and I'm sure I won't start sobbing into his chest, I open my eyes again. "You cheated."

He's not smiling anymore. In fact, he looks confused. "What do you mean?"

"Our game. All the questions and answers! We were on a level playing field, and you ruined it. How are we supposed to be friends now, when you have such an advantage?"

"I—" He shakes his head, looking stunned. "I didn't mean to make you mad. Honestly. It was a joke."

I fish my keys out of the black abyss that is my purse and wrench open my car door. "That's what all the stalkers say."

He recoils like I slapped him. After a pause, he takes a deep breath. "Can I drive you? I don't want you to—"

"To what? Have a swooning fit while I'm driving and black out? I'm not that fragile, Rafael, and I don't need you to save me." I hop inside the driver's seat, slam the door shut, and pull out of the parking lot as quickly as I can, heart pounding in my ears. As badly as I want to, I don't look into the rearview mirror. Not even a glance.

My hands have stopped shaking and my breathing has slowed by the time I get home. After I turn off the engine, I look into the rearview mirror. Mascara runs down my cheeks, away from my blotchy, red eyes. I don't want Mom to see me like this, but there's no way to avoid it. My mind is too busy reeling from my conversation with Rafael to think of an excuse, and the heat forces me out of the car before I can pull myself together. The only option is to keep my head down and make a beeline around several full garment racks.

"Claire! Is that you?" Mom's voice reaches me before my feet hit the stairs.

"Yep."

"How was school?"

A nightmare, actually. Thanks for that.

"Fine." I remove the emotion from my voice, hoping she'll leave me alone.

"Come here! I need your opinion on these shoes I just bought."

"I don't care!" I yell. And then, even though my brain is ordering my mouth to stop, I keep going. "Can't you make a decision without me? That's what you've been doing for the last seventeen years."

"What is going on with you?" A chair scrapes across the kitchen tile and she walks into the foyer. When she sees me standing on the stairs, all puffy and red and covered in mascara, the look on her face changes from annoyance to worry. "What's wrong? Why are you crying?"

"I'm not crying."

"Why *were* you crying? Is this about the video?"

"No. And yes. It's about everything in my entire stupid life." I stomp up to my room, slam the door, open my laptop, and get online.

The cursor blinks black and white in the rectangle box, waiting for instructions. My fingers wander across the keyboard without my permission until I'm staring at a home page that is familiar and foreign to me at the same time. I'm responsible for the front-end coding and design of the blog, but I never bother to actually read the content anymore. Reading it makes me feel weird and frustrated, and I find I'm happier when I ignore it. But since I'm already angry at Mom and Rafael and life in general, I let my eyes skim the page.

It's a thing of beauty. I can't deny it. Before Mom let me take over the design of the blog, it was cluttered with pictures and text and links. Now it's simple and streamlined. It's so user-friendly that even people Mom's age can navigate it, which I guess is the point. But once I stop admiring my own handiwork, I focus on the most recent post, and I'm not as thrilled about what I see.

It's a picture of the three of us from Labor Day weekend. We're sitting on the edge of a dock with our feet dangling off the edge. People see it and think they're looking at a fun family day at the lake, but it's just a catalogue image meant to sell swimsuits. (Now on clearance!) Below the picture are links to the items we're wearing, and every click is a paycheck for Mom. But what she's really capitalizing on is not a desire for cute swimwear. When I look at these pictures all I see is "For Sale: Perfect family. Perfect body. Perfect Mom. Perfect daughters. Perfect life." Too bad there's no way to buy what she's truly selling.

It's nothing but a series of pretty images that make other people jealous and resentful. If only there was a way to make people realize the blog is a lie big enough to fill the internet.

Mom and Poppy would be out of a job.

But at least I'd finally be free.

—Four Months of Ignored Voicemail—

July 24 @ 9:39 AM from 480-555-2718

"Hi this is Ryan from Arizona Solar Group—"

Message Deleted

July 27 @ 7:52 PM from Erica Mitchell

"Hey Claire. It's Erica. I'm sorry about everything that's been going on—"

Message Deleted

July 31 @ 9:52 PM from Mom

"If you would answer my texts I wouldn't have to—"

Message Deleted

August 7 @ 11:03 AM from Poppy

"Hey. I'm in the checkout line at Target and this creepy guy won't stop telling me how pretty I look. Gag. So I'm calling you so I look busy and hopefully he'll get the hint . . . I know you'll never listen to this so I guess I can say whatever—OMG! Have you seen this month's cover of *MyStyle*? Poor Kylie. Oh! My turn to checkout. See ya."

Message Deleted

August 16 @ 8:42 PM from Emily Cavanaugh

"Erica told me she tried—"

Message Deleted

Chapter 10

*B*EEEEEEP.

My heart thumps in my chest as a car horn tears me from my sleep. The haunting image of a blue minivan fills my mind, and I shake my head to clear it. I feel fuzzy and disoriented the way I always do after a nap. It's like my body knows I'm not supposed to be asleep at this hour and reacts by scrambling my brain. The clock next to my bed reads 5:45 p.m.

My phone beeps, and my brain struggles to untangle itself. The sound that woke me from my nightmare was my phone, not a car horn. I press my hand to my chest and command my heart to slow down. When it complies, I grab my backpack from the foot of my bed, unzip the front pocket and pull out my phone.

One voicemail. From "Rafael's Abuela."

He begged me not to save his number that way, but I had to. No phone, no contact. That made him scowl.

I groan and fall into my pillow, pulling another one over my face. The mere thought of talking to Rafael makes me burn with embarrassment. On the other hand, I'd be lying if I said a part of me didn't want to see him, even if I'm still furious over his fake resume. I take a deep breath, pull the pillow off my face, and dial my voicemail. It takes three tries to remember my passcode.

"You have twelve missed messages."

Ugh. I delete them as quickly as it'll let me, but after the fifth message I get impatient and hang up. Before I have the chance to overanalyze the situation, I press dial on his grandma's number.

He answers after one ring. "Thanks for calling me back."

"What do you want?"

"Did you listen to my message?"

"No. Voicemail is annoying."

"Why?" He sounds baffled, and I wish I could see his expression.

"It's just . . . it's a lot of work, trust me."

"I want to apologize."

I wait for the apology. It doesn't come. "You're bad at this."

"I want to do it in person. We need a real conversation, and you need to see my puppy dog expression. It's good, I promise."

I allow myself a small smile. It's a good sign that he's still joking around with me. Maybe he won't hate me forever. But there's still a chance I'll hate him forever, so. It's early to get excited.

"You have my address from my resume?"

"Yeah. But I can burn it, if it makes you feel better." He has the good sense to sound embarrassed.

"Meet me at the park by my house."

I wash my face, reapply my makeup, change my clothes, and walk downstairs to face the firing squad. "Feeling better?" Mom asks.

"Yeah. Sorry I yelled at you. It was a stressful day at school." This is basically a hostage negotiation, and I'll say whatever I have to say.

She smiles. A peace offering. "Dinner is ready."

"I'm going to go for a walk. I have a headache and need fresh air."

She tilts her head and frowns. "You really should eat something."

I glance at Poppy, who is looking at me with her eyebrow raised. I nod slightly and she understands. Sometimes there's nothing better than having a twin sister.

She turns to Mom. "Didn't you want to show me those pictures you were editing today? I still have that video to edit tonight, and homework, so we should probably look at them now."

"Oh, right!" Mom gets up and clears a spot at the table for her computer.

"So, I'm going to go. I'll eat when I get home." I walk toward the front door before she can stop me.

"Be safe. Don't go far," she calls, her head already bent over the screen.

The park is a short walk from my house. The sun is setting, but it's still warm outside. Rafael is sitting on a picnic table under a ramada when I spot him. We make eye contact, and I see a ghost of a smile. I wave, and then I don't know what to do. Do I hold eye contact as I close the distance between us? I'm still pretty far away and that seems weird. I look at the ground and pretend I'm intensely interested in the line of ants marching down the sidewalk. When I'm only a few feet away from the ramada, I risk another glance. His eyes are still on me.

"Hey." I hope the sun is low enough to mask the heat creeping into my cheeks.

"Well if it isn't no-last-name-necessary Just Claire."

I lean against the side of the ramada and fold my arms.

"Bad joke. Sorry."

I still don't say anything.

"Are you going to sit down? You didn't come all this way just to turn around and go home, did you?"

"It's only, like, a five-minute walk from my house," I tell him as I move to sit on the second picnic table, across from him. But he's right. Now that I'm here, we may as well talk about it. We face each other, our legs dangling off the tables.

"I'm sorry."

"Go on."

"I acted like a stalker and read your entire life story and then threw that information in your face like it would impress you. Not to make excuses, but I have been away from the internet for way too long. I don't know how to act like a normal person around you." He shakes his head and runs his hands over his face and through his hair. "And that resume! I can't believe I did that. Sometimes I try too hard to be funny and totally bomb."

I can't help but laugh. "I'm sorry too, for lying, and hiding the truth. But for what it's worth, I don't really think you're a stalker. Not compared to some others I've seen."

"The fact that you have to say that means I've clearly done something wrong." He shakes his head and groans.

"I kind of assume everyone is at least a low-level internet stalker."

Rafael's lips twitch. "At least you're still humble."

I lean back on my palms and try to figure out a way to explain this to him without sounding conceited. "If the information is out there, I have to assume people know it. There's no way to tell if someone reads the blog just by looking at them, so I have to assume everyone knows everything about me."

Rafael nods his head. "What a weird way to live."

"You have no idea."

"So . . ." He draws out the word, as if he doesn't want to say whatever comes after it.

"So . . .?"

"Is that the reason you lied to me?"

"Pretty much. It was nice having a friend who would actually give me a blank slate."

He rubs his hand over his jaw and looks at me with a confused expression.

"I'm sorry," I say. "It was a pretty rotten way to begin a friendship."

His face falls, and I can't help but think he looks disappointed, although I'm not sure why. That's when it occurs to me that he might not forgive me. I didn't realize how much I want him to until now.

"I get it. It's fine." He runs his hand over his face again. "When you put it that way, I understand why you didn't tell me about the online stuff. What I don't get is why you lied about the other stuff, like your sister and your hobbies. You had to know I would find out the truth sooner or later."

Lying to him seemed like a good idea at the time, but putting my reasons into words isn't easy. I look down at my feet and give it my best shot. "I almost never meet someone who doesn't have a preconceived notion about me. With you, I didn't have to be Ashley's daughter or Poppy's sister or the girl whose life revolves around fashion. It was the first time in my life I could write my own story."

Rafael goes quiet again. It takes every ounce of self-control I have not to fill the silence with awkward rambling. As usual, my self-control fails me. "Just say whatever you're thinking."

"You said it was your first chance to tell your own story. I guess I don't understand why the story you chose to tell was a lie."

"What else was I supposed to say? Everything true about me has already been written."

"I don't buy that for a second."

"Why not? It's the truth. You said it yourself. You want to know what I was like as a baby? What I did for my ninth birthday? How many days of school I missed in the seventh grade because I had mono? It's all there. Every mundane detail."

A look of frustration flits across Rafael's face. "You're honestly telling me that everything in that blog is a true picture of you?" His normally friendly voice has a rough edge I can't quite place.

I shrug because I don't know what to say. As much as I hate the blog and its glossy-magazine feel, I can't help but think it's all I am. "I may not want to be seventeen years of pictures and stories all neatly packaged with a bow for the whole world to see, but those stories and pictures *are* my life."

Rafael stands up and walks toward me in two long strides. My legs, which had been swinging back and forth, freeze. In fact, my entire body freezes while my stomach ties itself in knots. He holds his hands out in front of him, like he's thinking about resting them on my legs, and my throat goes drier than the desert around me. After a fraction of a second that feels like twenty, he stuffs his hands in the front pocket of his jeans. My shoulders deflate in disappointment. I tilt my head back until our eyes meet.

"You're completely missing the point." His quiet voice sends goosebumps scattering across my skin. "As far as I can tell, you didn't write any of those stories or post any of those pictures. The things your mom wrote about you may feel true to her, but that doesn't mean they feel true to *you*. She writes about you swimming for ten years of your life and then, in your senior year of high school, you 'can't fit it in your schedule anymore' and you 'have other interests.' I have a feeling your truth would sound different than that."

"No one has ever cared what I have to say." I've never said these words out loud before, but they feel right in my mouth. I can't unsay them, and I can't unhear them. And I can't forgive Mom for turning me into a silent prop in her online world.

"I care." He leans toward me, just a couple of inches, but it's enough for the sound of his breath to drown out the cicadas in the surrounding trees.

If we were in a movie, this would be the part where he kisses me, or I kiss him. But my life has always resembled a boring reality show more than a romantic comedy, and instead of waiting for the kiss, I hear myself asking a question, even though I'm afraid of the answer. "Do you think I'm shallow?"

"Why would you ask that?" His chest moves slowly in and out, way too close for comfort. I tuck my hands under my thighs so I won't be tempted to touch him and focus instead on the smell of his spearmint gum.

"The fake resume you wrote . . . all that stuff about modeling and braiding my hair. Is that what you think of me?" I chew on my lip while I wait for his answer.

"It was a bad joke. I promise I've never thought that about you."

"Okay. Well, good, I guess."

He leans closer and touches his forehead to mine, closing his eyes. Mine shut automatically.

This is it. The romantic-comedy moment I've been waiting for.

"Do you want to know what I think about you, Just Claire?"

My heart stops. My mouth doesn't. "You know that's not my name, right?"

Moment officially killed. People this awkward shouldn't be allowed in the outside world, interacting with other humans. I slowly open my eyes and cringe.

He leans back and studies me with a frown. If I wasn't sitting on my hands, I'd reach out and smooth it away. I doubt that would fix the moment, but it would be something. And sitting here with him in the dark, I can't seem to make my body or my mouth do anything I want them to. If only I could figure out the right thing to do, or say, or not say.

My phone beeps. I don't even stop to consider whether I should ignore it before pulling it out of my pocket.

"It's just my mom checking in." I look up at him.

Rafael takes a step back and crosses his hands behind his head. Something in the gesture feels final. "If I tell you something, do you promise not to get mad?"

"I promise."

"I'm so jealous of you."

Promise rescinded. "How can you say that after the conversation we just had?" A painful lump rises in the back of my throat. I feel stupid for confiding in him and more than a little betrayed.

"I'm not jealous of your internet fame or whatever. I'm jealous of how much your mom loves you."

"She loves how much money I make for her."

He shakes his head. "Have you ever read the Twin Tuesday posts? They're a love letter to you and your sister."

"Right. A love letter sponsored by Allegra Esposito."

"Why do you hate fame so much?" He looks genuinely curious.

"You mean besides the annoying photo shoots, the embarrassing blog posts, and the total lack of privacy?"

"Yeah, besides that."

"Poppy's better at it than I am." I shrug. It sounds so trivial, but it's true. "When we started our vlog, we had the same goals. Followers and money and fame. *Influence.* Somewhere along the way, I realized it was better to change my goals than spend a lifetime in second place."

"If it weren't for Poppy, you'd want the fame?"

"No. Living for internet clicks is a one-way ticket to misery."

He gives me a hard look, but whatever he's thinking, he doesn't say it. His face clears and he pulls his keys out of his pocket. "I know it doesn't feel like it right now, but you're one of the lucky ones. I should go home. I'll drop you off."

I want to take him up on the offer, but after dodging his kiss multiple times, I'm too embarrassed to be in an enclosed space with him. I'll just screw things up worse than I already have. "It's just down the street. I'll walk."

He swings his keys once around his fingers before saying "Thanks for meeting me. Good night." I watch him walk all the way to his car.

As I'm lying in bed that night, his words echo in my head. *You're one of the lucky ones.* I know a lot of people would agree with him, but I don't. Nothing about my life feels particularly lucky right now.

Incoming Texts from Poppy

Poppy

We need to talk about which of the new sponsorship offers we're interested in.

Me

Are you serious?

Poppy

Not the mouthwash. Duh.

We don't want our brand to be "bird breath."

Me

Gee thanks.

Poppy

But those Sun + Sky shirts are pretty cute.

Me

Molly used way too many exclamation points in her email.

Poppy

So?

Me

She! Sounded! Like! She! Was! On! Drugs!

Poppy

You're on drugs. I'm taking the free shirts.

Me

Fine.

I like the gray.

Poppy

!!!!!!!!!!!!!!!!

Chapter 11

"Good morning, sunshine," Poppy says through a mouthful of cereal as I walk into the kitchen. "You're looking very 'racoon goals' today." She gestures to the mascara smudges circling my eyes. "Last night didn't go well?" She tilts her head sympathetically.

"Why do you say that?"

"Your face. Your mood. Your refusal to talk to me when you got home last night." She ticks off the reasons on her fingers, but then her voice softens. "Did he see the video?"

"Yep. And read *way* too many Twin Tuesday posts." I pour milk over my cereal and swirl it around with a spoon.

"Ouch."

"No kidding."

I spent most of the night lying awake, thinking about Rafael and what it would have been like if he had kissed me, and *why did I have to keep babbling when he was obviously trying to kiss me?*

When I wasn't thinking about Rafael, I was thinking about the blog.

And Instagram.

And our YouTube channel.

Holy crap, how are people not sick of us yet?

I have to quit. That's all there is to it. The plan was always to quit next fall when I go to college, but everything that has happened over the last few weeks has made it painfully obvious that I can't wait that long. I feel bad bailing on Poppy, but I'll lose my mind if I have to keep pretending I'm obsessed with clothes and splashing my life across the internet for everyone to see.

"Eat," Poppy commands. "You're going to need your strength. Mom wants us to pull the Halloween boxes out of storage."

I perk up in my chair and resolve to tell Poppy the truth another day. Halloween Decorating Day is my favorite family tradition, and I don't want to ruin it. I've spent seventeen years in the Dixon family circus, pulling out can wait one more day. We celebrate Halloween the way some families celebrate Christmas. Our entire house gets decked out from top to bottom. The setup is different every year, but we never skimp on the creepy sound effects or fake blood. I've never loved being scared, but I can't deny it's fun to be the one scaring people.

"Where is she?"

"Some top secret conference call. She locked me out."

After breakfast, we navigate our way through the dark closet under the stairs and pull out dozens of boxes. The light in the closet is burned out, so I can only hope we got the right ones. As I'm setting down the last box, Mom finally emerges from her office.

"What was that about?" I ask. She smiles and mimes zipping her lips. Sometimes there are not enough eyerolls for this woman.

We spend the morning listening to our Halloween playlist, snacking on candy corn, and admiring each other's work. Mom takes down all the normal décor. She pulls picture frames off the wall and boxes up candles and other random knickknacks that litter our shelves and side tables. Poppy follows behind her with an arsenal of skulls, pumpkins, and potion bottles.

I grab the spiderwebs and spend the better part of an hour stringing them along our front porch until they look creepy, not cheesy. After that, I finish the yard with headstones and skeletons. When I'm done, I stand across the street and admire my work with a smile. I'm sticky with sweat, but the house looks great.

"It might be your best work yet." Mom puts her arm around me and squeezes.

"Thanks!" I lean my head on her shoulder before I remember that I'm mad at her and shrug away from the embrace. "I'm going to take a picture." I run inside, grab my phone, and snap a few shots from different angles.

Poppy glances at my phone. "You should send one to Rafael."

"Not possible. He doesn't have a phone."

"*Still?*" She collapses onto the couch.

Part of me wants to defend him, but the other part agrees with her.

"His grandma has a phone, right? Call him."

Ugh. I never should have shared that information.

"Call who?" Mom walks into the room.

"Her boyfriend."

Mom turns to me with an expression of genuine shock. *How flattering.*

"You have a boyfriend?"

"NO!" I say, too forcefully. "I mean, no. It's just a boy from school."

"Do you like him?"

"No," I say at the same time Poppy says "Yes."

"Do you want to invite him over for movie night?"

I'm about to say no again, but I stop myself. *Do* I want to invite him over? Maybe. I definitely want to see him again, at least so I can smooth things over after last night. Movie night is a safe, platonic way to do that. I spin my phone in my fingers and sink into the couch while I think about it. My thumb hovers over the call button, when my gaze catches the grim reaper leering at me from the wall. It feels like an omen.

"Oh my gosh, enough with the angsty indecision." Poppy snatches my phone from my hand, presses the call button, and holds it to her ear. I could try to stop her, but the truth this, I don't want to. I want to talk to him. Not tomorrow, or Monday at school, but right now.

"It's not ringing. It's beeping. Why's it beeping?"

"Busy signal," Mom says.

Poppy tosses it back to me. "Lucky you. Saved by the busy signal."

Mom and Poppy resume their normal activities (setting up the perfect Insta shot) while I call every ten minutes for the next hour. I groan at the now-familiar sound of the busy signal and end another call. Disappointment spreads through my body like a viral video. It's quick and visceral. But unlike the infamous bird video, I can stop this.

"What are you doing?" Poppy calls after me as I pick up my car keys and bag. I don't bother to explain myself. The instant I stop to examine this decision is the instant I chicken out.

I find Rafael's address on the resume in my email inbox. Google Maps directs me to his abuela's house on the other side of Gilbert. As I make the fifteen-minute drive, my heart pounds. First, with excitement. Then, with nervous anticipation. And finally, as I pull up to the curb in front of the small single-story house, with dread.

What spirit possessed me and brought me here? It must have been the grim reaper. It's the only explanation.

"This is so stupid," I say out loud as I approach the front steps, but I'm not sure what I'm talking about. The fact that I'm here? That I'm so nervous? Or that Rafael insists on living in the nineties and now I have to make a fool out of myself just to say hi?

The front door opens. An old woman with wrinkled skin frowns at me. "Can I help you?"

I open and close my mouth wordlessly, like a puppet.

She raises an eyebrow, reminding me so much of Rafael. "Your phone was busy," I say lamely.

She smiles, and it lights her entire face. "You're here for Rafael?"

I nod mutely and she ushers me into the sunny house. She directs me to a school-bus-yellow kitchen table and sets a tall glass of something icy and red in front of me. It's fruity and delicious.

"Rafael!" His name is followed by a long string of words that my Intro to Spanish class has not equipped me to understand. A minute later Rafael appears in shorts and a T-shirt, his hair scruffy and un-styled. My palms begin to sweat.

"This young lady's been trying to call you, mijo." Her tone is gently scolding. She turns to me. "I told him to get a phone."

"You did?"

"¡Claro! What's he going to do if he's in a car accident?"

"Exactly!"

She shakes her head with a wry smile. They exchange a few sentences in Spanish before she disappears down the hall off the side of the kitchen.

"Hey." He runs a hand self-consciously through his hair. It's the first time I've seen him anything but confident, and it relaxes me. We can be awkward together.

"First of all, you have to get a phone."

He wrinkles his nose. "If I had a phone, you wouldn't be sitting in my kitchen right now, which would be a real shame."

I bite back a smile. "This is my last house call. Next time your phone is busy, I'm moving on to the next guy."

I expect him to call me out on this outrageous lie, but he doesn't. Obviously. He's way too nice. He leans a hip against the kitchen counter and folds his arms over his chest. We lock eyes, and I'm determined not to look away, no matter how loaded this silence gets.

"I want to be able to text you."

"Why?" His shoulders lean toward me, but his feet stay planted. He gazes at me as if the answer is vital. My palms sweat and my heart thumps violently in my chest.

I want to ask if this is how all his friendships go, but I don't want him to know how thoroughly I've been charmed by his presence in my life. It's imperative to remember that this is his plan. *Move to town. Make people like him.* He never said anything about returning those feelings.

"Because that's what friends do."

His shoulders slump. It was clearly not the right thing to say.

"Because how else am I supposed to invite you over tonight?"

He silently points to the old telephone sitting on the counter. It has a spirally cord and everything.

"It was busy."

He nudges the phone, knocking it securely in its cradle. It was off the hook the whole time. "What time should I come over?"

"Pizza and a movie at six. Bring a phone."

He shakes his head with a laugh as I show myself out the front door.

I'm high on my own courage when I get back home. I can't even suppress my smile when Mom and Poppy try to rope me into organizing boxes of clothes. We're sent so many things from sponsors that it's impossible to wear them all, let alone fit them in our closets. I offer to put away the Halloween boxes while they sort through the newest offerings, deciding what to keep, what to donate, and what to feature on the vlog.

"Rafael's coming over tonight," I announce casually as I pick up the first box.

Poppy's jaw drops. "I'm impressed."

I struggle to suppress a smile. To be perfectly honest, I am too.

The empty boxes slide easily into the closet, and as I work, my mind wanders to my latest coding project. I finished the 15-puzzle and moved on to creating a Sierpinski triangle. By the time I get to the last box, I'm itching to get back to my room and get to work. I shove the box and am surprised by its resistance. Unlike the others, it's still taped down. I peel back the tape and open the top flap. Inside is a stack of books with blank covers. I pick up the one off the top and flip through it. The pages are filled with small, neat handwriting that looks familiar. It's obviously a journal, but whose is it? My heart stutters as I realize it may have belonged to my dad.

My hands tremble as I turn to the first page.

I'm not pregnant.

Well. I think it's safe to say my dad didn't write this, and if Poppy harbored any secrets about a possible pregnancy, there's no way she would use such a crappy hiding place. This must have been written by Mom. The yellow tinted pages are evidence of its age.

I didn't realize she ever kept a physical journal. What could she possibly write in here that isn't already in the blog? Judging by the dates scrawled on the corner of the pages, it's from the year that Poppy and I were born. She was already blogging then, but she didn't have nearly as large an audience as she does now. The way she tells it, her readers were mostly her family and women she knew from high school and college. I scan through the stack of books below this one and see more journals dating back to her high school years.

Footsteps thump down the stairs. I close the box and shove it in the closet, keeping the most recent journal with me.

Poppy walks around the corner. "Wow. That was fast. What, are you trying to impress a hot guy or something?"

I hold the journal behind my back as she walks past me into the kitchen. When she's out of sight, I run up the stairs and hide the journal under my pillow. Mom's been sharing my secrets with the world for seventeen years. It's time to find out some of hers.

From: ihateyou@gmail.com
To: poppyandclaire@dixondaily.com
Subject: you suck

i can't believe anyone cares about you. you literally
contribute nothing to society.

Block this email address
Future messages from ihateyou@gmail.com will be marked
as Spam.

Chapter 12

"I'm excited to meet Rafael. Poppy won't tell me much about him, except that Emily, Erica, and Olivia all think he's 'hot.'" Mom smiles from her usual spot in front of her computer, happy to play the part of a "cool mom."

I can't help but laugh, even though she's so devastatingly embarrassing at times like this. "About that." I sit down next to her and brace myself for this conversation. "We need to talk."

She frowns and closes her laptop. "What's going on?"

"No pictures of Rafael. No mention of tonight on the blog. As far as the internet is concerned, Rafael doesn't exist." I can hear the waver in my voice, but I try to sound assertive. Just because Rafael knows about the business doesn't mean he should have to be caught up in it. I don't want him to be a pawn in Mom's online game. He deserves better than that.

"Okay."

"Really?" This was not at all the response I expected.

"Sure. Is that what you looked so stressed about?" She laughs. "I don't blog or Instagram every person I meet."

I'm so shocked, I don't know what to say. In the weeks leading up to prom, she followed Jackson and me around with her camera like she was doing an anthropological study. Now that it's obvious Jackson and I aren't together, I thought she would jump at the chance to feature a new pseudo-boyfriend.

The doorbell rings and we both stand to get it.

"I think I'm early," Rafael says as I open the door. He follows this statement with a smile that liquefies my bones. He's wearing dark jeans and a button up shirt with the sleeves rolled to his elbows. It's a *good* look. Unlike this morning, his hair is styled in his specific undone way. I'm starting to suspect his hair always looks good.

"Don't worry," Mom says from behind me. "We love early in this house."

What?

Obviously, I should have added a rule about not saying embarrassing things tonight. She opens the door wider and stands back to let Rafael in.

"Wait!" I hold out my hands, blocking him from entering. "Did you get it?"

He rolls his eyes and pulls a small silver block out of his front pocket.

"What's that?"

"It's a phone!" He flips it open and grins at the tiny, one-inch screen and old school keypad.

"It's a brick."

"It receives texts," he says.

"Emojis?"

"You never specified emojis," he says, which, unfortunately, is true. His dark eyes sparkle, clearly pleased with the loophole.

Mom watches this exchange with a baffled expression. She raises both her eyebrows at me, and it takes me a few seconds to realize what she wants.

"Mom, this is Rafael. Rafael, this is my mom." I'm not used to making introductions. It's rare I meet someone who doesn't know my mom better than they know me.

Rafael sticks out his hand, and she shakes it. "Nice to meet you, Mrs. Dixon."

"Call me Ashley. I'm glad you could make it tonight."

"Happy to be here."

I try to think of a witty reply, but I've got nothing. He looks out of place in my house. Amazing, but out of place, like when a gossip magazine posts a picture of a celebrity in line at Starbucks. *Hot high school boy visits friend's house. He's just like us!*

"Do you want us to pick up the pizza?" I ask Mom, hoping for an excuse to get out of the house.

"Poppy already left." She heads toward the kitchen. "I have some work to finish up, but feel free to make yourself at home, Rafael."

"This place looks amazing." Rafael takes in the decorations, and I'm relieved that he doesn't seem weirded out. "Can I see the rest?"

I take him on a nervous and rambling tour of the house, where I point out the most obvious things. "That's a ghost.

That's a pumpkin. That's a black cat." I sound like a flight attendant identifying exit windows.

"I lived in India, and Mexico, and Turkey, and Greece. Not outer space," Rafael reminds me with a laugh.

We tour the house (minus my room, because it's messy and filled with, like, bras and stuff), and end up in the living room. He sits on the couch and leans his head back to take in the grim reaper. "Festive!"

"Halloween is my favorite holiday," I say from the corner of the room. I was afraid it would seem weird if I sat next to him, but now I feel weird standing on one side of the room while he sits on the other. I move toward the big ottoman and sit on it cross-legged, facing him.

"Why Halloween?"

"There's no pressure to buy the right gift or make the perfect meal or say the right thing. It's nothing but fun. I love the idea that for one night a year, I can be anyone or anything I want."

He nods. "I never thought about it that way."

"Plus, candy corn is, hands down, the best food on the planet. Let's get some." I lead him into the kitchen, where Mom is editing the pictures of us in the trench coats.

"Is this for your Instagram?" Rafael looks at the screen over her shoulder.

"Yes. I'm editing pictures for a sponsor."

"What's a sponsor?"

"It's pretty boring." I move toward the living room again, hoping he'll follow me. Instead, he pulls up a chair next to Mom and sits down.

Mom pulls up a picture of Poppy and me. "These coats were sent by a clothing line. It's our job to post pictures of us wearing them."

"How many pictures?" He looks genuinely interested, but maybe he's just being polite. Either way, I'm not about to leave him alone with my mom, so I pull up a chair and sit next to him. I open the container of candy corn and toss a handful in my mouth. Rafael reaches over and grabs a few pieces, brushing his hand against mine in the process. My skin warms at his touch.

"It depends on the sponsor. Usually a few different pictures spaced out over a couple of days. And then I'll caption the pictures with a sentence about how much we love the company."

"Do you?" Rafael looks to me for an answer.

I shrug and swallow a mouthful of candy corn. "They're cute, but it's too hot here to wear them."

"But the company pays you to wear them anyway?" Rafael turns back to Mom.

She nods her head. "They send a paycheck, and we get to keep the product. It's pretty simple once you get the hang of it." She scrolls through the blog. "If the company likes us and we help them to sell a lot of clothes, they'll hire us again. You'd never realize it by looking at the blog, but it's the business side of things that takes up most of my time. Some people think fashion blogs are nothing but pretty pictures and empty words, but it's a lot more than that."

"What about the tech side of things?" Rafael asks. "I know next to nothing about the internet, but that's probably a lot of work too."

"That's all Claire. She's been in charge of our web design for the last few years."

"Seriously?" Rafael turns to me. "That's impressive."

"It's easy to impress the guy who knows next to nothing about the internet."

He smiles and turns back to the screen, where Mom is now sorting through pictures from dinner. "Are all your posts sponsored?"

"Not all of them."

"If you have too many sponsored posts and not enough normal posts, people get mad," I explain. "People don't want to feel like they're constantly being sold something, even if it's true."

"Claire hates participating in sponsored posts, but it's part of the job," Mom says.

"You mean it's part of my life. Let's go pick a movie." I stand up and, this time, Rafael follows me.

"How'd you get web design skills? And don't say it's not a big deal, because it is." He sits on the couch. I sit next to him, leaving at least a foot of space between us, and fold my legs under me. I hold out the candy corn, and he takes another handful.

I sit back and think about it. I've been doing this for so long, it's almost hard to remember a time when I wasn't helping with the blog. "I started with Scratch when I was little, probably six or seven—"

"What's Scratch?" he asks. Sometimes I forget that he's been away from technology so long that he doesn't know the basic stuff.

"You really want to know? Because I've been told I can get a little . . . enthusiastic when I start talking about this. 'Boring' is another word people use."

"I'm interested," Rafael says, and I know he's just talking about our conversation, but my traitorous skin blushes anyway.

"It's this incredible program that is designed to teach computer coding to kids. Do you want to see it? It's easier to explain that way. Wait here!" Before he can answer, I'm taking the stairs two at a time. I return seconds later with my laptop in my hands. "Okay," I say, sitting next to him and showing him the screen. "You can animate anything with this, videos or games or whatever."

I click on the "Create" button at the top of the page. "So, say you're creating a story, and you want this cat to walk across the screen and then say, 'Hello.' Here's how you do it." I show him how to snap together building blocks of code to control the cat's actions. There are blocks that controls the cat's movements, blocks to control his appearance, and blocks that allow him to make sounds. I drag a few of the blocks together to create a simple animation. "Isn't that amazing?"

He nods his head slowly. "Yeah . . . but I'm confused."

"No! It's easy! *Kids* can do it. And it's not just for fun either. It helps them communicate and it teaches computer literacy and problem-solving skills. It's being used in schools all over the country!" I pause for a breath and Rafael starts laughing. "I'm totally boring you, aren't I?"

"I can't remember the last time I was less bored."

As I'm trying to figure out whether or not that's a good thing (it is!), he picks up a piece of candy corn and bites off the white and orange part. When he's done, he eats the yellow.

"Why are you doing that?"

"Doing what?"

"Eating them like that."

"The yellow part tastes the best. I'm saving it for last."

"It all tastes the same," I say. Then I eat a piece his way, just to make sure. "Yep. Definitely the same."

The front door opens and Poppy walks inside. "Get it while it's hot!" she says as she walks into the room with two pizza boxes and a bag of cheesy bread.

Ten minutes later, we're all assembled in front of the TV with pizza, soda, and bags of candy corn. Rafael and I are sitting next to each other, slightly closer than before, but still not close enough to touch.

"What are we watching?" Mom asks as she browses through the options on our video streaming service.

"*The Orphanage?*" Poppy suggests.

"No way." I shake my head. "Too scary."

"I thought you wanted a scary movie," Rafael says.

"Not really," Poppy says as she rolls her eyes. "Claire hates being scared."

"You love Halloween but hate being scared?" Rafael looks at me with his eyebrows raised and a small smirk on his face.

"Pretty much," I say and take a bite of pizza.

"We could spend the next twenty minutes looking at movie options while our food gets cold, or we could skip

to the inevitable end of this conversation and save ourselves the trouble," I say. Mom apparently agrees because
she grabs our old copy of *Halloweentown* and puts it in the
Blu-ray.

"Never heard of it," Rafael says.

"You'll love it," I promise.

"You probably won't," Poppy says. "Unless you like
cheesy old kids movies.

"Don't pretend like you don't love it, Pop." I turn to face
Rafael. "It's hilarious. Trust me."

"I do trust you," he says with a wink.

I spend most of the movie watching Rafael watch the
movie, throwing sideways glances at him to see if he's enjoying it. It's only after the movie starts that I realize Poppy
is right. It's seriously outdated and probably dumb if you
don't have a sentimental attachment to it like I do. He
doesn't seem to mind though.

It's hard to focus on the movie when I'm sitting so close
to him. His arms are crossed so there's no way to accidentally brush my hand against his. At one point, he uncrosses
them and my heart picks up speed. He scratches his cheek.

False alarm.

After that, I spend an unhealthy amount of time trying
to decide if I should brush my knee against his, but I don't.
Of course I don't. Making the first move like that requires
a bravery I can only dream of.

Driving to his house today was an admission that I like
him as a friend. Holding his hand would be something so
much bigger. Something I'm not even sure he wants. Not
in the same way I do. I still don't know how many girls he's

kissed in the dark, how many of them still think about him long after he left and moved on.

I breathe a sigh of relief as the credits roll. If I have to spend any more time next to Rafael, in the dark, *with my family*, I'll explode. Mom opens the game cupboard and pulls out our ancient version of *Clue*. "Who wants to play?" She shakes the box in front of her and smiles at the three of us.

"I don't think so, Mom." No one could argue that I haven't put in my share of family time today.

"Come on. *Clue* is your favorite!"

Either my mother is trying to keep Rafael and me from spending time alone or she's oblivious. I shoot Poppy a pleading look. "I think I'm going to go call Brayden," Poppy says as she stands and brushes crumbs off her pants onto the carpet.

"Not while we have a guest!" Mom says. "Let's play. It'll be fun."

Poppy gives me a look that says, *I tried*, and I return one that says, *Not that hard*. She sits next to Mom who is already opening on the box and shuffling cards. So, this is happening.

Rafael and I sit next to them on the floor, and we play *Clue* for the next two and a half hours. I win the first two games, but Rafael wins the third. When we finish, it's almost eleven o'clock.

"Another game?" Mom asks as she stifles a yawn.

"Not for me." Poppy jumps up. "I'm going to go call Brayden before he goes to sleep. See you later, Rafael." She leans in to me and says "This will give Mom something to blog about" in a voice that is way too loud. I pretend not to hear and hope that Rafael is slightly deaf.

"I guess I should go to bed too. It was nice to meet you, Rafael," Mom says as we all stand up. I stretch my body, which is stiff from lying on my stomach on the carpet for so long. "Come say goodnight before you go to bed, Claire." She leaves the room.

As soon as she's gone, I turn to Rafael. "I'm sorry my mom hijacked the night and forced you to stay for so long."

He shakes his head. "It was fun. I had a really good night."

"Me too." My stomach flips nervously. I'm starting to think that being with Rafael makes everything more fun, including boring school classes and spending Saturday night with my family.

He rubs the back of his neck with his hand, making me wonder if he's as nervous around me as I am around him. "Should I expect to see my face on your mom's blog next week?"

Crap. I guess that means I can cross "slightly deaf" off the list of things I know about Rafael.

"Definitely not." I bend down and clean up the game, hoping that he'll let the subject drop. I grab our plates and empty cups and bring them into the kitchen.

"What was Poppy talking about?" Rafael follows me. I put the dishes in the sink and when I turn around, he's standing inches away from me with a small smirk on his face. I lean back against the counter and put my hands up on the edge of the sink.

"It's nothing." I'm unable to think of a believable lie with him staring at me like that. I can hardly think about anything at all with him staring at me like that.

"I won't tell anyone." His smirk turns into a grin, making my knees wobble. I tighten my grip on the sink. He raises his eyebrows, making it clear that he's willing to wait as long as it takes. It's a battle of wills in who can go the longest without talking, and I know I don't stand a chance.

"Fine." I exhale. The sooner I get this over with, the sooner we can forget about it. "On her best day, Mom's nosy. On her worst, she's an invasive exhibitionist. But don't worry, I already told her, under no circumstances are you allowed anywhere near her blog or Instagram or You-Tube or any of it."

The effect of my words is instantaneous. He steps back. "You don't want people to know we're hanging out?" His face falls, all traces of a smile vanishing in an instant.

"It's none of their business."

"Oh. Okay." He looks down at his shoes. Over my shoulder. Up at the ceiling. It's the first time he's ever had trouble meeting my eyes, and that realization is crushing.

"But I do like spending time with you!" I insist. I need to do something to save this moment, but I don't know what to do. I let go of the sink, no longer weak at the knees. My hand drops to my side, hanging loosely beside me as if it doesn't belong there. I have no idea what to do with my body, like an alien who was just beamed here from outer space, not a girl with seventeen years of practice commanding my arms and hands and mouth.

I look at his hand. I could reach across the space between us and grab it, but I have no idea if he wants me to do that. If he did, wouldn't it be obvious? The last time I held a boy's hand was on the ride home from prom with Jackson. In a rare moment of bravery, I grabbed his hand and held onto it the entire ride home. I was so sure he wanted me to. I was so sure he was going to kiss me.

I look at Rafael, and suddenly those twelve inches between us feel insurmountable. It might as well be twelve miles. "You want to play another game? Or watch something else?"

"Nah. It's okay. I should go." He finally meets my gaze. Frustration clouds his expression.

We don't say anything as we walk to the front porch. It's dark outside except for the glow that comes from a trio of life-sized witches who are stooped low over a cauldron. The one in the middle is stirring a potion with a long wooden stick in her hands. I have a sudden urge to crawl inside the giant cauldron and let them cook me in their potion, just so I can avoid the awkward goodbye that's coming. Once again, I've ruined everything with my big mouth. For the second night in a row, he's leaving with confused eyes, and I'm left with a lump in the back of my throat.

"Good night, Claire." Rafael hesitates and extends his hand into the space between us, waiting for me to shake it. I look at him in disbelief. "I thought I could use some more practice." He drops his hand and forces a laugh that sounds awkward and jerky until it's drowned out by a cackle from the witches behind us. He jumps and then laughs at himself, for real this time, and shakes his head.

"Motion sensor," I explain.

"Right. Well. Night." He nods at me before jogging toward his car, glancing sideways at the witches as he goes.

A *handshake.*

He tried to give me a good night *handshake.* Suddenly, a high five doesn't seem so terrible.

Incoming Text Messages During the Closing Credits of Halloweentown

Rafael

Now you have my number *and* you can text me. Happy?

Me

Very.

Rafael

I'll probably throw this brick away tonight.

Me

You won't. You'll become an addict like the rest of us.

Rafael

I think your mom is watching us.

Me

Hence the beauty of the text message.

Rafael:

Hence! This is all very sophisticated.

Me

What'd you expect?

Rafael

smh

c u l8r

Me

No. Stop.

Chapter 13

I can't sleep.

I close my eyes, and my mind drifts off and rewinds the night until I'm in the kitchen with Rafael. In my imagination, my back is pressed up against the kitchen sink. The smell of spearmint gum is as strong as if he were actually there with me. Headlights from a car pass through my window. I squeeze my eyes shut tighter to keep the fantasy from slipping away. I say something flirty and funny before leaning in for a kiss.

If only real life was as easy as a daydream.

With a sigh, I flick on the lamp by my bed, pick up *Know Your Onions*, and try to lose myself in its pages. But images of Rafael's hurt expression won't leave me alone. Nausea floods my stomach as I replay the moment when he stuck out his hand for me to shake.

It's the same nausea I got the day Parker Evans found those pictures of me with the braces and the acne and lumpy, lopsided boobs. At twelve years old, I had the brilliant idea to stuff my bra with toilet paper. When Mom took my picture, I thought it was because I suddenly looked more mature. Not because I looked like a silly little girl playing dress up, and she wanted pictures to post online. When Parker passed those pictures around school, I felt humiliated. Worse than that, I felt exposed. Suddenly, I didn't just *feel* awkward. I *was* awkward. Full stop. Parker had the receipts, the tangible proof that I was a loser, and it was proof that every kid at school could carry in their pocket. There was no hiding from it.

My embarrassing doorstep scene with Rafael may not have been caught on camera, but I still feel humiliated, like anyone who looks at me will see how pathetic I am. My cell phone sits on the table next to my bed, mocking me with silence. No texts. No calls. No direct messages or likes or comments or any of it. Ugh. Thanks to social media, there are so many ways to be ignored.

Rafael probably hates me now, which is understandable. I invited him here to watch a lame, old movie with my family and then made him play board games *with my family*. And then, because none of that was bad enough, I basically told him I'm ashamed to be seen with him.

I'm the worst.

I pull my pillow over my face and groan. My head hits something hard. I toss the pillow aside and grab Mom's journal, tilting it toward the light for a better look.

Holding it in my hands makes me feel uneasy. My gut tells me she wouldn't want me to read it. The entire reason people keep journals is to write down the things they can't say out loud. She doesn't like people to know her real secrets. Her life is misleading that way. Thousands of people double tap her pictures every day and think they know Ashley Dixon, but they don't know that she dyes her gray hair, edits her smile lines, and drinks diet soda for breakfast. They don't know that she cries herself to sleep at night when she misses my dad. They don't know that one of her perfect daughters is sitting here in bed thinking about betraying her privacy.

Privacy. As if that word has any meaning in our house. Poppy and I have never had any, so maybe it's not the worst thing in the world to take some of Mom's.

January 15

I'm not pregnant. I think Jason is more disappointed than I am. Logically, I know we're still young and we have plenty of time to get pregnant, but it's still hard not to be disappointed after another failed month. There's nothing I want more than to hold my baby in my arms. It's all I've ever wanted. Even when I was in high school I knew I wanted to be a mom.

In high school, my mom ran track and wrote for the school newspaper. I close my eyes and picture a younger version of Mom doing normal teenage stuff, but the image doesn't compute. All I can see is my forty-two-year-old mom running around a track with a baby strapped to her body in one of those slings. I can't think of her as anything other than a mom. Apparently, neither could she. It's so weird that she thought about babies when she was my age. Sometimes it's hard to believe we're related.

I turn to the next page.

January 17

I'm so mad at Jason I can't see straight. We got into a fight about something stupid over dinner. I don't remember what started it, but then everything spiraled out of control. Before I knew it, we were yelling at each other and I told him that he's working way too much and that he never wants to spend time with me and then he got mad at me and said I don't appreciate the fact that he's in school full time and working. By this time, I was crying into my spaghetti and he stormed out the front door.

I know it wasn't fair to blame him for working so much but I get so lonely sitting here all night waiting for him to come home. When I have a baby, it will be better. I'll be able to spend my time with her (or him). If I ever have a baby. I'm starting to doubt it will ever happen.

This is the kind of thing that Mom would never write in the blog, because it's not perfect. Messy, uncomfortable, real life has never been Ashley Dixon's forte.

My eyes begin to droop near the end of January. I slip the journal back under my pillow and finally nod off to sleep.

My hands are jittery by the time I get to school on Monday, but it turns out I don't need to be nervous. Rafael acts as if nothing ever happened, like he forgot all about the weekend.

Relief washes over me when he sits next to me at lunch, but paranoia is hot on its heels. Despite the way our nights ended, there was also a lot about the weekend that was really great. Eating candy corn, teaching him how to use Scratch, and the thump of my heart when he got close to me in the park come to mind. I don't want him to forget all of that. Is it possible that three minutes of awkwardness were enough to trump two evenings spent together?

Rafael is friendly and funny at lunch, but he keeps a careful distance from me and spends most of his time talking to Poppy and Olivia. At least he's still talking to me. Despite everything I've done, he's making an effort to be my friend.

The week drags. One school day seems to multiply into a hundred, and by the time the final bell rings I'm itchy with the anticipation of getting home to read Mom's journal. You couldn't pay me to read her blog, but for some reason, I can't make myself put down her book of secret thoughts. I lock myself in my room and read until my eyes start to burn. In early March, she finds out she's pregnant. From then on, she writes about being sick, how happy she is, and lists of baby names.

It's the most interesting part of my life until Friday morning at breakfast.

"Jackson's in town this weekend. I invited him and Cami over for dinner tonight." Mom washes down a bite of toast with a sip of Diet Coke.

I choke on my cereal. "What? Why is he in town?" I didn't think I'd have to deal with him until Thanksgiving break.

"He totaled his car. Everyone is fine, thank goodness, but Cami's taking him to buy a new one. I'm surprised he didn't tell you."

"We don't really talk anymore." I turn to Poppy. "Did you know he was coming home this weekend?"

She shakes her head. "Please. I talk to the boy less than you do."

"Not possible," I mumble into my breakfast, remembering the unanswered texts and the others with bare-bones responses. My body is trained to blush when Jackson's name comes up, and the familiar heat starts creeping into my chest. It's a bad habit that's impossible to shake.

Mom frowns. "You have been friends for so long. You should try to stay in touch."

"Emily and Erica and I are hanging out after dinner." Poppy turns to me. "You can come, if you want."

"Hard pass."

"They're not who you think they are." Her voice is firm, but I'm not interested in rehashing an argument we've have a hundred times.

"Jackson will be bored if you leave, Claire," Mom says. "And anyway, Cami told me he's excited to see you."

I sit up a little straighter. "Really? He said that?"

Poppy narrows her eyes. "I thought you didn't care what he thinks."

I silently curse my skin for blushing without my consent. "I don't."

Judging by the way Poppy rolls her eyes, she doesn't believe me. I can't say that I blame her.

"Have you ever been to Boo! At the Zoo?" Rafael asks from across the lunch table, where Olivia is sitting by his side. I try not to be jealous of their close proximity but fail spectacularly. Poppy is next to me, folding a car wash flyer into one of those cootie catchers we used to play with when we were kids.

I shake my head. "What is it?"

"I need a marker." Poppy opens my bag and paws through it until she finds a teal Sharpie. She pulls the cap off with her teeth and begins scribbling fortunes on the small paper square.

"It's a Fall Festival-type thing at the Phoenix Zoo this weekend. They have lights in the animal exhibits and music and food. Want to go with me?" Rafael's eyes light up the way they did the first day I met him, and he looks more excited than he has all week.

Poppy whistles under her breath as she continues to write.

I ignore her and focus on Rafael, thrilled that he's asking me on a date.

He turns to Olivia. "You and Poppy should come too."

Poppy's head snaps up from her fortunes in time to see my smile slip off my face. He's *not* asking me on a date. It takes a few seconds for my mouth to catch up with my brain and realize I still want to say yes. How could I say anything other than yes? A night at a Halloween festival with Rafael is bound to be a blast, even if it's not a date.

"We can't. We have a family dinner tonight." Poppy's voice brings me back to reality and layers on extra level of disappointment. She scribbles another fortune.

"On a Friday?" His eyes dart between us.

"With family friends," I clarify, hoping he'll realize that I'm not blowing him off. "Someone is coming in from out of town."

"Can you get out of it?"

I shake my head. "Sorry."

"I'm free tonight," Olivia says.

Poppy puts the cap back on the Sharpie and folds the origami cootie catcher. She pinches the bottom between her index fingers and thumbs and holds it out to Olivia. "You're first!"

Olivia points to one of the quadrants and Poppy pulls it back to see which one she chose.

"Smiley face?" I ask, staring at the face-like blob with a gap tooth.

"Jack-o'-lantern. Duh. H-A-L-L-O-W-E-E-N." Each time she says a letter, she moves her fingers to open the cootie catcher up and down or side to side. Olivia chooses one of the inside quadrants. Poppy opens it and shoots me a look.

"What does it say?" Olivia cranes her neck to read the fortune. Rafael laughs and puts his hands behind his head, clearly amused by our venture into elementary school entertainment.

"Something spooky will happen to you this weekend," Poppy reads in a low, husky voice.

"Ooh. Sounds intriguing. What do you think, Rafael?"

He looks at me, and I turn away from his gaze so he won't see my jealousy. "Definitely! We should hang. It'll be fun," he says to Olivia.

"Your turn." Poppy thrusts the cootie catcher at me, nudging my nose with the sharp paper corners. I don't feel like playing anymore, but I point to one of Poppy's sketches anyway.

"B-O-N-E-S." Her fingers move the paper back and forth.

Rafael leans his chair forward on its two front legs to see the picture. "Dinosaur?"

"Dog skeleton," Poppy says as she opens a paper flap. I choose a quadrant for her to read. "You will have a romantic weekend with an old flame. Interesting."

I jump at the sound of Rafael's chair slamming back to the floor. He picks up a French fry and jams it in his mouth.

After we've left the cafeteria, I grab Poppy's hand before she can run to class. "What the hell? Is that really what my fortune said?" I'm dimly aware that it sounds like I believe in fortunes, but what I believe in is Poppy's inclination to meddle.

She shrugs. "I'm trying to help you."

"Well, stop."

"Why are you so worked up?"

Because I have to spend the weekend with Jackson. Because Rafael is going out with Olivia. Because I cannot stop reading my mom's secret journal even though I know she wouldn't want me to. "I . . . I don't know. Just mind your own business, okay?"

"Poppy's Paper Fortunes make no promises." She winks and saunters off, leaving me with nothing but an uneasy feeling.

Incoming Text Messages

Jackson

Guess who's coming to town?

Me

Sorry about your accident. Glad you're okay.

Jackson

Thanks

You'll be around Friday? I think we're coming for dinner.

Me

Would we even be friends if it weren't for our moms?

Jackson

What?

Me

Never mind. I'll be here.

Jackson

Cool. See you soon!

Chapter 14

Butterflies bang painfully against my ribs when I open the door and see Jackson standing in front of me. He looks just as good as he did the last time I saw him.

No. He looks better. Older, even though it's only been a few months.

Sun-bleached curls fall across his forehead. He's wearing flip-flops, shorts, and a tank top. His ever-present uniform. He flashes a smile, revealing the whitest teeth I've ever seen outside of a toothpaste commercial.

"Hey, Clarabelle." The nickname from my childhood catches me off guard, and suddenly he's pulling me in for a hug. Behind him, Cami steps into the house. She's almost six feet tall with an athletic body that she developed running marathons. Her dark blonde hair is pulled back into a ponytail, and her teeth glisten as white as Jackson's. Mom and Poppy walk into the room, and in a matter of seconds everyone is saying hi and hugging each other and acting like we're long-lost relatives at a family reunion.

The sun sets over our swimming pool while we eat burgers on the patio. Everyone chats happily as we pass the food around, and it feels like no time has passed, especially when Jackson puts his arm around me and pulls me close for the benefit of Mom's camera. Mom and Cami gossip about the neighbors, while Jackson and Poppy argue over the merits of Arizona State versus UC San Diego. I close my eyes and can almost make myself believe that it's last spring, that prom hasn't happened yet, and that Jackson still lives in the house down the street instead of in a dorm room by the ocean.

I'm hit with a vivid memory of two summers ago. Jackson was stretched out on a pool floatie, his golden abs on glorious display, his damp curls falling over his forehead. I pretended to need a drink, but when I climbed out of the pool I snuck a picture of him. Not because I wanted it for myself (though I did), but because I wanted other people to see it.

Poppy was the first to notice the Jackson Effect. The way pictures of him got more likes and comments than any others. My status rose simply by Jackson's proximity. It was the first time in my life I was getting more attention than Poppy. I pretended not to care, but in that moment, I knew my facade was a lie. Poppy could never compete with that picture. Jackson was my ticket to first place.

Cami lifts her glass and looks at Mom conspiratorially. "Have you told the girls the news yet?"

Poppy raises an eyebrow at me. I shake my head in response.

Mom glances at me. "I was going to wait until it was official, but I guess I can tell you now." She takes a drink, pausing for dramatic effect. "When you girls reached one million subscribers, I put out some feelers and the most amazing opportunity fell in our laps."

I shift in my chair uneasily. Mom's had this Cheshire-cat grin before, and it always leads to something bad.

"STARR Network wants to film a Poppy and Claire reality show!" She claps her hands together. Poppy flies out of her chair and tackle-hugs Mom.

"Why?" *An entire show about our lives? Don't people know enough about us?*

"Your vlog is funny and stylish and they love the way you play off each other. And the way that video of you went viral?" She shakes her head, smiling at the memory of my humiliation. "They think it could be a hit!"

Poppy pulls me up and throws her arms around me. "Can you believe it?"

I look at Mom. "When would this happen?"

"They want to film for ten weeks next fall."

"What about school?"

"Who cares about school?" Poppy laughs in my ear. I push her arms off me.

"You could take a couple classes, but nothing that keeps you too busy," Mom answers.

I sink back into my chair as everyone around me celebrates a future I don't want.

"Let's get the wine!" Cami and Mom disappear inside. A giddy Poppy follows soon after to meet up with her friends, leaving Jackson and me alone on the porch.

"Wow. Can you believe that?" I shake my head, dazed by the speed with which my entire future has changed.

He puts his elbows on his knees and leans forward over his clasped hands. "It's pretty exciting."

"Is it?" If Jackson thinks this is something I'll be excited about, he doesn't know me at all. Maybe he never did.

He drums his fingers on his legs as silence falls between us. It seems almost impossible that we used to have so much to say to each other. Now that he's in college, we have nothing in common.

"So . . . you're getting a new car?" I finally say, when it's clear that Jackson is just as lost for words as I am.

"Yeah!" His eyes light up. "I test-drove the new Mustang in California and it's unreal. You would not believe the horsepower on that thing."

I smile without really listening. Jackson goes on about different car makes and models for the next fifteen minutes while my mind spins with the news of the reality show. It's a perfect metaphor for my life. Mom makes a decision, Poppy's thrilled about it, and by the time the dust settles, contracts have already been signed.

My term was supposed to be up in eleven months. I'd love to tell Poppy there is no way in hell I'm forgoing my college experience for the chance at becoming a Kardashian, but she'd be crushed. Mom made it clear they want both of us. A packaged deal. If I refuse to play along, Poppy will miss out on the opportunity of a lifetime. But if I do it, I'll lose another part of myself in pursuit of . . . what? More fans and followers? The constant need to look over my shoulder?

Every few minutes, I smile at Jackson and nod to show him that I'm listening, but I think he would keep talking even if I didn't. He doesn't seem to care that I'm here at all, which gives me a chance to look at him in a way I couldn't do near the end of our friendship, because my cheeks would've burst into flames. I take in his blond curls and his white teeth, and I can't deny it. He's still hot. Really freaking hot.

But I'm not in love with him anymore.

Not even a little bit.

We're sitting in the dark by ourselves, and I'm not nervous or excited. He hasn't said anything slightly amusing. Did I used to think he was funny? Or was my entire crush based on the fact that he made me feel special? He made me feel seen, but not in the way Rafael does. When I was with Jackson, I knew other people were watching. Envying.

I glance at the clock and see that Mom and Cami have been gone way too long. I wouldn't put it past Mom to leave us alone in an effort to get us to "reconnect."

Jackson clears his throat and looks at me, clearly waiting for something.

"Uh . . . sorry. What did you say?"

"What's going on in your life? Are you dating anyone?"

I wince at his attempt at casual conversation. "Um. Nope."

"Look. I know this is awkward, but I just want to apologize for taking you to prom last year."

"Apologize?"

"Yeah. I knew you liked me . . . I shouldn't have lead you on like that."

"Why did you?"

He ducks his head and stares at his hands. "Mom told me to. I think our moms have this fantasy we'll get together someday. It's stupid, I know. I should have just told her that I wasn't interested."

My stomach sinks. It's surprisingly easy to hear him say he never had romantic feelings for me, but the other part, the part about our parents, makes me feel ashamed. "It's not entirely her fault."

"What do you mean?" His gaze meets mine.

"Our followers got this idea that we should be a couple, and Mom wanted to keep them interested . . . but I did too. I didn't realize it until tonight, but I used you. I'm sorry you got sucked into that mess."

"California is pretty far removed from the mess. You should move out there if the reality show doesn't work out."

I sit back in my chair with a sigh. I don't know if I want to go to California, but I loved having the option of removing myself from it all. In the course of one dinner, my entire future shrank. The only thing on my horizon is a camera.

If I thought my memories of prom were tainted by an awkward goodnight high five, that's nothing compared to the betrayal I feel now that I know the date was orchestrated by our mothers. Sure, I used Jackson too. But only because Mom put me in the position of having to compete with my twin sister. Add that to the fact that she's literally been shopping me around to TV networks without my consent, and any trace of guilt I felt for reading Mom's journal vanishes that night as I open the pages.

I read all about her pregnancy. It's weird to see her write "the baby" when it should say "the babies," although it's not new information for me. Years ago, she told Poppy and me that we were a surprise. Well, one of us was, anyway. Money was tight, my parents didn't have health insurance, and they could not afford to have any ultrasounds done while she was pregnant. When she went to the hospital, she assumed she would come home with one baby. And then—surprise! Twins!

The confusing thing is that she doesn't mention money troubles in her journal, and it seems like she went to plenty of doctor's appointments. I turn to an entry dated November 23. My birthday.

A piece of paper that had been tucked in between the pages of the journal falls to my lap.

Ashley,

You're living the life I want. If I can't have it, maybe this baby girl can.

I don't want her.

I hope you do.

I read the note again. And then again. I read it half a dozen times, trying to make sense of the words, but it's like the letter and Mom's journal are pieces from two different jigsaw puzzles.

I turn my eyes to the entry dated November 23.

My baby girl is here. She's the most beautiful thing I have ever seen.

That's it. Nothing else. I read it again.

Her baby girl. Singular. One baby. I pick up the note and read it again. It's difficult to see the words through the tears that are pooling behind my eyes. It doesn't matter though. I already have them memorized.

I don't want her.
I hope you do.

A tear breaks free and falls onto the page, blurring the old, blue ink.

I close the journal, unsure if I want to know what comes next. Ten seconds later, I open it again, knowing I don't really have a choice.

The next entry is dated November 24. The handwriting is a messy scribble, as if Mom was writing in a hurry.

I don't know where to start. We still don't have a name. Jason likes Poppy. I like Claire. You'd think we would have chosen before the baby was born but every time I tried to talk about it with Jason, he would laugh and kiss me. "Whatever name we don't use, we'll use it for the next one."

We planned on having six babies. When we got married I wanted four. He wanted five. For some reason, six was the compromise.

It took almost three years to get pregnant. They were the longest and hardest years of my life. I started to doubt whether there would be one baby, let alone six. But then she came. My miracle baby came and I believed again. We planned for six.

Labor was a blur. It happened so quickly, I don't remember it. One minute, I was being checked into the hospital and the next minute, I was pushing and then my room was full of doctors and nurses. There was blood everywhere. I've never seen Jason so scared in my entire life.

Seconds later, I was wheeled out of the delivery room and into an operating room.

Placenta Accreta.

That's what they called it. I know because Jason wrote it down so he could tell me. It basically means there was a problem with the placenta and there was too much blood. The baby and I are both lucky to be alive. It also means that I won't be able to have any more babies.

We have to choose a name and I don't know how to do it.

November 25

Mom called today and left a voicemail asking about how I'm feeling. I still haven't told her I had the baby. I haven't told anyone yet. No one knows we're here. I haven't posted any pictures online and I haven't written in the blog. I don't know how. I don't know what to say. I don't know what to name this sweet baby girl. I think I'm still in shock. I can't stop crying.

November 27. Thanksgiving.

Today is a day of miracles.

November 28

I finally have time to write down everything that happened yesterday. It's so incredible, I still can't believe it. Jason was down in the cafeteria getting breakfast while I was taking a shower in my room. When I came out of the shower, there were two baby girls in my room. Two! I know, it sounds insane, but the second I saw this new baby, I knew she was meant for me. It was as strong as the feeling I had after giving birth. But I'm getting ahead of myself. Inside the clear bassinet thing that the hospital uses to wheel babies around was a note from her mom saying she didn't want her. Before I could do anything, Jason came back into the room and paged for help. The nurses contacted hospital administrators, who apologized a million times for the fact that this happened. But I didn't want them to apologize! I just kept asking to talk to the baby's mother, and finally they let me. When I got to her room, I recognized her a little. Her name is Brittany and we went to high school together. She said she can't take care of the baby and she kept meaning to find a family to adopt her but never got around to it. And then when she was in labor, she saw me being checked in, and she recognized me right away because she reads my blog! I KNOW. Anyway, she knows how hard it was for Jason and me to get pregnant and she thinks it was like, fate, that we delivered in the same hospital and she wants us to raise her baby girl. Everyone thinks Jason and I are out of our minds, but the hospital called in some lawyers and we all signed papers and Jason and I are officially and legally parents of the TWO most amazing baby girls I have ever seen.

The clip of footsteps echoes on the tile hall outside my bedroom. Either Mom or Poppy passes my door, then turns around and backtracks to my room.

I stop breathing.

The footsteps pause again, and my door handle starts to twist. My brain is screaming at my hands to hide the journal and the letter, but I can't make my body move. If it's Poppy, I'm caught red-handed. If it's my mom, I'm dead.

I press my hands to my chest, trying to quiet my racing heart so it won't be heard from behind the closed door. Every sense in my body is heightened, like I'm anticipating an attack. The handle slides back into place, and the footsteps return down the hall and into Poppy's room, where the door shuts. I sag back into my pillows as relief blossoms through me.

I should tell her what I found. I mean, obviously. This is a secret too big to keep. I'm shocked Mom hid it for this long. Tell the internet when Poppy had her first date, sure. Tell them you picked up a spare daughter as a replacement for the ones you couldn't have? Nah. Who needs to know that?

Images from my childhood flash through my mind, and the truth is so obvious my chest aches. I've heard countless strangers coo over how much Poppy looks like Mom, only to be shocked when they find out we're twins. I always assumed my looks came from Dad. I never stopped to examine a photograph to find out if that was true.

All the times I didn't fit in. All the times Mom favored Poppy over me. I assumed it was just for clicks. More clicks equals more money. Even if I hated it, even if I fought against it, I understood why Mom favored the internet's golden child. I never dared to think the reason I feel left out is because I *actually* don't belong with this family.

I have to tell Poppy. She would do the same for me because, despite our differences, she's always been a good sister.

KARA McDOWELL

My brain orders my legs to move, but they listen to my heart instead. I'm not ready for this conversation. I hide the journal under my bed and pull the covers over my head.

Maybe that makes me a bad sister, but I'm not going to worry about that right now, because it turns out Poppy and I aren't sisters after all.

Email from a fan

From: trevorsgirl@gmail.com
To: poppyandclaire@dixondaily.com
Subject: I LOVE YOU!

Hi Claire!
I saw that Jackson is in town this weekend. It must be so nice to spend time together after so many months apart! You guys are total relationship goals. My boyfriend and I are doing the long-distance thing. He's in Ohio, I'm in Pennsylvania, and it's so hard. I just miss him all the time. Do you have any advice on how to make it work? I'm worried we won't last the whole four years of college, but I don't know what I'd do without him.

Thanks in advance!
Bianca!

P.S. I love your vlog!!

Chapter 15

The Valley of the Sun is urban sprawl at its finest. The Phoenix metropolitan area has pushed its way across the dry desert landscape in every direction, crawling toward the low, dusty mountains that surround the city. Lights from buildings, cars, and streetlamps twinkle below me for miles, like stars that were poured from the sky. The sun is just about done for the day, leaving a textbook Arizona sunset ablaze with reds, purples, oranges, and pinks so vivid, it looks like God tripped over paint cans. It's even more spectacular from my seat in the dark foothills of the Sonoran Desert, where the saguaro cacti are a dark outline against the horizon.

It's Sunday night, and this is the first time I've left my bedroom all weekend. On Saturday morning, I shut myself in my room, claiming sickness. One glance in the mirror confirmed I looked the part. Despite the many hours of sleep I've gotten over the last two days, when I woke up this evening, I looked and felt restless. My skin was humming, commanding my body to move. I threw on a pair of jeans and a T-shirt and rushed out of the house.

An invisible force pushed me into my car, telling me to go. I rolled the windows down, turned the music up loud, and hopped onto the nearest freeway. Without realizing it, I drove north toward the mountain foothills. The road up the mountain is long and twisty. Paloverde trees and desert shrubs threw shadows on the ground. I turned off onto a street lined with large homes and parked my car on the road, flashing back to my first time here with Poppy and the rest of the swim team. It was the last day of freshman year, and we were drunk on warm night air and the feeling of freedom.

One of the older girls showed us how to climb over a locked gate and sneak through a private backyard to get to the face of the foothills. From there, we climbed until we reached a flat stretch of rock where we could sit and gaze over the city. It felt like the top of the world.

Now, I sit on the same spot and gaze out over the valley. I've been back several times since that first night, but I always come alone because I love the feeling of being away from everyone and everything else. It's easier to breathe and easier to think up here. Unfortunately, that also means that the dark and scary thoughts that have tiptoed to the edge of my mind over the last two days finally have a place to put their feet up. Until now, I've pushed them away with the internet or TV or sleep. The glow of a screen makes it easy to avoid thinking.

The only lights I see now are the ones sprawled out in front of me. For the first time in six months, cool air grazes my cheeks. Despite everything that has happened this weekend, I breathe a small sigh of relief. I survived another suffocating Arizona summer. One of the things I was most looking forward to about college was getting out of this town. Now, it looks like my only choice is to stay here and continue to be the third wheel in the Ashley and Poppy Show.

For the millionth time, I wonder what my life would be like without Twin Tuesday or outfit photos or vlogs about makeup. For the first time, I realize this wasn't the life I was supposed to have. Maybe landing with the Dixons was just a weird fluke, and I should go home right now and tell them I quit.

But then I realize that quitting social media might *actually* mean quitting the family. By acknowledging I'm not really her daughter, Mom would finally have an excuse to admit that I'm not the daughter she wanted. I'm the difficult one who complains and rolls her eyes and can't keep her mouth shut. And Poppy. My heart squeezes painfully when I think about how it would hurt her if I quit. She knows what she wants, and she needs my help to get it.

I sigh and lay flat on my back. Stray pebbles dig into shoulders. My head is throbbing, and my body feels heavy and tired. Why did I think it was a good idea to come here? What I need is a distraction. Not a silent sky and an empty mountain.

As if on cue, my phone vibrates in my pocket.

Rafael

This just in: homework sucks.

I smile into the dark night sky. It's the first text since the movie night.

Me

He texts! It's a miracle!

Rafael

The jury is still out on whether I'll ever do it again.

Me

That's a lot of pressure on this one conversation.

Rafael

Don't disappoint me, Just Claire.

Me

You want to take a break from homework?

Rafael

Always.

Me

Are you opposed to trespassing?

Rafael

Never.

I send him my location, close my eyes, and wait.

It's not long before I hear a car approach. I keep my eyes closed and focus on steady breathing. A door slams. Footsteps crunch across gravel. And then, faster than I would have thought possible, I hear him panting.

Panting?

My eyes fly open as I sit up. Rafael puts his hand on his side and bends over, breathing heavily. He holds up a finger, asking me to wait for him to catch his breath.

I jump up, unsure of what to do. I can't believe I asked him to drive thirty minutes and climb up the side of a small mountain just to see me. He probably thinks I'm a lunatic. I bite my lip, thinking of ways to get out of this situation, when he glances up at me with a sparkle in his eyes. He straightens his back and takes in our surroundings. My shoulders relax as I realize he was messing with me.

"Are you going to murder me and bury my body in the desert?" he teases.

"Not unless you deserve it." I slip off my flip-flops, and we both sit down.

I'm afraid he's going to ask why I'm here or, even worse, why *he's* here. But he doesn't. He looks out over the valley and whistles.

"*This.* Is a view."

"It's my favorite spot in the city."

"I can see why." He leans back on his hands. "How'd you find it?"

"A few summers ago, Poppy and I spent the day at Saguaro Lake with the swim team. Afterward, we drove up here to eat shaved ice and watch the sun set. It was love at first sight. I've been coming back on my own ever since."

"Always by yourself?" His gaze turns to me in the dark.

"Until now."

One corner of his mouth pulls up in a smile. I try to return it but it's half-hearted at best. Rafael's expression softens. "What happened with the swim team?"

I consider his question as I look at the lights below us. I asked him to come, the least I can do is answer his question. "Do you know what an online troll is?" He shakes his head. "It's someone who spends time 'trolling' the internet, looking for ways to make people mad or start arguments."

"What? Why?"

"Boredom. Jealousy. Straight up nastiness. Who knows? Poppy and I have always received mean comments on our pictures and videos, but last year, things got *really* bad. The worst of it came from one person who would leave horrible insults on everything we posted and send terrible emails. No matter how many times we blocked the person, they would register under a new username and start over. Eventually I figured out it was two of our swim team friends, Emily and Erica." I pause, suddenly worried about how petty this must sound to a boy whose entire life revolves around helping less fortunate people.

"How'd you find out?"

"They left a comment containing information I only ever told them," I say, hoping he doesn't ask for specifics. It was posted on a vlog Poppy and I made last summer called "How to Get Ready for a Date." I still remember their comment word for word. *What a joke. Poppy's such a slut all she has to do is open her legs, and Claire's such a prude even her boyfriend won't touch more than the palm of her hand.* They were the only ones who knew about Jackson and the prom high five.

"That *really* sucks," Rafael says and I'm relieved to hear him say it. "What'd you do?"

"I quit the team, because I had zero interest in spending time with those girls."

"And Poppy?"

"She swears they didn't do it, but she's such a people pleaser, I'll bet she never confronted them about it."

"I'm sorry," he says, and I can feel the sincerity in his voice. For some reason, the sound of it brings tears to my eyes. He focuses on my face again, but I keep my gaze on the lights below.

"Mom told me to develop thicker skin, and I swear that hurt worse than any of the online garbage. I trusted her to understand how much I was hurting, but it was like she only wanted me to toughen up so I would keep posting."

Rafael sits up. "That's terrible. She never should have said that." He turns his body to face me, and I put my arms around my legs and rest my head sideways on my knees to look at him. His face is so earnest. I'm struck by the horrifying thought that he feels sorry for me, that he drove here out of pity.

"Whatever. It's not a big deal," I lie, so he doesn't feel obligated to spend time with me or comfort me. And then, before I make a conscious decision to tell him, I add, "She's not my mom."

"That's harsh."

Everything about the journal and the letter and the abandoned baby comes spilling out. The silence that follows stretches out before us and fills the empty sky. I imagine stars scooting out of the way to make room for it, falling into recently darkened windows and lighting them up again.

"What are you thinking?" I ask after several minutes.

He waits a beat and then responds. "I've lived all over the world and seen every kind of mom you can imagine. I've seen moms with dozens of filthy kids running around their feet and naked babies strapped to their backs. I've seen moms go hungry so their children have something to eat. I've seen them cry and yell and hit and pray. Even the best ones seem a little unhinged at times."

"Is this supposed to make me feel better?"

"I just can't help but think, unhinged or not, the good moms are the ones who stay. The ones who keep trying day in and day out." He picks up a handful of small rocks and tosses them one by one down the hill.

"Well, that doesn't apply to me then." I imagine a woman with my hair and freckles wheeling me into a stranger's hospital room and running.

"I'm not talking about your birth mother. I'm talking about Ashley. She did more than stay. She took you in. She wanted you." Rafael turns to me again and gives me a hard look. A twinge of sadness lurks behind it.

My insides squirm as I flash back to the time he told me about his parents. Never once in our game of questions and answers did I ask about his feelings toward them. "Does your dad ever talk about her?

He shakes his head. "Never."

"Have you ever tried to find her?"

"It wouldn't be that hard; even if I couldn't get my dad to tell me her name, she was stationed in Greece with Doctors Without Borders the year I was born. But why should I care about her when she never cared about me?"

I turn back to the lights. "What was it like, growing up without her?" I lost my dad a long time ago, but it's not even close to the same thing.

"My dad gets restless easily. It's why he continues to re-up with Doctors Without Borders year after year, instead of settling down in his own practice. Every time I felt comfortable in a new country, he'd uproot us, and I'd have to start all over again. It's not all bad. I've seen a lot of cool places and met a bunch of amazing people, but honestly? I'd give it all up to stay in one spot and make connections that last. I bet half of my childhood friends don't remember me."

"You sound like my friend Nora." I have the connections and stability they both crave, but more and more, my life feels stifling. Not comforting.

We watch the lights dance for several minutes before Rafael speaks again. "I answered your question, which means it's my turn to ask one."

I roll my eyes and nudge him with my shoulder. "Let's not keep score." Somewhere between the stuffy cafeteria and this open mountain, we've moved beyond that.

"How are you holding up? You don't look nearly as freaked as I would have expected."

"You didn't see me yesterday." I spent the entire day in tears, crying until my eyes were swollen and sore and my limbs felt like they weighed a thousand pounds. The tears took everything out of me, and by the time they ran out, I felt hollow.

Rafael jumps to his feet. "Come on. I have an idea." He holds out his hand to help me up. His warm fingers wrap around mine, and my skin buzzes, wiping away the tired and empty feeling that's been plaguing me all weekend. His eyes dart to our hands. A quick squeeze, and he drops mine. I slip on my flip-flops and bounce on my toes, ready for whatever the night has in store.

"Let's go." I take off down the hill, his laugh following close behind.

Incoming Text Messages

SATURDAY MORNING

Poppy

Sorry you're sick! Feel better! xoxo

We're still filming today, right?

SATURDAY AFTERNOON

Poppy

We're way behind schedule!

Our Top Five Trends for Fall video is scheduled to drop Monday.

Mom

Do you think you'll be good for outfit photos in the morning?

SATURDAY NIGHT

Poppy

Suck it up! Unlock your door!

Mom

You can push the video to Tuesday but no later. The sponsors need it posted ASAP.

SUNDAY AFTERNOON

Mom

Have you thought any more about the mouthwash?
Did they mention how much money they were
offering?

Poppy

UGH!!!!!!!!!!!!!!!!!!!!!!!!!!!!!!!!!!!

Chapter 16

"Don't worry. We won't do anything too destructive," Rafael promises with a mischievous wink as he opens the dairy fridge and pulls out two cartons of eggs.

Once we made it down the mountain, I left my car on the side of the road and hopped in his. At his request, I directed him to the nearest grocery store. Now, he carries the eggs to the checkout counter with a whistle and a bounce in his step that contradict his words. If a cop saw us right now, I doubt they'd believe we were on our way to make omelets. Fortunately, the small store is dead. The aisles are empty with the exception of a few employees pushing mops.

"You look familiar," the cashier says. Her name tag says Ariel, and she looks about my age. She has black, shoulder-length hair with hot pink tips. Instinctively, I shake my hair from behind my ears and let it fall in front of my face. Rafael looks at me but doesn't say anything. He takes his wallet out of the back pocket of his jeans to pay for the eggs, but Ariel hasn't scanned them yet.

"I definitely know you." She squints at me, and I'm wondering if I can lie my way out of this. "You're the clothes girl! The one in the bird poop video!" she exclaims. "Which one are you?"

It always surprises me how often people say this, considering Poppy and I don't look much alike. The pain hits me square in the chest as I remember. *We're not even sisters!* People should be able to tell us apart.

"Sorry. Wrong person," I say.

She narrows her eyes in disbelief. Rafael looks at me with a question on his face. He wants to help but doesn't know what to say.

"Can I take your picture?" She pulls her phone out of her apron pocket.

"She said you're mistaken." Rafael's rough voice is a warning shot. He opens his wallet and takes out a five-dollar bill. Without waiting for the cashier to ring up the eggs, he places the money on the counter, grabs the eggs and my hand, and pulls me into the night.

We drive south, crossing from Mesa back into Gilbert. I roll my window down and watch the wobbly sugar skull attached to his dashboard. Rafael hands me his phone, which is hooked up to his car speakers through Bluetooth. "What are you in the mood for?" I ask, scanning his music library.

To my complete surprise and delight, he says, "You choose." I thought it was an unwritten law of the universe that the driver controls the music. I look at the carton of eggs on my lap and pick something loud and angry that gets my blood pumping.

"I had no idea Gilbert had so much farmland," Rafael says over the music as we turn off onto a dirt road.

It's easy to forget Gilbert's country roots. The majority of our town is just like every other desert suburb: lots of little houses in a row, lawns that are watered around the clock to keep them green, and churches and elementary schools on every corner.

And then the wind rolls in.

The wind rolls in, and with it comes the smell of manure from a nearby dairy farm. It's horrible, but it's home. It reminds me that all I have to do is get in my car and drive a few miles south, and I will be surrounded by empty fields that grow corn in the summer and turn into mazes in the fall. It's easier to breathe out here, just like in the mountain foothills. I never realize how restless those houses and churches and schools make me feel until I leave them behind.

"I love it out here," I tell Rafael. "It's such a contradiction."

"What do you mean?"

"The idea of farming in the desert is so ridiculous. These people are creating life where it shouldn't exist."

Rafael pulls the car off to the shoulder of the road at a four-way stop and turns it off. "These farms aren't the only contradictions out here tonight."

"What are you talking about?"

"You. You have a million online followers, or subscribers, or whatever they're called. Everyone wants to be friends with Claire Dixon."

"But . . . ?"

"But you don't like people very much."

"That's not true!"

He laughs and shakes his head. "Yes, it is. But we can talk about that another time." He reaches his hand across the car. My breath hitches against my ribs as I brace myself for contact that never comes. He picks one of the cartons of eggs off my lap and opens his door. "Come on. Let's do this."

I take the second carton of eggs and follow him into the middle of the empty intersection. We're alone in a sea of farmland.

"What exactly are we doing?" I ask, even though the answer is pretty clear.

"We're getting angry. You first." He nudges my arm with his carton of eggs.

"Where do I throw it?" My stomach turns over in nervous excitement.

Rafael laughs again. "Anywhere you want."

I close my eyes. I have never done anything remotely rebellious in my entire life. It could be because I'm a good kid, or it could be because I've never had the opportunity. I've had a camera in my face and the threat of embarrassing my family since the moment Mom signed the adoption papers and brought me into her life.

But Rafael is right. *I am angry.* I'm angry at my birth mom for abandoning me, at my parents for lying to me, at Poppy for being the perfect daughter, and at STARR Network for wanting to put me on TV for people to gawk at, like some bearded lady in the circus.

I open my eyes and pick an egg from the carton. It feels cool, smooth, and fragile in my hand, like one touch from me could turn it to dust. I rub my thumb across the shell and look up at Rafael. His arms are crossed, and he watches me with interest, probably curious to see if I'll actually go through with his ridiculous plan. My heart thumps faster and faster, but I don't know if it's because of the egg in my hand or the look on Rafael's face. A breeze blows through his hair, and I want to reach out and run my fingers through it. An ache runs through my hand and arm and down into my stomach, and I know I have to do something. If I keep standing here and staring at him like this, he's going to know how badly I want to touch him. Or worse, I may reach out and actually do it. I take a breath, and before I can talk myself out of it, I send the egg sailing over Rafael's head. It hits a stop sign with a splat.

Rafael cups his hands around his mouth and cheers loudly. "I knew you could do it!" He opens his carton and throws an egg at the back of the stop sign across the intersection. Another satisfying splat. This time I whoop and holler for him. Before I know it, we're both tossing our eggs left and right. We get all four stop signs. Then Rafael starts throwing them as high as he can straight up in the air, and I chuck them hard against the ground. I feel like a little kid again, completely free and unrestrained.

It's over as quickly as it started, and we're both laughing so hard, we're crying. I snap a picture of the vandalized stop sign from my seat on the trunk of Rafael's car.

He leans over my shoulder to see the dark, blurry picture. "Are you going to post it?"

"Nope."

"Why not?"

"It's not 'on brand.'" People would be confused. It's bad quality, for one thing. It's bad content, for another. No one wants to know how angry I am.

All I want is to be a normal kid who can post whatever normal, boring crap I please without worrying about disappointing my family or upsetting hundreds of thousands of strangers. It's a simple wish, and I hate how impossible it feels.

I smile at Rafael. "Thanks. That was very therapeutic."

"I was hoping you'd like it."

"Do you do this often?"

"Every Sunday night," he teases as he nudges his shoulder against mine.

I shake my head in mock horror. "I knew you were a bad influence."

He scoots close enough that our legs are almost touching. "This is a big moment, your first act of juvenile delinquency. What would your mother say?"

My whole body stiffens.

Rafael's expression freezes as he realizes what he said. "I'm so sorry. I was just trying to make a joke. I'm so stupid." He scoots back across the trunk of the car and turns toward me. I don't respond because I'm afraid that if I say anything, my tears of laughter will take a less happy turn.

Rafael rakes his hands through his hair. "I'm an idiot. Really."

"You think I don't know that?" I look at him sideways and pull up half my mouth in a smile.

Relief washes over his face but is quickly replaced by anguish. He reaches his hand out slowly and wipes a stray tear from my cheek. He looks like he wants to say something but he hesitates. I stay quiet. He'll eventually put his thoughts into words. He always does.

"I know we haven't known each other for long, but I'm sorry you're hurting. I wish there was something I could do to help." His thumb lingers on my cheek for a moment longer than necessary before he pulls it away and averts his eyes from mine.

"The fact that you're here is enough." Just having him here makes the pain a little more bearable, because I no longer feel alone. I slide toward him, and he does the same. I lean my head on his shoulder and stare down a long dirt road. It's almost enough to make me forget that the biggest of my problems are asleep in a house not so many miles away.

Poppy's Ten Commandments for Posting

1. Thou shalt never post a picture with bad lighting.
2. Use hashtags sparingly. (Long hashtags are only acceptable when they are funny.)
3. Post at peak times (morning, after school, after dinner).
4. Do not post on Friday or Saturday night.
5. No blurry photos.
6. Do not post more than twice a day.
7. Post mostly pictures with faces in them. (They get thirty-eight percent more likes!)
8. Insta-clipsing (the art of posting a picture where you look better than everyone else) is acceptable—within reason.

8b. Never post a picture if someone else in it has a double chin or sweaty pit stains. Karma's a bitch.

9. Nothing sad. No complaining.
10. If a picture gets less than five thousand likes within the first two hours, take it down immediately because it's embarrassing and bad.

Chapter 17

Olivia

I had soooo much fun with Raf on Friday! He's the best.

I wake up to the most obnoxious text from Olivia on Monday morning, and I have one more thing to add to my growing list of worries. It was only after we said goodbye that I remembered his Friday night date with Olivia. In the midst of my total meltdown, it slipped my mind. I plan to casually ask him about it at lunch, but the right moment never appears. He doesn't bring it up.

He does seem more agitated and distracted than usual. Less like Rafael. When I ask him about it during College Prep, he insists that he's fine. After that he starts acting more like his usual self, leaning over my shoulder and whispering jokes while Ms. Grant lectures us about the importance of dressing like professionals. She surveys us over the top of her glasses and makes a tutting noise. The majority of the class is in flip-flops and shorts, and a few of the girls are wearing pajama pants. Apparently, Ms. Grant disapproves.

Time all but stops when I'm at home. I shoved Mom's journal under my bed and haven't looked at it since. The swim team has a big meet coming up this weekend and preparing for it demands all of Poppy's attention, which means after the fall trends vlog is done, we don't film any new ones. I spend most of my free time in my room, logging into BITES, but I can't bring myself to post. I finally have a story that will top six brothers sharing a hundred-square-foot bedroom and @SIGNOFTHETIMES's cryptic "rowboat, poop, dragon," but I'm no longer interested in winning the "My Life Sucks Worse Than Yours" competition. I preferred it when my biggest problem was an annoying wardrobe.

With all my problems at home, lunch and seventh period quickly become the highlight of my week. I'm thrilled when Ms. Grant tells us to choose a partner in class on Thursday. As she's explaining the activity, Poppy reaches her hand across the aisle and knocks off my flip-flop. She silences my question with a pointed look and swats Rafael's pen off his desk, then quickly buries her head in her bag.

"Hey!" Rafael glances sideways at Poppy before bending to pick up his pen, and I realize what Poppy is up to. I lean over to slip my sandal back on, meeting Rafael's eye at desk level.

Bless you, Poppy. I can practically feel her triumph radiating through the room, and I decide not to let it go to waste.

"Partner?" I ask.

He shakes his head in fake disapproval. "If I didn't know better, I'd think you two planned that."

"Good thing you know better."

He smiles in reply. I'm not sure he believes me, and I'm not sure I want him to.

"You could've just asked me." He sits back and props his feet on my desk.

I roll my eyes and nudge them off. "It's like you don't know me all," I tease.

His lips part in question, but he shakes it off without a word.

We're doing mock interviews again, this time for college admissions. Rafael and I practice interview questions for a few minutes, but the activity quickly breaks down. People around us start talking about their weekend plans and whether or not Highland stands a chance in Friday's football game.

"Where do you want to go to school?" I set the paper down on my desk and settle back into my chair.

"Everywhere!" He grins and sits up straighter. "I'm trying to narrow it down, but I have eleven schools left on my list."

A fierce stab of envy shoots through me. "What schools?

"NYU, Columbia, BU, Georgetown, Northwestern, Tulane, Berkeley," he counts them off on his fingers. "Places like that."

I sit back, stunned. "Wow. That's . . . impressive."

He shrugs. "Some of them are a long shot, but they all have good pre-med programs."

"You want to be a doctor?"

"Maybe. My dad wants me to be a doctor. There are worse things I could do. What about you?

"Probably Arizona State."

"Why?"

"That's where Poppy's going."

He raises his eyebrows. "You don't have to go where Poppy goes."

If only that were true. My fingers trace a pattern over the curse words that have been carved in pen on my desk. "There's a possibility that we'll film a reality show next fall. We'd have to live in the same city, and they want us close to home, so Mom can make cameo appearances."

His head rears back in a mixture of disgust and surprise. "Do you *want* to be in a reality TV show?

I look across the room to make sure Poppy is well out of earshot. "No." My answer is automatic.

"Then why would you do that to yourself?"

"I'm doing it for Poppy. It's her dream come true."

He sighs and shakes his head. "You once told me Poppy is a people pleaser. But that's not true at all. She's a Poppy pleaser. You're the one who always wants to make other people happy, but you deserve to be happy too."

I can't possibly explain my thought process to him in a way he'll understand. I barely understand it myself. The Poppy-and-Claire brand is the only connection we have left. Half the time, I'm afraid quitting will rob her of her dream. The other half, I'm afraid she'll bail on me the second she finds out we're not really sisters. I don't know which scenario scares me more.

"You're becoming a doctor because it's what your dad wants."

He shakes his head. "That's different. I've given myself choices by applying to lots of schools. You're not giving yourself options. You're just sticking with the one school in the one city that's closest to home, all so your sister can live out her fame fantasies?"

"I never said ASU was the only place I applied. I just said I would probably end up there."

"Oh? So where else did you apply, *Just Claire?*" Based on the tone in his voice, he knows I'm lying. He crosses his arms on his desk and leans forward. I consider doing the same just to bring myself a few inches closer to him.

"UC San Diego."

"Why there?"

My face flames. *Why did I tell him that?* First of all, it's a lie. I filled out the application but never submitted it. When Jackson got accepted last year, I thought it would be amazing if we went to school together. I imagined us studying on the beach, walking to class together, eating in the dining hall, and falling in love. I completed the application over the summer, but the soonest I could submit was this fall. By that time, I had given up on most of my Jackson fantasies. After last weekend, those fantasies are gone for good.

Rafael is still waiting for an answer. "I like the beach," I mumble as I watch Parker Evans play darts with a pile of sharpened pencils and the ceiling.

"You're a terrible liar." Rafael follows my gaze over his shoulder.

"Fine," I admit. "I have a friend who goes to UCSD. But it doesn't matter, because I'm staying here."

A pencil falls from the ceiling and lands on the edge of Rafael's desk. Before Parker has the chance to grab it, Rafael picks it up and breaks it in half with one hand. "Have you talked to anyone about your mom's journal yet?" he asks, and I'm thrown by the sudden change in conversation.

"You mean Poppy?"

"Poppy. Or anyone."

"No, just you. Why?"

Rafael looks at me hard. It's a face I recognize well by now. It's a face that means he has something to say, but he's waiting to say it.

"I think you should," he says at last. He runs his hands over his face. It's a frustrated gesture but his expression is resigned. He picks up the paper of interview questions. "We should get back to work. What do you want to study in school?"

Disappointment and curiosity course through me, battling for attention. Rafael has decided not to say whatever he's thinking, and I can't even pretend to guess what it is.

A curvy blonde woman is waiting to accost Poppy and me as soon as Poppy gets home from swim practice. She introduces herself as Stella, and the bangles on her arms clink together as she greets us with a tight hug. Stella's an executive from STARR Network, here to deliver our contracts and talk to us about ideas for the reality show. I expect a big pitch before getting down to the nitty-gritty, but to her credit, she slides the contracts across the dining room table as soon as we're all sitting down with something to drink.

I glance at the papers and a rush of nausea rises in my throat.

"Where do I sign?" Poppy flips straight to the last page and picks up a pen.

"Aren't you going to read it?" I ask, desperate for some way to slow the train barreling straight at me.

"I'm sure Mom read it," she says.

"Claire's *right*. You *should* know *what* you're getting into." Stella reads through the contract line by line, putting oddly strong emphasis on way too many words. She goes slow to makes sure we *understand* how long filming will *need* to take place (*ten* weeks), how often the cameras will be with us (*always*), and when we're allowed to take off our mics (in the *bathroom*). Poppy nods along with everything, and I realize Rafael is right. She's not trying to please this woman, she's genuinely thrilled about what she's hearing.

"What's this?" I ask, pointing to the "Scandal Clause."

"If, at any time *before, during,* or *after* filming, either of you gets involved in a *scandal* or embarrasses the show or network in *any* way, we have the right to terminate your contract *without* payment."

"Isn't scandal and drama what you guys live for?"

"That's not *on brand* for you two. We're pushing you as *'girls next door.'* Girls should want to *be* you, and guys should want to *bring you home* to meet their moms," Stella says with a wink. The urge to vomit resurfaces.

"What about Lena's story?" I ask Mom, remembering the *MyStyle* piece that's supposed to run next month.

"I've promised her an exclusive interview ahead of the show in exchange for scrapping the story," Mom says. "She's excited about it."

I turn back to Stella. "What's the goal here? One or two seasons and then we're done?" I can't keep the note of hope out of my voice, and judging by Stella's expression, she hears it too.

"The goal is to make *really* great TV that lasts a *long* time. The two of you together will be ratings *gold*. And when that happens, *you'll* become household names. We're talking *Kardashian-level* fame. If you get a haircut, we want it on CNN."

Every feature on Poppy's face lights up. "I'm sold."

"Wait." I turn to Poppy, desperate to change her mind. "Do you really want to be like the Kardashians?"

"Do I really want to be a business mogul with literally dozens of companies, products, TV shows, and franchises to my name? Yes."

"But why?" I shoot a look at Stella, wondering how much she knows, and lower my voice. "After what happened when we were younger, why would you put yourself in that position? You know how dangerous it can be."

"Influence. *Power.*" She signs the contract and slides it across the table to Stella, seizing her power and stealing mine with one swift movement.

Stella pats my hand. "Take a few days to *think* about it. Whatever you need to feel *comfortable* with the idea."

Poppy's obviously in heaven, but I have a feeling it'll take more than a few days for me to feel comfortable with this.

I knock on Poppy's open door later that night. She's wearing headphones and painting her toenails black and teal in preparation for the swim meet. She looks up, sees my bowl of ice cream, and points to the door.

Instead of leaving, I sit in her desk chair and prop my feet up on her bed.

"Want a bite?" I hold out a spoonful of Rocky Road. She always cuts sugar out of her diet before a big race, and she hates when I taunt her with it.

She pulls off her headphones. "You're the devil."

"I love you too," I say through a mouthful.

She shakes a bottle of teal toenail polish and props her foot on a textbook to protect her bed from the getting stained.

I came to talk about the show, but I feel myself chickening out. I spin around in her chair, taking in her shelves of ribbons, trophies, and swim team pictures. This year's picture earned a prime spot above her desk, and I feel a stab of sadness when I realize I'm not in it. It's not that I miss swimming, but it's weird that she's doing it without me.

But in reality, it's not weird, because we're not related. In another life, we'd just be two girls with dark hair who kind of resemble each other if you squint your eyes, not twins who spend nearly every waking moment together. I take a breath, and spin back to face her. "I don't want to do the show."

She doesn't look up from her toes. "Why not?"

"I want to go to college."

"You *can* go to college."

"I want to go away."

"Then let's go!" She moves her foot and flips open the history textbook until she finds a map of the United States in a chapter about the Louisiana Purchase. "Pick some-where." She pushes the book toward me.

I push it back. "It's not that simple."

"Make it a condition of signing your contract with STARR. I don't care where we go, as long as we're doing the show together."

Together.

I close my eyes and imagine Poppy and I in a new city. San Francisco, Chicago, New Orleans. It doesn't matter where. We're sharing an apartment, or a dorm room, and I'm in school, and life is good. And then I pan out and see the cameras and the microphones and all the damn people intruding on my life. My heart beats faster just thinking about it.

There's no destination on *any* map, past or present, that would be enough to convince me to sign away my future. I have to make Poppy understand that. But how do I reject the future she's planned for us without rejecting *her*?

She puts the top back on the nail polish and blows on her toes. "Is this about Rafael?"

I sit up, surprised by the change in direction. "No. Why?"

"You never had a problem with our life until you met him."

"If you believe that, you haven't been paying attention." Does she honestly not remember all the photo shoots I grumbled my way through? All the times I tried to avoid filming our vlog? How uncomfortable I get any time I'm approached by someone I don't know?

"He went out with Olivia on Friday night."

"I know. They went to Boo! At the Zoo."

"No, they went to a movie."

A wave of relief rushes through me as I realize Rafael must have planned Boo! At the Zoo specifically for me. Just as quickly, however, the relief is replaced with unease. If they saw a movie, that means they sat next to each other, *in the dark*, for two solid hours. And I bet Olivia didn't bring along her mom and sister for company. She probably giggled and twirled her hair and hid her face in his shoulder during the scary scenes. I put down my ice cream, no longer hungry.

"He can see a movie with whoever he wants." I don't want Poppy to know how much the idea of Rafael and Olivia bothers me, but I sound too defensive.

"I'm sure." She rolls her eyes and stretches her legs out, smacking her feet against my bowl. "I know you don't have any dating experience, and I just don't want you to get hurt. Or to plan your future around someone who's not interested." Her voice drips with sarcasm as she rubs salt in an old wound.

"At least I'm not sexting some guy I've never met." As soon as the words are out of my mouth, I regret them. Her eyes flash with anger. I've gone too far.

"Did seeing Jackson make you finally realize he never liked you? And that you embarrassed yourself for years by following him around like a puppy dog?"

The words hit my chest like oncoming traffic. That's the thing about sisters, best friends, roommates, and especially someone who is all of the above. They know which words will hurt the worst. I have to say something, anything, to show her that she hasn't hurt me, she hasn't won. So I lie.

"Actually, Jackson kissed me. He told me that moving away made him realize that he does have feelings for me."

Poppy narrows her eyes as she weighs the unlikelihood of what I said against the fact that we never lie to each other. "Then why have you been in such a bad mood all week?"

"Because he left. Obviously." I stare her down, refusing to blink first.

She caves. "Good for you, I guess. I'll tell Olivia that Rafael is all hers." Jealousy flares in my stomach, and it takes all I have not to lash out against Poppy. "I was just trying to be a good sister." She picks up her headphones.

Her last words set off my alarm. It's such a lie. She wasn't trying to be a good sister. She was trying to get under my skin. *And she's not even your real sister*, I remind myself. My heart is pumping faster now, and I know I shouldn't say these next words but I say them anyway. "Don't bother. We're not really sisters anyway."

"Yeah. Okay. Please leave my room."

"I'm serious. And I can prove it."

BITES Forum

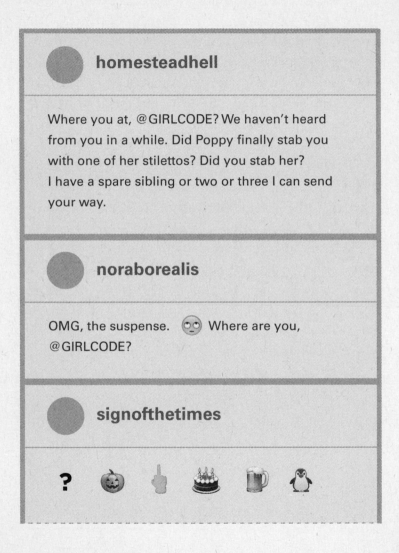

homesteadhell

Where you at, @GIRLCODE? We haven't heard from you in a while. Did Poppy finally stab you with one of her stilettos? Did you stab her? I have a spare sibling or two or three I can send your way.

noraborealis

OMG, the suspense. 🙄 Where are you, @GIRLCODE?

signofthetimes

? 🎃 🖕 🎂 🍺 🐧

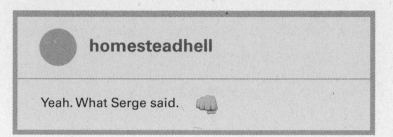

homesteadhell

Yeah. What Serge said.

Chapter 18

Poppy closes the journal and tosses it on the bed, her face unreadable. I'm prepared for a meltdown. While she was reading, I retrieved a box of tissues from the bathroom and the bag of candy corn I keep in my desk drawer. I look at her expectantly. She doesn't say or do anything. That's when I begin to worry she's in shock.

"I know this is a lot to take in. I was stunned too." I offer her the candy corn, thinking that now is as good a time as any to break her swim diet.

She pushes the candy out of her face. "I don't care."

"What?"

"I don't care. Why should I?" She doesn't sound shocked or upset. She sounds bored.

"Um, maybe because I just told you that our entire lives have been a lie."

She shrugs and bites her fingernail. "It doesn't change anything."

"How can you say that?"

"Because it's true. I don't want to know which one I am."

Typical Poppy, only looking at this from her point of view. "That's because we both know you're really a Dixon, and I'm the charity case our mom couldn't refuse."

"We don't know that."

I pick up my phone and scroll through my photo gallery until I find a picture of the three of us together. I shoved it under Poppy's nose. "Yes. We do." She takes the phone out of my hand and examines the picture for a long time.

"Maybe," she finally says as she hands the phone back to me. The word crashes on my ears. Ever since I discovered Mom's journal, there has been no question in my mind that I'm the one that doesn't belong. But hearing Poppy say it hurts worse than I would've thought possible.

I look at the picture on my phone. Mom stands in between Poppy and me with her arms around us. It was taken last May after graduation. We were waiting for Jackson to fight his way through seven hundred other graduating seniors so we could congratulate him. Mom's hair is her signature auburn, which I now realize she probably dyes to obscure the fact that she looks so much like Poppy. They both have the same hazel eyes on a heart-shaped face with perfectly proportional mouths and noses. Less than half an inch separates our heights in this photo, but that's because I was wearing three-inch wedges. My hair is darker than Poppy's, and my round face is covered in freckles. My eyes are blue, and my smile takes up too much of my face.

It's so obvious to me now. I can't understand how Mom got away with her lie for so many years. She didn't just convince Poppy and me; she convinced countless readers. I feel like all I have to do is post this picture online with the caption LOOK AT US, and people will discover the truth. But I know it's not that simple. You can't undo a lifetime of lies with one picture. This isn't an easily toppled house of cards. It's a freaking fortress.

"I don't care, and you shouldn't either. Why should you care about some woman who obviously didn't want you?" Poppy's voice brings me back to our conversation.

"Because she's my *mother*." I cannot believe that she doesn't understand the magnitude of this information.

"No, she's not. Ashley Dixon is your mother." Poppy stands up. "Our lives are amazing. We couldn't ask for anything else. Don't mess that up just because you're in some huff about your DNA."

Hot tears prick at the corners of my eyes. Poppy and I have always had a connection, an ability to read each other's minds and know exactly what the other person is feeling. But right now, it's like we're trying to communicate through a jammed router. Maybe our "connection" was so fragile that it vanished once we discovered we're not biologically related. I take a deep breath and try again. "Can you just think about how I feel for one second?"

"As soon as you start thinking about someone other than yourself, I'll start thinking about you." She slams the door on her way out.

It's one a.m. and I'm still awake, scrolling through the BITES message board without really reading it. That was not the way I wanted to tell Poppy. I never should have thrown that information in her face in the middle of an argument. How did I expect her to react? It's not like I took the news very gracefully myself. No, I cried my eyes out, locked myself in my bedroom for twenty-four hours, drove up a mountain, and then egged a dirt road. Different people have different reactions. When confronted with the information that one of us was abandoned by our biological mother and adopted into this family, I freaked out. Poppy didn't care. That's not weird or anything.

Except it is. It's so weird.

When I'm all caught up on the BITES message board, I switch over to our YouTube channel and read the comments on our "One Million Subscribers Thank You" vlog. Emily and Erica are back at it again with a new username, calling us "navel-gazing special snowflakes." It's meant to be hurtful, but I can't help but laugh at that one. My entire life, family, and future are falling apart before my eyes, and they think they're going to hurt me by calling me a snowflake? I can tune that noise out all day.

I flip back to BITES and enter my contribution to the one-up game.

---

girlcode

My family wants to make me into the next Kardashian. Reality show and all.

It's less than ten minutes before Nora requests a video chat and is smiling at me from my computer screen. It's already morning where she is. Or maybe it's still yesterday? Either way, she's swinging on a hammock with mountains behind her, her dark hair fanned out in a halo around her face. "Tell me everything," she demands through a puff of smoke. Her parents must be out; she once told me they'd sent her to a convent if they found out she smokes weed.

I give her a quick recap of Stella's visit.

"You have to get out of it." Nora's voice is insistent. I'm so grateful to have her as a friend. She's been around long enough to understand what participating in the show will cost me.

"Poppy would hate me."

She pauses, considering this. "Tell me about the scandal clause again."

"They won't film the show if we get involved in any scandal or drama. It's not 'on brand.'"

"Then there's only one choice."

I raise my eyebrows.

"You have to *create* a scandal." She leans back against her hammock with a satisfied smirk on her face.

"Poppy would know it was me, and she'd be furious."

"Good point." She scratches a mosquito bite on her cheek while thinking. "Too bad you don't have a relative who's dumb or racist or sexist or something. That's the way *real* celebrities get into trouble."

The screen goes black when I end the call, but Nora's words sit with me for a long time. I try to push it away, but once the idea grabs hold of my brain, I can't ignore it. The fact is, I *do* have a hidden relative with a history of making bad decisions, and maybe she could do the PR damage I need.

I open Google and type everything I know about my birth mother: *Arizona Highland High School Brittany*. My hands are shaking as I press enter.

Email from Stella

From: starrstella@gmail.com
To: poppyandclaire@dixondaily.com
Subject: Checking in!

Hello Girls!
I hope you both are doing well. I just wanted to check in and see if there is ANYTHING AT ALL I can do for you. Do NOT hesitate to let me know if you have any questions or concerns. I'm here for YOU!

Best Wishes,
Stella

P.S. I DO hope you are staying out of trouble! The Dixon brand is squeaky clean, and it's why we LOVE you!

Chapter 19

"Let's go in." Rafael grabs my hand and tugs me toward the haunted house.

"No way," I say but let him lead me to the front doors so I don't have to let go of his hand.

"Oh, come on! It won't be that bad. Besides, I need a break from the heat." He squints into the fading sunlight. "It still feels like summer."

He's not wrong. It was ninety-eight degrees today, which may feel like a relief in July, but is absolutely criminal at a Halloween festival. The heat is hanging on tighter than ever this year, like a lingering sunburn that still stings days after I've forgotten about it. "A couple years ago it was ninety degrees on Thanksgiving."

"And you want to stay here for college." His cocks an eyebrow, daring me to argue. Instead, I pull my hand away and cross my arms over my chest.

"You can go in. I'll wait out here." I lean against the side of the temporary haunted house that stands in the center of Howl-O-Ween. We missed Boo! At The Zoo, but this weekend's festivities are even scarier.

Lucky me.

I throw Rafael a smile but refuse to budge. He pretends to scowl, but it's a poor imitation of his actual upset face, which includes less smirk and more raking his hands through his hair.

"Was your childhood traumatized? What happened the last time you went into a haunted house?"

I ignore his first question and answer the second one. "I've never been in a haunted house."

His eyes widen in genuine surprise. "Are you serious?"

"Afraid so."

"That's it, you have to try it at least once." His eyes get big and soft as he clasps his hands in front of his chest, pleading with me. Behind him, a man with a chainsaw runs out of the house, chasing after a group of shrieking kids. When the chainsaw man retreats back into the shadows, they burst into laughter, all begin talking at once, and race to the front doors to go through again.

"I'm sorry, but I don't see what's so fun about being scared."

"Remind me why you love Halloween again."

"Candy corn, costumes, pumpkins." I tick the reasons off on my fingers. "And I look good in orange."

"Watch out for birds, Claire!" a voice shouts from somewhere to our left. I stand up straight and scan the crowd but there are so many people here that it's impossible to tell who's speaking. My entire body freezes until several seconds after the laughter has faded away.

"Don't listen to them." Rafael scans the crowd also, with just as little success.

My neck breaks out in a cold sweat as people jostle around us. I press my back against the haunted house to put distance between me and the crowd, but it doesn't get any easier to breathe. There are too many people, too much noise, and not enough personal space.

I grab Rafael's hand. "I need to get out of here." The closest escape is the front doors of the haunted house. I yank them open and dart into the dark with Rafael behind me.

It's warmer inside, but it's dark and quiet and blessedly free of people. My heart slows to a normal pace as my shoulders relax and I drop Rafael's hand. We're in a cramped room with three black walls and a handle-less black door in front of us. It's not long before it begins to feel *too* quiet and dark, and my shoulders tense up again. Somewhere in the heart of the house, a door creaks and footsteps tread lightly, sending a chill up my arms. The door in front of us cracks open, sending a shaft of dim light into the room. A hand appears, and one finger crooks to motion us forward.

"We can leave if you want." Rafael's breath is hot on my neck.

I swallow. Leaving means venturing back into a crowd of strangers who hold the unfair advantage of knowing my face and all the embarrassing parts of my history. They always see me before I see them and I hate it. I shake my head. "I want to stay."

He reaches for my hand at the same time I reach for his. He takes a small step forward and pulls the door open wide enough for us to slip through.

The haunted house offers an acre of skinny hallways that twist and turn like a maze. They're so narrow that we're forced to walk single file. Every time a new turn appears, I'm so terrified of what monster is lurking just out of sight that I ask Rafael to go first.

By the time we turn down the third hall, we still haven't seen anyone, and I begin to wonder if the actors are on break. I listen for any sound, but all I can hear is our slow footsteps and my blood pumping in my ears. At a fork in the hall, Rafael stops. "Which way?"

I squint to the left and right. A few dim lightbulbs hang on wires from the ceiling, spaced far apart, so we can't see much. My heart thumps steadily over the sound of our footsteps. Goosebumps erupt across my skin as my brain registers that we're both standing still.

The footsteps don't belong to us.

"There's someone in here."

"You want me to go look?"

"Yes. No. Don't leave." I squeeze his hand as the hair on the back of my neck stands up. Something reaches up from behind and brushes a lock of my hair off my shoulder. I scream and throw myself into Rafael's arms as man in a dark mask dashes back down the hall and into an invisible door in the wall.

My body trembles as fear electrifies my veins. If Rafael wasn't anchoring my body to his, I'd probably collapse. He holds me until my breathing slows and my legs regain their strength. Then, at my urging, we switch places and I lead. Maybe it'll be better if I see what's coming.

The hallways open up into rooms with different scenes inside. One is decorated like a little girl's nursery with creepy dolls and a woman sunk into a rocking chair. She has long, gray hair and dark shadows under her eyes. I expect her to jump out at us, but she just sits and stares while slowly rocking. It's worse than if she'd jumped.

Further on, people sneak out of closets and men with axes in their hands chase us down pitch black hallways. Those things are scary, but to my surprise, they're not the scariest part of the haunted house. When we're being chased, I know it'll end as soon as we turn the corner and find a new horror. The quiet and empty hallways are much worse. They flood my body with dread and adrenaline, because I never know what is coming next. That's when my imagination goes into overdrive and creates scarier monsters than the ones employed by the Phoenix Zoo. My monster always drives a blue minivan and calls Poppy by name.

I lose all sense of time in the haunted house, but we've been weaving our way through the halls for quite a while when we reach a small, empty room with no doors. The only way out is the way we came in.

"What now?" I ask.

"I guess we have to go back." Rafael looks around the dark room. "Wait, this is a door." He shows me the outline of a black door like the one that held the man in the mask.

"I'm getting tired of these doors without handles on our side."

"Maybe we're supposed to wait," he says.

"For what?" I look up and am surprised to find his face inches from mine. His chest expands and brushes against my body with every breath. My own air catches in my throat as I meet his eyes and inhale his spearmint breath. He's so close, but not nearly close enough. Once again, electricity jolts through me, awakening all the nerve endings in my body. It's scarier—and better, so much better, than the chills provided by the hired actors. Rafael's eyes are searching as we wait. Pressure builds in my chest, but I'm not tempted to say anything to ruin the moment. Not this time. He leans in and I exhale a sigh of relief, anticipating his lips on mine—just as the roar of a chainsaw rips through the silence.

The door springs open. We run through it as the man with the chainsaw chases us outside into the last few minutes of fading sunlight. I collapse onto the nearest bench and struggle to catch my breath. I'm relieved and jittery and disappointed, I can't stop the laughter that bursts from my lips.

Rafael sits next to me. "I told you you'd have fun."

"Who says I had fun?" I try and fail to keep my smile under control.

"Oh, please. You loved it."

"It was tolerable."

Rafael shakes his head. "You're ridiculous, Just Claire. But hey, are you hungry?" He nods toward a row of food trucks behind us. "I smell something fried and delicious with our names on it."

"What's the biggest misconception about Poppy?" Rafael licks his mint chocolate chip cone.

"You mean besides the thigh gap thing?"

He stops mid-lick and turns to me with a horrified expression. "The what?"

"You don't want to know." I'd rather him stay blissfully unaware. "Okay, my turn. What's your favorite food?"

"Boring."

"Not for someone who's lived all over the world. I stand by my question."

"Abuela's tamales. Dad and I would sometimes come to Arizona for a week at Christmas, and man, I could eat my body weight in those things."

My mouth waters at the thought, despite the double scoop of cookies 'n cream in my hand. "Your turn."

"Don't hate me for this one." He smiles wickedly, and my heart picks up speed. "I watched one of your earliest vlogs."

"Uh oh . . ."

"The one where you bleached Poppy's hair. And left the bleach in too long? And it fell out in clumps?"

"I remember." I casually lick my cone, praying this doesn't go where I think it's going.

"A lot of the comments say you did it on purpose."

"What's the question?"

"Did you?"

"Rafael!" I smack him on the shoulder. "I can't believe you would accuse me of such treachery."

"That's not an answer," he accuses with a smile. I bite my lip at the sight of his dimples.

"There might be *some* truth—"

"I knew it!" He roars with laughter.

I shake my head at the memory. I didn't want her hair to fall out per se, but I also didn't dissuade her from buying the cheapest box of bleach in the drugstore. And okay, maybe I forgot to remind her to wash it out. But it's her fault for getting distracted by a text message from Cooper Clawson, the cutest boy in eighth grade. "The joke was on me, because the damage resulted in a pixie cut that *everyone* loved. Even the trolls couldn't deny how cute she looked."

"Eh. Not as cute as some." He winks, and my insides feel all melty, like the ice cream slipping down my tongue.

After three hours and two loops around the zoo, we walk toward the exit. My feet hurt, I'm hot and sweaty, but this is the happiest I have been all week. I step off the curb and scan the animal signs affixed to light poles in the parking lot.

"Where did we park? Was it the cheetah section? Or the tortoise?"

"Hey! Can I get some help?" I turn to see a middle-aged man leaning out of a blue van, and am overwhelmed by a terrifying sense of déjà vu.

Poppy! I need your help! I close my eyes and see the face of the woman who called to us from the driver's seat. She looked so nice. So normal.

Rafael walks toward the van. "What's up?" I watch him go but can't make my feet follow. I want to yell at him to stop and tell him it's not safe, even though I know he'll be fine. Rafael is eighteen years old and six feet tall, not your typical kidnapping victim. The parking lot is full of people leaving for the night. There are parents with small children and ASU students holding hands and teenagers in big groups. Rafael is safe. I'm safe. I repeat the words over and over in my head, as if that'll make me believe they're true.

Rafael jogs to me as the van drives away. "He wanted an opinion whether or not the festival is too scary for his kids. I told him to steer clear of the haunted house and they'd be fine. I'm pretty sure we're in the cheetah section." He nods to the left and continues toward his car.

He turns around when he realizes I'm not walking with him. "Are you okay?" He moves toward me with his eyebrows knit together. "You're shaking! Are you cold?" He puts his hands on my arms and rubs them, despite the warm weather. "What's going on?"

I shake my head. This is so not the place to talk about it. "Let's go."

When we're sitting in his car with the air conditioning blasting, Rafael turns to me. "What happened back there? You looked more scared than you did in the haunted house."

I hesitate, but only for a moment. My mom isn't here to hijack my story and make it about her. Poppy's not here to guilt me into silence. It's just me and Rafael in this car, and the story comes out with surprising ease. I've never talked about this with anyone before, but the longer I talk, the more I have to say.

One of my favorite things about Rafael is how well he listens. He doesn't make a single joke the entire time, and he ignores every alert from his phone. I tell him every detail; the woman calling Poppy's name, me pulling Poppy out of the van, and bony but strong fingers latching around my wrists.

Rafael's hands twitch at his sides, like he wants to reach out to me. Instead he runs them over his face. "I get it now."

"Get what?" I wipe my tears and come away with mascara-streaked fingers.

"You. Your animosity toward the internet. The way you get uncomfortable when strangers talk to you. The way you seem lighter, more relaxed, when no one is around." He shakes his head and then he looks at me. "I wish I could say something more helpful, but man . . ." he rakes a hand through his hair. "People suck. Including your mom, no offense, for keeping you on the internet. I'm so sorry." His eyes lock on mine.

The sincerity of his words settles on me like a blanket. No one has ever said that before. If my mom said it in the days and weeks following the incident, I don't remember. With the exception of the interview with Lena, we haven't talked about it in years.

"It helps more than you realize."

I no longer feel like crying, not when I'm in a dark car with Rafael. It'd be easy lose myself in his ready smile and devastating hair, if I wanted to. And I want to.

My past is a lie. Things at home are a mess. The future I planned for myself is slipping away. But right now, all I want is to be closer to the boy who makes me feel light, even with all of the darkness.

My heart thumps wildly in my chest, louder than the bass from a nearby pickup. I shift my body toward him. Inch by inch, he mirrors my movements, until we're both leaning over the center consol.

Rafael touches his forehead to mine and closes his eyes. Our noses touch, both of them cold from the air conditioning. A soft sigh escapes his lips, and I can't wait another second. I lean into him and close the gap between us.

In the second before my lips meet his, he jerks back.

"Sorry! I'm sorry!" My face heats beneath the icy cold blast of air coming from the dashboard. Forget the too-small dress at Fashion week. Forget the viral video. *This* is the most humiliating moment of my life.

I open my purse and dig around frantically for tissues to dry my face. While I awkwardly fumble around in the passenger seat, Rafael doesn't say a word. When the mascara situation is under control, I look at him again. He leans against the headrest with his eyes closed. There's a look of pain on his face.

"Um, Rafael?" My voice is almost a whisper. He takes a deep breath, opens his eyes and turns to me. "I'm really sorry. I shouldn't have assumed."

"Don't apologize. It's my fault. I shouldn't have . . . I shouldn't have gotten so close. I'm sorry. I just don't want either of us to do something we'll regret."

Oh.

I have no idea what I expected him to say, but it wasn't that. If there's one thing about Rafael I can count on, it's his ability to surprise me every time.

COMMENTS ON OUR TOP FIVE TRENDS FOR FALL VLOG

MADI 3 days ago

Ok but you guys are literal sister goals I'm obsessed

LISA 3 days ago

omg I have that sweater I'm famous

KIERA 3 days ago

you both are sooooo beautiful I want your life

CHARLI 3 days ago

what's your intro song?

NATALIE 3 days ago

Hi Claire and Poppy I just found your channel last week
and I have to say that you two are so pretty and inspiring
and I want to be just like you!

LINDSAY 3 days ago

What size are those jeans? And how tall are you and how
much do you weigh thanks so much

KRYSTAL 3 days ago

When are you going to do another fan meet up in AZ?!?!

BIANCA 3 days ago

Damn you two SLAY. GOALS.

NADIA 3 days ago

Your life is literally perfect.

Chapter 20

As it turns out, being good with web design and coding isn't much help when it comes to finding my birth mom. My internet searches don't turn up anything helpful, because it seems like approximately half the girls who went to school with my mom were named Brittany. I don't go to school with any girls named Brittany, but there's a Bryttannie. I don't know which is worse. I spend the rest of the week scanning social media sites and profiles for anything relevant but it's no use. Without a last name, I have no idea what or who I'm looking for.

Mom would know. But even if I asked, she wouldn't help me. If she wanted me to have a relationship with my birth mother, she wouldn't have smothered the truth under thousands upon thousands of disingenuous words about our perfect life. No, this is something I have to do on my own.

What I really need is proof that I'm adopted. Once I get my hands on my birth certificate or adoption papers, I should be able to find my mom's full name. If this were a Lifetime movie, I'd probably go to the hospital where I was born and find the nurse who was in the room when I was delivered. She'd be old and wise and she would cry with me while she told me the story of my birth and how much I look like my real mother. And, okay, my life may be as staged and fake as they come, but in a boring way, not in a Lifetime movie way.

If my life were a Disney movie, I'd be Claire, Regular Girl by day and Claire, Computer Hacker by night. I'd hack into the hospital database and find all the information I need while wearing a hoodie and black fingernail polish. I'm embarrassed to admit this, but I totally watched twenty minutes of an hour-long video called "Introduction to Hacking" before I realized that I don't have the necessary skills to pull that off.

Nor do I have the skills required to be a normal human being around Rafael. We have an unspoken agreement to pretend the almost-kiss this weekend never happened, but we both try so hard to make things *friendly* and *normal* that the results are almost painful. He forces himself to joke around with me at lunch, and I force myself to laugh. Poppy and Olivia exchange glances. Under normal circumstances, Poppy would corner me and demand to know what is going on. Because she's still mad at me, she rolls her eyes and talks to Olivia instead.

Contrary to prevailing opinion, my life is *not* super fun and perfect all the time.

Just when I think things can't get worse, Olivia invites Rafael to a Halloween party. Poppy has been talking about her sexy strawberry costume for weeks. When I pointed out that strawberries aren't a particularly attractive fruit, she told me I don't "understand Halloween" and huffed away, red platform boots in hand.

Rafael hesitates when Olivia invites him and looks at me. "Are you going?"

"I don't know." I wasn't actually invited to the party this year, and I raise my eyebrows at Poppy to see if she plans to confirm this fact.

"Claire has a thing against teenage Halloween. Sexy fruit offends her," she says.

Rafael looks amused. "Me too. Last night, my dad served bananas with dinner . . . totally inappropriate." He shakes his head.

I burst out laughing. Poppy glares at me and flips her hair over her shoulder. The gesture is so over-the-top "mean girl" that I start laughing again.

"I think I'll skip the party this year," I tell Rafael. The truth is, I don't want to go. Last year's party was just an endless stream of look-how-cute-my-costume-is selfies.

Yawn.

I'd rather have actual fun than spend hours posing for pictures that only make it *look* like I'm having fun. But it still hurts that Poppy is so obviously excluding me, because we've always been together on Halloween.

"Yeah, I'm not sure 'High School Party' is really my scene," Rafael says.

"Oh, come on. You don't want to just sit at home alone all night, do you?" Olivia puts her hand on his arm and bats her eyelashes. I bite my lip to keep from laughing. Apparently, Poppy is not the only one taking notes from high school movies.

Rafael moves his arm away. "I'll hang with Claire. I hear she's the real Halloween aficionado." He flashes me a genuine smile for the first time since Saturday and my heart races. He's giving me another chance to be his friend, and I'm determined not to screw it up this time.

"Well, if that gets boring," Olivia shoots me a look, "you can always change your mind."

"Wait up!" Olivia runs up the stairs to catch up with me that afternoon. After her stunning display of friendship at lunch, I decided to skip our usual meeting at the drinking fountain and go straight to class. Clearly, she's not going to let me off that easily. Both her blonde pigtails and her sundress swing side to side as she hurries up the steps.

She falls into step next to me when we reach the top of the stairs. I resist the temptation to blow her off. This is just the way it is in high school. We're still supposed to be friendly to each other even though she was completely rude to me at lunch.

"You weren't at the drinking fountains today." It sounds like an accusation. So maybe we're not acting like friends anymore.

"Nope."

"What's the deal with you and Rafael?"

"What do you mean?"

"Do you like him? Or are you with Jackson?" She speaks slowly, like she's talking to a child. Poppy must have told her that Jackson and I are together, and I'll look like an idiot if I admit I was lying.

"Oh. Um, yeah."

"Yeah *what*?"

"What was the question again?" I check my phone for the time, hoping for the warning bell.

"Are. You. With. Jackson?"

"Yes." When I say this, her grimace turns into a sweet smile.

"Well then, you won't mind if I invite Rafael to the party again." Olivia pulls her phone out of her bag and walks away without another word.

"Don't you ever get tired of acting like a bitch?" I call after her.

She whips around and surveys me with a frown. "At least I'm the same bitch online as I am in real life," she accuses.

"I'm always the same person."

"If that were true, would we be having this conversation?" She gives me a pointed look before leaving again. This time, I let her go.

"You wore a costume!"

Rafael is standing on my doorstep in blue scrubs and a surgical cap. I'm fairly certain entire television franchises have been built around the idea that men look irresistible in scrubs. Rafael is no exception. I don't know what Olivia said to him, but I'm thrilled it wasn't enough to change his mind about the party.

"It's Halloween! I had to." He steps inside and I realize with a jolt that we're alone. After taking pictures of us in our costumes, Mom left for Cami's house and Poppy left for Olivia's. I grab the door handle just for something to do with my hands.

"I still can't believe you wore a costume!" I say, hoping my makeup will cover my flushed cheeks. Experience has taught me that Poppy, Olivia, and all the other girls at tonight's party will be costumed head to toe, with fully coordinated makeup and accessories, while the boys will point to their ball caps and claim to be dressed as baseball players.

Rafael shrugs. "I thought you would ostracize me if I didn't." He smiles with half of his mouth and shrugs his shoulder again, as if he doesn't know what else to say.

"Do you get it?" I gesture to my costume. I'm wearing a black dress with a large white spider sewed to the front and black fishnet stockings. Fake spiderwebs are strung through my hair, and when I raise my arms, webs fan out like wings. I've had it planned for weeks, and I hope he understands the reference. There's nothing worse than spending Halloween fielding endless questions about what you are. "It's a pun," I add, suddenly self-conscious.

"Don't tell me," he says. "Okay, spider, obviously." I raise my eyebrows as he continues. "But no! Okay, um . . . spiderweb . . . black widow . . . cobweb, something . . ." He trails off and looks at me sheepishly. "I'm useless." He rubs the back of his neck with his hand, and it's so cute, I'm almost grateful he didn't get it.

"Web designer."

What he lacks in ability to guess my costume, he more than makes up for with his enthusiastic grin. "You look great! Really." Our eyes meet and monstrous butterflies come to nest in my stomach.

Rafael clears his throat. "What's the plan for tonight? I'm expecting big things from Miss Halloween herself."

"Well, I don't want to overwhelm you with my genius . . . but I thought we'd pass out candy."

"Sounds wild." His voice is low and teasing and completely devastating.

"I'm just getting started. We can even bring the fire pit out to the driveway, and then, if we're feeling adventurous, we can walk around the neighborhood."

"Whoa. Mind blown."

He helps me drag the fire pit to the driveway and light a fire. It's warm enough outside that we don't need it, but my parents used to sit around the fire every Halloween when I was little. We wave to my neighbors, many of whom have gathered together on camping chairs around their own fires. With a stroke of brilliance, Rafael starts melting mini candy bars, and I run inside for graham crackers and marshmallows. We take turns inventing new s'mores combinations. As I take a bite of a peanut butter cup s'more with a deliciously roasted and gooey marshmallow, I think about Poppy and Olivia at a party surrounded by loud music and beer pong.

"Sorry if this is lame in comparison to a big party." I unwrap another graham cracker and pass half to him.

His fingers brush against mine as he grabs the cracker. A flame surges through my body.

"It's not lame. I kind of love how much you love this holiday."

Love. My head spins as my cheeks redden underneath the eyeliner web spanning my cheek.

The dark and the stars and the heat from the fire break down my inhibitions enough to try to get some answers.

"Olivia will be disappointed." I watch him over the flickering embers, trying to gauge his reaction.

He shakes his head. "I have a feeling she'll recover. Besides, there's nowhere else I'd rather be right now." His smoky eyes rival the fire.

My fingers fumble with a marshmallow as I thread it on a roasting stick. I thrust it directly into the flames and set it ablaze. I have no patience for a slow burn.

If Rafael doesn't want to kiss me, why does he say things like that? And why is he here with me instead hanging out with any of the other amazing girls at school?

"Tell me about the other girls."

"What do you mean?" He frowns.

"Did you have a girlfriend in India? Or Mexico? Or Turkey?"

"Not officially. But yeah, there were a few girls I hung out with."

I raise my eyebrows.

"Not at the same time! Why are you asking about this?"

I pull the marshmallow out, and blow out the flames before grabbing the charred mess with my fingers.

"Ow!" The sticky goo burns my skin.

Rafael grimaces. "Did you get burned?"

I sigh. "I'm not sure yet."

The Five Kinds of Halloween Pictures You See on Social Media

1. The "I Spent Two Hours on This Makeup, Please Appreciate" selfie
2. The "Take This Blatantly Unsexy Object and Make It a Sexy Costume" selfie
3. The "Girl Group Costume" picture
4. The "I'm Too Cool for This, but I'm Here Anyway" selfie
5. The "Couples Costume" picture—the Holy Grail of social media

Chapter 21

The morning after Halloween, I run out of toothpaste, which is how I find myself in Poppy's room for the first time in weeks. To be perfectly honest, I consider *not* brushing my teeth, but there are some lines I won't cross. Oral hygiene is one of those lines.

"You could knock next time," Poppy says from her position sitting cross-legged on the bathroom counter, where she's applying mascara with her mouth open. The same way I do it. The same way our mom does it. I push the thought from my mind.

The same way *her* mom does it.

She doesn't look at me. The last few weeks have been tense. She won't come right out and say she's mad, but it's obvious.

"We should talk." I didn't plan on saying that, but now that I have, I decide to go with it. I'm sick of fighting with her.

"About what?" She switches the mascara wand to the other hand.

"About what I read in Mom's journal." This is the first time I've broached the subject since our first and last conversation about it.

Poppy freezes for a second. She quickly starts back up with the mascara again, but I can see a shake in her usually steady hand. "Crap." She picks up a Q-tip, runs it under the tap, and wipes off a black smudge underneath her eye. "Whatever. I told you I don't care," she says to the mirror.

"Honestly? That's all you have to say to me right now?"

"*Honestly*, I don't think it's a big deal. So we're not biologically related. So what? We're still sisters. Your still our mom's daughter. One white lie can't erase the eighteen years of history we have as a family." She rubs her lips together and leans into the mirror to examine her lip gloss.

We're still sisters. Her words echo in my head. We're still sisters. Are we? We haven't been acting like it lately. We haven't even been acting like friends.

"What's wrong?" she asks. For the first time since I entered her room, she gives me her full attention.

"Nothing. Why?"

"You're chewing on your lip so hard you're going to draw blood." She tilts her head to the side and studies me with a concerned expression and pursed lips.

"Oh. It's . . . it's nothing." I can't do it. I can't tell her that I'm looking for my birth mother in an attempt to prove the thing Poppy's trying so hard to avoid, and possibly sabotage the future of our reality show.

"Is it Jackson? Rafael?" she asks.

"What? No!"

"I'm not blind. You spend all of your time with Rafael, and you never talk about Jackson. What's going on?"

"There's nothing to tell. We're just friends." He made that perfectly clear when he almost sprained his neck dodging my kiss. But I can't tell Poppy the whole story, because it's humiliating and things are so weird between us.

"Sure. I definitely believe that you're randomly and secretly dating Jackson while spending all your time mooning over your 'just friend' Rafael. Or, like we learned in science class, the simplest answer is the right one, and you're a big liar." Her expression dares me to contradict her.

I grab the toothpaste and leave, but I'm still thinking about our conversation while I brush my teeth. I once read an article about words that have no English equivalent. The Inuit have a word for when you're so excited for someone to come over that you keep opening your door to check for them, and there's a word in Hawaiian that describes the action of scratching your head to help you remember something forgotten. *Pana po'o.* What I need is a word for when someone replays a conversation in their head, giving them the chance to say all the witty and amazing things they should've said the first time. If I could go back three minutes, I'd tell Poppy that if the simplest answer is the right one, I would have known years ago that we weren't really sisters because she's a shallow automaton and I'm . . . well, I'm still trying to figure out exactly what I am when her words hit me again.

The simplest answer is the right one.

I don't need to hack hospital files or track down the wizened old nurse who delivered me. All I need is some good old-fashioned snooping.

I make a big show of putting away the Halloween decorations while Poppy and Mom brainstorm holiday vlog topics. Once I'm satisfied that they know exactly what I'm doing, I pull the closet door closed and flip on a flashlight app on my phone. Then I dig.

The box of journals doesn't turn up anything. Neither does the trunk of old family photos or the box of my dad's clothes that Mom couldn't bear to part with. I'm starting to get discouraged when I take the top off a box of files. I thumb through sixteen years of taxes before reaching a thin file that says Medical Records. I lean my phone-flashlight against a box and open the folder with unsteady hands.

It doesn't take long to find it. Below a few hospital bills is a single sheet of paper.

On top is the logo for Gilbert Regional Medical Center. Below that it reads PROOF OF BIRTH.

It doesn't look like any birth certificate I've ever seen in movies. There's no official seal on the bottom or anything. Just a few blank spaces filled in with messy handwriting.

This is to certify that: Baby Girl Dewitt
Was Born on: November 22, 2000
Name of Mother: Brittany Dewitt
Name of Father:
Delivering Physician: Eric Barney, M.D.

Below that are official adoption papers signed by my parents, making them the legal guardians of Claire Dixon.

I place the two papers side by side and stare at them. Relief courses through my body at this evidence that I really am the adopted one. Poppy needs this life more than I do. If our roles were reversed, she would have a lot more to say than "I don't care." Plus, it's liberating to finally have an explanation for why my life has felt so hard the last few years. I know I'm lucky to live in a nice house in a nice neighborhood. My closet is overflowing with free clothes. Any other teenage girl would kill to be me. But it's never really felt *right*, and now I know why.

I read the Proof of Birth paper again and focus on the date. According to this paper, I was born on November 22. Poppy and I have always celebrated our birthday on November 23. It's weird that *this* is the thing that makes me cry. For some reason, the thought of my parents ignoring my true birthday hurts worse than the confirmation that I'm adopted. It's another lie on the increasingly long list.

I sigh as I slip the papers back into the box. It's not much, but it's a start. I retreat to my room and lock the door. Armed with a full name and a determination to find my real family, it's time to get to work.

I spend the night Googling endless variations of "Brittany Dewitt Gilbert Arizona," starting with the obituaries. It feels morbid, but I want to get the bad news out of the way first—just in case. I breathe a heavy sigh of relief when nothing turns up and focus my attention elsewhere.

Next, I search at least a dozen social networking sites and find plenty of women named Brittany Dewitt, but none of the profiles scream forty-year-old woman-who-abandoned-her-baby-in-a-stranger's-hospital-room. Not that I have any idea what that type of woman would look like. I suppose there's every likelihood that my real mom is one of these women beaming at me from her profile picture. She could be the brunette standing on top of a mountain or the blonde blowing out birthday candles with a party hat strapped crookedly to her head. It's been eighteen years since she had me, and it would be silly to assume that the memory of me is anything but an annoying gnat she swats away when it intrudes on her happy life with her loving husband and perfect children.

I sigh and drop my face on the keyboard. My forehead presses on the letter h, spilling it at least twenty-five times in the search bar. I've been at this for hours and my brain feels like mush. I'm at a complete and utter dead end. I need help. Normally, I'd ask Poppy, but I know she wouldn't want to be involved with this. I'm tempted to ask Rafael, but Halloween finally put us back to a normal place, and I don't want to threaten that by bringing up all my baggage again. With the two of them ruled out and given my miniscule social circle, there's only one place left to turn.

I was hoping that Gideon or Nora would be on BITES chat, but the only one around is Serge. It's a long shot, but I send him a message explaining my predicament, and he immediately replies.

signofthetimes

☠

girlcode

Already checked the obits.

signofthetimes

👽

He's either suggesting my birth mother is an alien, or was abducted by aliens, or . . . something else entirely. I'm never really sure with him.

girlcode

I doubt it.

signofthetimes

girlcode

I can't begin to guess what you're getting at.

Serge breaks from tradition to send me a link. I click on it and am taken to a family history website that is specifically designed to help people find their family members. It's worth a shot, at least. I stretch my arms over my head and then shake them loose, ready for another marathon session of snooping.

I type Brittany Dewitt into the search box, chose "Arizona" from a drop-down menu, and click a button that says "Search Records." Fifteen seconds later, I have a list of two dozen records that match Brittany Dewitt, including birth years for each. Halfway down the list, I see a birth year that matches my mom's. I click it, and am given everything I could ever want to know about this particular Brittany Dewitt, including her address.

It's almost scary how easy that was to find. I didn't have to pay, or give the website my name, or anything. I simply searched her name, and it spat out a list of addresses spanning the last twenty years. I'm also given access to several people who are listed as "possible relatives." I glance over the strange-to-me names. As far as I know, one of these men could be my father. Or not. I might never know.

My fingers fly over the keyboard without permission from my brain, and before I have consciously made the decision whether or not I wanted to find her, I have a street map of her last known address pulled up on my screen. It's a home in Superior, a ghost of a town east of Gilbert that I know by name and not much else.

I stare at that address for a long time, unsure of what I want to do with it.

Directions to 623 Copper Street, Superior, Arizona

Head east on E Guadalupe Rd
   0.6 miles

Turn left onto S Power Rd
   1.5 miles

Use the right 2 lanes to turn right to merge onto US-60 E toward Globe
   38.2 miles

Take exit 227 for AZ-177
   0.2 miles

Turn left onto AZ-177 N/Ray Rd
   167 feet

Continue straight onto S Magma Ave
   0.2 miles

Take S Magma Ave to W Copper St
   2 minutes (0.6 miles)

Chapter 22

Days blur into weeks. I don't sleep. Brittany Dewitt's address fuses itself onto my brain as if my life depends on remembering it. Every morning on my way to school and every afternoon on my way home, the urge to skip town nearly overcomes me. Once, I missed all of first period because I drove right by the school and was halfway to Superior before I chickened out and turned around. It's the last thing on my mind at night and the first thing I think about every morning.

Originally, I was hoping to find her as a means of getting out of signing my contract with STARR Network. But I have no idea if that would even work. The ink dried on Poppy's contract weeks ago, and every day that passes without me signing mine puts more distance between us. I want to make Poppy happy, but I'm not sure how much of my future I'm willing to compromise for her. If she's not looking out for my happiness, should I be concerned about hers?

Just when I'm starting to feel like I'll explode if I have to think about my family for one more second, distraction arrives on a Wednesday afternoon in the form of Rafael Luna.

"I brought you a present!" He leans against my doorframe with his hands behind his back.

I sit up from my sprawled position on my bed, where I was doing my homework, surprised to see him standing in my room. Or nearly in my room, anyway.

"Your mom let me in. I told her it was a surprise." He grins.

"But my birthday is not until Sunday!" *Saturday*, I mentally correct myself. My birthday is before Poppy's, making me a whole day older than she is. One day might not sound like a big deal, but when you're a twin, every second counts.

"I couldn't wait. Close your eyes!" he instructs, and I comply. "I didn't wrap it for reasons that will become clear in a few seconds." He takes my arm and pulls me to my feet, then puts his hands on my shoulders and leads me across the room. My legs bump into my desk chair, and a slight pressure from Rafael's hands indicates I should sit down.

Sitting, I ask, "Can I look?"

"Not yet." His arm brushes against mine as he leans forward, sending a shiver tumbling down my spine. My curiosity is tugged to the surface when I hear his fingers tapping against my keyboard.

"Now?"

"Patience is a virtue." Rafael's voice is close to my right ear and the intoxicating scent of spearmint hits me.

"Not one of mine."

The tapping stops, starts, stops. Hands cover my eyes, blocking out all the light in the room. He clears his throat. "Are you ready?" My limbs weaken at the nervous tremor in his voice.

I nod my head under his hands and he pulls them away. My computer screen is logged onto the Scratch website I showed him weeks ago.

"Okay, don't laugh. I'm brand new at this." He clicks on a project titled "Happy Birthday, Claire," and it's only then that I realize what he's doing.

"You didn't!" I look at him but he keeps his eyes on the screen.

"Whenever you're ready." He gestures to the computer.

I click to start the animation and jaunty music plays from the speakers. A boy appears on the screen, with a thought bubble above his head that says, "I have no friends." He turns his head left and right then shrugs his shoulders.

"That's me," Rafael explains helpfully.

A girl with long brown hair, a face full of freckles, and a laptop walks into the picture.

"That's you!"

I nudge him in the arm to make him stop talking.

"I'm Rafael!" the boy says, in Rafael's actual voice.

"I'm Claire!" the girl says, in a high-pitched version of Rafael's voice. I immediately crack up laughing. Then, for reasons that can't be explained, they both start hopping up and down as pumpkins rain from the sky. After thirty seconds of this, they're transported to a room filled with balloons and eighteen floating birthday cakes. Animated Rafael says, "Happy Birthday, Claire!"

As soon as it's over, I immediately watch it again. By the third viewing, I'm laughing so hard, I'm crying. When I finally turn back to Rafael, he looks at me like he's bracing himself for a punch in the face.

"I love it!"

"You do?" The lines around his eyes smooth and he smiles.

"It's amazing. I can't believe you learned Scratch for me." And then, out of nowhere, I develop a lump the size of a pumpkin in my throat. "I can't believe you took the time to do this." He turns to me so we're eye to eye. He crosses his arms and rests them on my knees. It's the first time he's touched me since Howl-O-Ween, and as soon as he does, the space between us shrinks and expands simultaneously. My hands hang limply by my side, waiting for an order from my brain. He's close enough that my breath catches in my chest, but not close enough for me to be sure what he's thinking.

"I hope it's okay that I did." His eyes lock on mine, and I get the feeling he's trying to gauge my reaction to his words. My first instinct is to put my hands around his neck and lean forward and kiss him, but last time I did that, it ended in disaster. So instead, I spring to my feet, knocking him backwards in the process. He puts his hands out to catch his balance.

"Of course!" I smile in a fake, overly happy way that would make Mom and her camera proud.

He turns back to my computer and exits out of Scratch, revealing another tab open to the map of Brittany Dewitt's address. I should have gotten rid of it a long time ago, but at this point it may as well be the background image on my computer. "What's this?"

"My birth mother's address."

"What? How did you find her?"

"You can find anyone with Google and enough time." I shudder at the truth of this statement, and wonder how easy it is to find *my* address on the internet.

"Are you going to go see her?"

"I haven't decided yet."

"Wow. That's huge."

"Not as huge as your animation. It's the best birthday present I've ever gotten." I shut my computer, hoping to let the subject drop. I don't feel like talking about my birth mother, and I want him to understand how much I love his present.

"Didn't your Mom buy you a Mercedes last year?"

I wrinkle my nose, realizing how spoiled that makes me sound. He interprets my reaction as a slight against my mom.

He shakes his head. "I know things are kind of confusing and messed up right now, and maybe it's not my place to say this, but I'd give your mom a break." His eyes look sad, the way they did that night at the park when we first talked about the blog.

"When you said you were jealous of me . . . what did you mean by that?"

"Isn't it obvious? I'm jealous of how much your mom cares. I know you don't see it, but everyone else does."

"I'm sorry about your mom."

"It's not her. I could care less about her. It's my dad."

"You don't think he loves you?"

Rafael runs his hand through his hair and sits on my bed. He leans against my headboard and stretches his long legs out across the duvet. The sight of him there hitches my breath.

"Loves me, sure. Likes me? I don't know. We never spend time together, because he's always working. The other day, I asked him if I had a baby book. How pathetic is that? I wanted some proof that he cared to remember anything about my life."

"It's not pathetic."

"Says the girl whose every move is documented for the rest of time."

"Or until the internet explodes."

"Or that."

"So what'd your dad say?"

"He said he couldn't remember. How's that for ironic?"

I sit down next to him, and we both lean back against the headboard. He closes his eyes.

"Aren't we a pair of tragic childhoods." Now that Brittany Dewitt's address isn't glowing at me from my computer screen, my body relaxes. I close my eyes and drop my head on Rafael's shoulder without thinking about whether or not I should or what message I'm sending. I'm too tired to worry about any of that right now. Every inch of my body feels exhausted.

"We should probably start our homework," Rafael says. And maybe I'm imagining it, but he doesn't sound very committed.

"Definitely," I agree but don't move. I doubt my body could move if I wanted it to.

"Hey Claire. Can I ask you something?"

"Mm-hmm."

"Are you falling asleep?"

"Mm-hmm."

"Go to sleep. We can talk later."

Incoming Texts

Unknown number

Hi Claire! This is Stella from STARR Network!
How are you doing?

Me

I haven't decided yet about the show.

Unknown number

What's your biggest hesitation?

Me

All of it?

Unknown number

Poppy told me you want to go away to school. We're
currently planning to rent you a home in Tempe and film
near ASU, but we can certainly discuss other locations.

Me

I want to be a normal college student.

Unknown number

Oh honey, I think that ship has sailed.

Me

Can Poppy do it without me?

Unknown number

Absolutely not! We want you both and won't
settle for anything less!

Keep thinking! I'll be in touch soon!

Chapter 23

I wake up on Saturday morning to a steady drumming sound. It takes me several seconds to identify it as rain against my window. I stay in bed and listen with my eyes closed. This is the first rain we've gotten since monsoon season ended in September. Autumn in Arizona doesn't involve a lot of rain. When I was little, I used to wish for a rainy birthday the way most kids wish for a white Christmas. It never happened though. Arizona always gives me clear skies for my birthday.

My eyes fly open. I grab my phone and check the date, just to make sure I'm not wrong. Saturday, November 22. According to the Proof of Birth document I found, today is my birthday. I'm eighteen years old. Officially an adult. I glance at my panda-print pajama bottoms and feel the opposite of mature.

I wonder what my birth certificate says. It must say November 23, because that's what my driver's license says. How did my parents convince the court to change my birthday? Is that even legal? I'm overcome by a sick feeling that the blog paid not only for this house and everything in it, but also for some kind of bribe that convinced a judge to change my actual birthday on a legal document.

Despite the pounding rain, the house feels unnaturally quiet. I investigate and discover a note taped to the milk in the refrigerator.

> *Claire Bear,*
>
> *State Swimming Championships today!*
>
> *You should come cheer for your sister! (Bring an extra umbrella if you do.)*
>
> *We'll be home late.*
>
> *Love you!*
> *—Mom*

Outside, a gray blanket of clouds covers Gilbert. Poor Poppy. Swimming in the rain isn't so bad, but sitting in the rain for hours while waiting for your next race is a nightmare. Swim meets are long and unbearable even in the best weather. I love my sister, but I'm not about to spend my birthday hunched under an umbrella for her.

My birthday. I shake my head, unable to wrap my mind around the thought. I wonder if Mom remembers she had my birthday changed, or if she tucked that information neatly away in a box of things she doesn't think about anymore.

I collapse on the couch and turn on the TV. As I mindlessly flip through the channels, I can't help but think this is a really pathetic way to celebrate my eighteenth. No cake. No party. No presents. No friends. I won't even get those insincere birthday wishes on my social media page that I roll my eyes at but secretly love, because no one knows that today is the day they're supposed to write them.

It's too bad my biological mother doesn't have a social media page of her own, because she would know why today is special. I'd send her a private message, and she'd know just the right thing to say. She'd understand me in a way Ashley Dixon never could.

That's when it hits me, and I know exactly how to celebrate. I'm going to see the one person who might know and care that I was born eighteen years ago today.

"Are you going to tell me what's going on?" Rafael asks as he ducks into the passenger seat. He shakes his hair and rain splatters the inside of my car. It reminds me of a golden retriever after a bath—in an adorable, I-want-to-snuggle-him sort of way. "You sounded a little frantic on the phone."

"Birthday road trip." I put my foot on the gas and retrace my way out of his neighborhood.

"Road trip? Should I have brought a change of clothes? A toothbrush? Left my dad a note?"

He bends forward to tie his shoe, and I can't see his expression. *A toothbrush?* Did he really think I'd take him on an overnight road trip? I lean my head from side to side to crack my neck and shake the tension out of my body. He was joking. He had to be.

"We'll be home by tonight." I take the nearest freeway ramp and head east. "Turns out today's my birthday. Surprise!" I'm breathless and nervous as I push harder on the gas pedal. Now that I've made up my mind to go, I can't get there fast enough. I look sideways at Rafael and see him eyeing the speedometer. I'm going fifteen miles per hour over the speed limit.

"Oops." I back off the gas pedal. "Sorry."

"Where are we going?"

"To meet my mom."

Rafael closes his eyes and leans back against the head rest. It reminds me so much of the night in his car at the zoo that the knot in my stomach pulls itself tighter. My foot feels antsy again, but I resist the urge to slam on the gas. The roads are wet, and I don't want to do something dangerous.

"I was afraid of this." Rafael opens his eyes and looks at me.

"What?" I check the speedometer again. "I'm only going sixty-five now, I swear."

"Not that. I was afraid of you going to meet your birth mom."

"You don't think I should?"

"I don't think you're ready."

"Why not?" I can't believe that he's trying to tell me that I'm not ready to meet my own mother.

"I don't think you're going for the right reasons."

My hands clench the steering wheel. "What does that mean?"

"I think you're going because you're mad at your family. And you have every right to be. But that doesn't mean you should rush off and try to find some replacement family without talking to them about it first."

"I tried to talk to Poppy," I say, remembering the time I told her about Mom's journal. "She doesn't want to hear it."

"What about your mom?"

"I can't talk to her."

"How do you know if you've never tried?"

I pause, trying to conjure up Mom's reaction to an honest conversation about my adoption. I don't know if she would deny it, or if she would listen to me. Should I have tried to talk to her before leaving? I push the thought aside. I just want to go. There has to be a way I can make Rafael understand that.

"Are you telling me that if you discovered that your mom lived less than fifty miles away, you wouldn't want to find her?"

"That's exactly what I'm saying."

"I don't believe you."

"You have a family that loves you so insanely much. I don't. I have a mom who left and a dad who's never around. But I can't say anything bad about him, not really, because he spends all of his time saving lives and doing charity work. When I complain about that taking priority over me, I sound like a dick." Rafael's angry voice fills my car, and it startles me to realize that I've never seen him like this before. I can't help but smile.

"You look pleased." He accuses.

"I've never seen The Unflappable Rafael Luna get upset before. It's kind of nice."

"Nice?"

"Yeah, it makes me feel less bonkers."

He rolls his eyes. "Glad to be of service."

I sigh and try again. "My life is weird. My family has literally depended on likes and pageviews since I can remember. It's always been an inescapable fact of life. Some people are born in Russia, some people are born to billionaires, I was born into the Dixon Family. I don't know if it's fair or not, but I've always assumed God or the Universe or whoever chose me for this life before I was born. And so I've played along. But now I find out that I wasn't *chosen* for this life. It was chosen *for me* by regular people who made regular mistakes. And that means maybe I can choose something else, you know? Maybe I don't have to schedule my life around photo shoots and sell my soul to a reality show.

"But how am I supposed to know where I'm going if I don't know where I came from? I've watched from a distance as Mom told my story for my entire life and I'm sick of it. I want to tell my own story. But I can't tell it unless I know how it started."

When Rafael doesn't respond, I glance over to see his reaction. "Now *you* look pleased."

"The first time I saw you reading a graphic design book in the cafeteria, wearing a t-shirt I *still* don't understand, I had to get to know you. I knew you had something to say, and I was right." He grins at me. "I like being right."

The clouds thin as we head east, revealing the brown and red hues of the Superstition Mountains. Miles of creosote bushes and cholla cacti dot the desert landscape outside the windows. By the time we pass a sign that says "Superior 10 Miles," the sky is blue in every direction and the sun is shining again. That's the way it is with rare Arizona rain-storms; they pass as quickly as they come. We roll down our windows and breathe in the smell of wet earth.

"Have you visited Superior before?" Rafael asks.

"Superior is not a place you visit. It's a place you drive through on your way to somewhere else."

"That bad?"

"That small. It's an old mining town that has all but been abandoned. The town is less than two square miles, and the population is less than three thousand."

"Thanks for the info, Wiki."

"I've been called worse," I say, and Rafael laughs. It sounds even better than rain on my window.

The mountains close in on us as we get closer, the cholla making way for dense patches of saguaros. I slow down when I see the "Entering Superior" sign. The small town is nestled in a valley at the base of a mesa butte.

"What are we looking for?" Rafael asks.

"Six twenty-three, Copper Street. Directions are saved on my phone." I nod to my phone in the center console.

Rafael picks it up and finds the directions. "What if she's not home?"

I hesitate, realizing this address might be a dead end.

"If we can't find her, we'll do the tourist thing. Then our trip won't be a total waste." He gestures to the right where a red shed sits in the parking lot of an old café. The sign out front reads "World's Smallest Museum."

"Artifacts of Ordinary Life," Rafael reads. "What do you think that means?"

"Toothbrushes?"

"Dirty dishes?"

"Socks," I reply in a strained voice. He's obviously trying to keep the mood light but the knot in my stomach is so big I feel it knocking my lungs aside as it moves into my chest. We both quiet down as we roll slowly through the nearly empty town. I turn left when I see a sign that says "Historic Superior." It's a convenient way to avoid my own history a little longer.

Historic Superior isn't much of a detour. It's one road, maybe half a mile long. Cafés, kitschy shops, and buildings with boarded-up windows line the street. Colorful murals adorn the brick walls. Some appear to be inspired by Native American culture, and the others are paintings of Jesus and Our Lady of Guadalupe. They have more life in them than the rest of the town put together.

The road ends with a government building at the top of the hill. I turn the car around and drive toward the main stretch of town, where a small turnoff leads to residential houses.

"Well. Here goes nothing." I spin the steering wheel and the car obeys.

I drive slowly through the neighborhood as Rafael uses my phone to direct me to Copper Street. The houses are old, with chain-linked fences and dirt yards displaying broken-down cars. The entire feel of this town is neglect. Like everyone who cared about it left or died, and now all that's left are the people who don't know how to leave. People like my birth mother.

Would I have ended up here if things had been different? If she hadn't wheeled me into Mom's hospital room and run? I try to picture life in one of these ramshackle houses. Driving to the small, red-brick schoolhouse that wouldn't hold a quarter of my graduating class. I can't fathom what it would be like.

Who would I be, if I wasn't Ashley Dixon's daughter, Poppy Dixon's sister?

Maybe my weird internet life isn't as bad as I make it out to be.

Sooner than I expect, Rafael nods toward a street sign. "There. On the left."

I turn and pull over to the side of the road, in front of the first house on the corner. My hands automatically reach for my phone, but instead of slipping it in my pocket, I turn it off. I don't want to be distracted by comments from fans or emails from people who are offended by my very existence. Not now. Not during something this important.

"Do you want me to stay in the car?"

I shake my head. "Please, come with me."

He reaches over the center console to squeeze my hand. We get out of the car and walk toward my future and my fate. Swaying in the breeze, a tire swing hangs from an old tree in the front yard. A scooter is lying on its side in the dirt, sending me into a panic that I'm about to meet a half sibling. One long-lost family member is all I can handle for today—if that. But before I can change my mind, Rafael reaches out his long arm and knocks.

A young boy with shaggy brown hair answers the door while holding an Xbox controller. "Who are you?"

"I'm looking for Brittany Dewitt." I clench my hands at my sides to keep them from shaking, but my voice is surprisingly loud and steady.

"She lives in the apartment over the garage." He turns around and looks at the TV screen, clearly itching to get back to his game.

"Can we see her?" I try to step inside, but he pushes the door forward, nudging my foot back outside.

"There's an entrance around back." He shuts the door in our faces.

Rafael looks at me with raised eyebrows, indicating that the next move is my decision. I nod to his unspoken question, and we walk around to the side of the house. The chain link fence is open. We push our way through and into the backyard, where a rickety set of wooden steps leads up to a door above the garage. We take them carefully, and when we reach the top, I'm the one who knocks.

Inside, feet shuffle across the floor. The door creaks open. A familiar face appears in the doorframe, although it's older and thinner than the one in my nightmares.

It's the woman who tried to kidnap me nine years ago.

Chapter 24

My vision blurs. I fight by the urge to vomit on the doorstep. I grip the railing until my knuckles turn white. Once my head stops spinning, and I'm positive I'm not going to collapse, I'm able to focus on her face.

The first thing I notice is the freckles, although they're faded. That must be how people feel when they meet me. First, they see the freckles; then, everything else. On my birth mother, everything else includes sallow-tinted skin, sunken eyes, and bones sticking out of her chest. Her dirty blonde hair hangs limply around her shoulders, begging for a wash. All of her could use a good wash, actually.

Her eyes dart back and forth as she looks at me, then Rafael, then back at me again. Without warning, she bursts into tears and pulls me into a hug.

"I knew you'd come." She squeezes me with a surprisingly strong grip, given how frail she appears. I look at Rafael. His eyes are as wide as mine feel, and I can tell he has no idea what to do. My natural instinct is to push myself as far from her as possible, but instead, I pat her awkwardly on the back as she sobs the same words over and over into my shoulder. "I knew you'd come."

Really? Cause I sure didn't. If I'd know what I'd be walking in to, I probably wouldn't be here at all.

After an unbearable length of time, she releases her hold on me and wipes the tears with her sleeve. Before I can move, she puts her hands on my shoulders and tugs me over the threshold. "I knew it was you the whole time. I swear, I knew it was you."

My attempt at a smile feels like a grimace. The apartment is dark and dirty. Cigarette butts, clothes, and food wrappers litter the floor.

Don't judge her, I scold myself. *You don't know what's she's been through.*

Rafael walks further into the apartment, stopping in the makeshift kitchen with his back toward us. A portable refrigerator sits next to a folding table and two chairs. He picks up a picture frame from the top of the refrigerator and studies it for a long time before setting it back in its place.

Brittany's hands are still on my shoulders. I try to shrug away, but she puts them on my face and leans close. "I always knew it was you." The scent of smoke is suffocating. Dread scatters across my skin. I wrap my arms around my stomach in a pathetic attempt to hold myself together.

Rafael turns, alarm written all over his face. I shake my head, warning him not to say anything. Brittany fixes her pleading eyes on mine. "I tried to take you first. You have to know that."

Either she's completely rewritten history, or she's a liar. "That's not true. You grabbed Poppy." My voice is defiant, because she's wrong. I still hear her scratchy voice calling Poppy's name when I lie in bed at night. She didn't want me. Like everyone else, she wanted my sister.

"No!" Her face falls. The toxic smell of her breath wafts over me, causing my stomach to swirl in angry protest. "I called for you, but you ignored me. Poppy was curious. She wanted to come. I knew if I took her, you'd follow. You have to believe me." Her eyes lock on mine and there's a glimmer of *something* that clashes with the rest of her appearance.

Life. Hope. *Affection?*

Half of my life. That's how long I've been clutching this memory in tight fists. It's not possible something slipped through my fingers. *Is it?*

Rafael crosses the room to my side. "What's going on?"

Brittany's shoulders slump in defeat. I can't bring myself to say the words.

He steps in front of her, forcing me to look at him. "Who is she?"

"I'm her mother." The words are a whisper, stitched together with heartbreak and regret.

Rafael keeps his focus on me. "Why do you recognize *her?*"

"She's the one who tried to kidnap me." Brittany flinches at the word. I do, too.

Rafael takes my hand in his. "We're leaving." His voice is calm, but his eyes are hard.

I yank my hand away. "Do what you want. I'm staying." He closes his eyes and clenches his jaw, but I don't care. I've waited eighteen years for answers, I'm not waiting another second.

I walk over to Brittany on unsteady legs and attempt a smile again. "Let's sit down." I move toward the table and glance at the picture Rafael was holding. I'm in a swimsuit and swim cap, holding a first-place ribbon and grinning for the camera. The old photograph from the blog is folded in half, erasing Poppy completely. I touch the frame gently with trembling fingers before looking at Brittany in awe. She was telling the truth.

"I have more." She pulls a large photo album from under her bed and thrusts it into my arms. My hands are still shaking as I open the book. When I see the first page, my stomach floods with acid. It's a scrapbook filled with pictures of me. Me as a baby. Me taking my first steps. Me on my first birthday. Some of the picture were always solo shots, but in many others, Poppy has literally been cut straight from the image. Page after page, I view my life through a lens that removes my mom and dad and sister. It's just me, smiling at nothing, arms thrown around thin air, celebrating birthdays and Christmases as if I sprung up from nowhere. Anxiety wraps its iron grip around my heart, and I can't move or speak or even breathe.

"I'm going to print out the ones I missed," Brittany says, referencing the gap in the timeline that I suspect represent the years she spent in prison. "As soon as I get time."

"You real busy these days?" Rafael's voice is icy. He stands behind my chair with his hands on the back of it. I look up to see him glowering at her while she studiously avoids his gaze.

I close the book and push it away from me. The room is stuffy and hot. Sweat soaks through my shirt.

Rafael's hands twitch and he folds his arms across his chest. He's seconds away from losing it, which will destroy any chance I have of connecting with my birth mother. I'm here to find my family, discover my roots, and hopefully see a path for my future. As much as I wanted him here, I can't do any of those things with Rafael breathing protectively down my neck.

"Can we go for a walk?" I ask Brittany. She smiles weakly and stands.

Rafael moves to follow us, but I shake my head. "I need to be alone with her." He looks like he wants to protest, and Brittany quietly slips out the door, leaving us behind in her apartment.

"You don't know if she's safe or mentally stable. I can't leave you alone with her."

I gesture around the dingy room. "She's had a hard life, sure, and this is weird and uncomfortable, but nothing here makes me scared for my safety."

He sighs. "If you're not back in thirty minutes, I'm coming to find you."

Thirty minutes isn't much, but I appreciate the fact that this is hard for him too. If the situation was reversed, I wouldn't be thrilled at the thought of leaving him alone with the person who almost destroyed his life. I nod and hand him my car key, and we stare at each other for a fraction of a second too long, tipping the moment from gentle understanding to tense and loaded silence. It seems like he wants to hug me, or maybe just stop me from leaving, but he doesn't do either. I'm disappointed and relieved.

Brittany waits for me in the yard. "You hungry?" When I nod, she says "Wait here," then opens the front door of the main floor of the house and returns a minute later with a black apron.

"Auntie Brittany!" A little girl in a diaper and small pigtails chases her out the door and throws her body around Brittany's leg. She giggles as Brittany lifts her legs and stomps around the yard.

"I'll be back soon," Brittany says as she detaches the girl and carries her back to the porch. The girl juts out her bottom lip and threatens to cry. "And I'll bring a treat. Broccoli is still your favorite, right?"

The girl shrieks in disgust until Brittany promises to return with a sugar cookie, a statement that is met with delighted squeals. She allows Brittany to usher her inside and shut the door.

I watch the whole encounter, speechless. How could this be the same person who dumped her baby, and returned nine years later to ruin her life? I don't sleep, or talk to strangers, or feel safe in public. *Because of her.* But she obviously loves that little girl (my cousin?!) and the girl feels the same. Brittany isn't unfit for motherhood . . . she was just unfit for *me*.

My mind and heart race as my feet robotically follow the path she leads to a café in Historic Superior. I barely listen as she narrates the walk, pointing out landmarks around town. She opens a heavy door in the back of the building and we weave through a small but busy kitchen filled with line cooks assembling sandwiches and ladling soup into bowls. I sit on a counter stool while she stands on the other side and ties the apron behind her back.

"I shouldn't have showed you the book." She sighs.

"You shouldn't have made it. You gave up your right to my life."

Cringing, she turns to scoop ice into a glass cup, then fills it with water, sticks a straw in it, and slides it in front of me, alongside a cookie from the bakery display. "Happy birthday."

At least someone remembers. I take a sip even though I'm not thirsty, my mind still stuck on the girl from the yard, on the life I could have had.

"Why did you do it?" I swirl the straw in my cup and avoid her eyes. I'm not even sure what "it" I'm referring to. Giving me up, or trying to take me back. She interprets it as the former.

"They were going to take you away."

My head snaps up.

"I failed the drug test." She methodically rolls forks and knives into flimsy white napkins and secures each set with a paper ring. "The nurse told me while I was in labor. She said to expect a visit from CPS after you were born, and that I wasn't allowed to breastfeed you, and that you'd have to be tested. They took you away to the nursery. I was standing in the hall, watching you through the window, when Ashley and her new baby were wheeled by. She didn't recognize me, but I read her blog, knew every detail of her perfect pregnancy and perfect life. And

I thought, *I'm going to see more of that little girl's life than my own baby's*. I snapped. If she could just take you for a little bit, until I could get my life together, I'd still know you." She swipes a tear from her cheek with the back of her hand and continues rolling.

I'm too stunned to respond.

She loved me.

She made a lot of really bad decisions, but she loved me.

"It was harder than I thought it'd be, watching you grow up from the other side of a screen. *She* was the one wrapping your presents and brushing your hair. And lying the whole time, pretending you were hers. Letting commenters compare you to Poppy. It made me sick." She spits the words. "I got worse instead of better, and I got tired of waiting." She looks at me for the first time since starting her story, and her eyes are filled with decades-old anger. She's so consumed by her own rage that she doesn't consider my own.

"I still have nightmares," I say.

"So do I." Her eyes are hard, and it's obvious I'm not getting an apology. But I ask for one anyway, because I'm desperate and sad and too pathetic for words.

"Do you regret it?"

"I regret not fighting for you when you were a baby."

My stomach sinks. Giving me up was the best thing she could have done for me, but *that's* the decision she would change. I let my head fall into my hands, suddenly exhausted.

"My dad?"

"Never knew about you. He moved on long before you were born."

Of course. Another dad I'll never know.

"You graduating soon?"

I nod, too tired to be amused by her attempt to pretend she doesn't know every detail of my life.

"Then what?"

I shrug. "Maybe a reality show. With Poppy." I may as well tell her. She'll find out eventually.

"You don't sound too happy about that."

"I'm not."

"Move here." She says it as if it's the most obvious solution in the world, but I can't mask the look of shock on my face. *Is she serious?*

"You don't belong in that world, with those people. You belong with me. I can get you a bed, and a job, and we can finally be the family we were always meant to be."

I squirm uncomfortably, because I've had some of those same thoughts. I don't belong in Mom and Poppy's world. But I don't belong in this one either.

This could have been my life, but it's not. This is her town. Her stuffy garage apartment. She could have been my family, but she's not. And not because she was too sick to take care of me as a baby. She forfeited any right to my life when she used violence to try to rip me away from the only family I'd ever known.

"Your boy is here." Brittany nods to the front door of the café. I spin on my stool to see Rafael hesitating, waiting for a signal from me. I hold up a finger and swivel back to Brittany. "He doesn't like me," she muses.

"Can you blame him?" The words slip out before I can stop them, and she freezes midroll. "I don't think I'll be moving here." My voice is strong, but my body winces in anticipation of her reaction.

Her face hardens. "Why did you come here?"

"I wanted to meet you."

"Well, congratulations! You met me. Now what? You're going to run away again? Just like last time?

"No, I just—"

"You came here just to show me how much you don't need me?"

"It's not that."

"You're just like Ashley." She shakes her head. "No appreciation for my sacrifices. Neither one of you spared a single thought for me in eighteen years. Ungrateful bitches, both of you." Her hands shake as she grasps a roll of silverware. My body freezes at the abrupt turn in mood.

"That's enough." Rafael crosses the small café in quick strides.

"What'd you say to me?" Brittany gives him a look of pure hatred that knocks the breath right out of me.

"The fact that Claire's even here is more than you deserve."

"Her coddled life is more than she deserves." She turns her steely glare from Rafael to me. "Get out of my town!" It's a threat as much as an order, and her entire body shakes with rage.

"Gladly." Rafael takes my hand and moves toward the door, but I'm paralyzed by indecision. All rational thought is telling me to get out of here, but my feet are welded to the floor. It can't end like this. This isn't how it was supposed to go. She's my family. My second chance. If I don't have her, what do I have?

Rafael looks at me in disbelief. "Let's go!"

"I . . . I . . ." I stare into Brittany's angry face, desperate for a hint of the affection and understanding I saw minutes ago.

"I said get out!" She shatters my cup against the floor, spewing glass and ice water at my feet.

I don't need to be told again.

Chapter 25

I wrench the car door open with trembling hands. My clumsy fingers fumble with the keys while Rafael impatiently taps an unsteady rhythm against the dashboard. I finally get the car started and slowly ease it down the road. Back in Historic Superior, I pull into the parking lot of an empty auto body shop, turn off the car, and crack my knuckles to relieve the tension coursing through my hands.

Rafael doesn't say anything. Doesn't even apologize. Before I realize it, I've stopped my deep breathing and my hands are shaking again.

"Why did you do that?" I ask.

"Do what?" He looks at me like I've lost my mind.

"Make her angry!" *She was opening up to me. We just needed more time.*

"In case you didn't notice, she's intensely unstable. I had to say something."

"I was handling it."

"No. You weren't." His face is calm but he fixes me with an intense stare. I can't deal with him looking at me like that, so I climb out of the car and slam my door. Rafael follows suit. We face each other across the hood of the car.

"You made everything so much worse. I can't believe you did that." I hurl the words across the car with as much venom as I can muster.

"Worse? *Worse?*" He raises his voice to match mine. "Listen to yourself! That woman went to prison for trying to kidnap you. It doesn't get worse!"

He didn't hear her story, so he can't understand the pain she's been through. "I shouldn't have brought you." It's not true. I'm glad he was there with me.

He pauses, and when he speaks again, his voice is quiet. "Why did you bring me?"

"I don't know. Obviously, it was a mistake." *Lie.*

"No, Claire. Why did you bring me?"

"You didn't have to come." *Lie. Lie. Lie.* I barely gave him a choice. I didn't even tell him where we were going until he was already in the car.

"I never said I didn't want to come. I said, why did you bring *me?*"

He's looking for a specific answer, but I don't know what it is. And if I did, I'm so mad I wouldn't give it to him. "Who else would I have brought? Poppy?"

"What about Jackson? He should be home for Thanksgiving in a few days, right?" His face is blank, his expression unreadable.

"What are you talking about? Why would I bring Jackson?"

"I don't know. Maybe because he's your boyfriend?"

"*What?*"

"You told me you want to go to school 'with a friend' in California. You defended long-distance relationships when I said I didn't believe in them. Your Instagram is covered in pictures of him."

"Old pictures." And even then, those pictures don't tell the full story. The relationship they flaunted was nothing more than an illusion. I thought Rafael understood that.

"Not all of them. You two were looking very friendly on the blog just last month. All the comments say you two are together and—"

"You read the blog? And the *comments*?" Hurt and anger compete for my attention.

"Sometimes." He shrugs like it's no big deal.

Anger wins. "I can't believe you would do that after everything I've told you!"

"You don't tell me anything! You never told me about Jackson. Instead you just string me along and try to kiss me and fall asleep on my shoulder all while you have a boyfriend."

"Jackson is not my boyfriend."

He raises his eyebrows in disbelief. "You said you didn't want people to see us together, and I assumed it was because you two were still dating. What else was I supposed to think?"

"He was never my boyfriend. You would have known that if you had bothered to ask me about it instead of trusting gossip written by strangers on the internet."

He puts his hands on the hood of the car and hangs his head with a sigh. "It wasn't just strangers. It was Poppy, too."

"You talked to Poppy? Instead of me?"

"I wanted to ask you so many times, but I was too nervous. I didn't want to scare you off. So, I asked Poppy. She told me that you and Jackson got together when he visited last month. She warned me not to interfere because you've been in love with him forever. It seemed like everyone knew but me. Even Olivia mentioned it one or two dozen times."

Okay, I shouldn't have lied to Poppy. But I refuse to let this be my fault. "It's not true. And like I said, you would have known that if you had talked to me instead of going behind my back and believing the crap you read online."

"It's hard not to believe something when the proof is in front of my eyes."

I think about Jackson with his arm around me at dinner last month and my mom with her camera, and I'm flooded with anger. "It's a lie! I've told you that! You're just like everyone else, except worse because you know how I feel about the blog but you trusted it anyway."

"You know what I don't understand? If you hate the blog so much, why don't you tell your mom to stop?"

"It's not that easy. She started it before I was born. It's her *life*."

"It might be her life but it doesn't have to be yours. You had no choice when you were little. I get that. But you definitely don't have to agree to that reality show."

"What about you? Had any honest conversations with your dad lately? Or are you going to stop whining about your relationship with him and just deal with it?"

Rafael's expression falls. If I'm trying to hurt him, I've succeeded. And I hate myself for it. I blink back my tears and brace myself for his response when something catches my eye across the empty parking lot, at the gas station next door.

No. *Someone.*

A teenage girl leans against the side of her old Volkswagen Beetle while she waits for it to fill up. She's close enough that I'm sure she's heard every word Rafael and I have hurled at each other. Worst of all, she has her camera phone pointed directly at us.

"Crap." I lock eyes with the girl, and she stumbles with her phone. It drops on the ground. She picks it up and shoves it in her pocket before she turns around and pulls the fuel nozzle out of the gas tank.

"Hey! Excuse me!" I run across the empty parking lot toward her. "Hey!" I yell again as she opens her car door. I reach out and hold it open before she can slam it shut. "What do you think you're doing?" My heart slams against my ribs as she glares up at me from behind her thick, black-framed glasses.

"Claire!" Rafael slides over stray pieces of gravel and comes to a stop next to me. "What's going on? Do you know her?"

"She was recording us. Or taking pictures. On her phone." The words come out in short spurts as I try to catch my breath.

"I was not." She doesn't look at either of us. Instead, she sticks her keys in the ignition and stares at the fuzzy purple dice hanging from her mirror.

"She's lying."

"So what? It's not illegal."

"Why were you taking pictures of us?" A hard edge has returned to Rafael's voice.

"I was waiting to see if a bird would show up." She smirks. "What are you doing here, anyway?"

"Give me your phone."

Good one. That'll definitely work.

To my surprise, she pulls it out of her pocket and dangles it in front of me with two fingertips. I reach for it, but as she swipes it back with a laugh it slips from her fingers and clatters to the ground. I lunge to grab it at the same time she does when Rafael pulls me away. His fingers grip my arms with just enough force to keep me from throwing myself at the girl.

She picks up her phone and glares at me again. "You're insane!" She slams the door shut and peels away. When her car is out of sight, Rafael releases his hold on me.

I turn on him with renewed anger, ready to go another round, but he holds up both of his hands. "Before you say anything, just know that I was trying to help."

"I don't need your help!"

"I didn't want you to do something you'd regret later." His eyes plead with me to believe him.

It's the same thing he said when he dodged my kiss in the car, and I'm sick of him trying to save me from regrets. "I wasn't going to attack her. I was just going to delete the pictures or video of us from her phone."

"Ten bucks says if you'd touched that phone, she would have called the police."

"With what?"

Rafael smiles at my joke but shakes his head.

"I'm not afraid of her," I say.

"I know. I'm actually kind of impressed."

"Why?"

He shrugs. "Last week, you would have been."

I think about Rafael's words on our silent drive home. A few weeks ago, I could barely make eye contact with a fangirl in the bathroom. Today, I chased down and yelled at a complete stranger without a trace a fear. It could be because I had so much adrenaline from meeting Brittany and fighting with Rafael, but I think there's more to it than that. Now that I know exactly who tried to kidnap me and why, I have no reason to be afraid of the rest of the world.

So why do I still feel so lousy?

"Pack a bag! We're celebrating!" Poppy accosts me as I enter the house. Around her neck is a shiny silver medal.

"Congrats on second place, but I'm not in the mood." I try to swerve around her, but she blocks my path. "We're not celebrating this." She rolls her eyes at the medal. Figures. She's never known what it's like to come in second. "We're going to Disneyland. Tonight!"

Mom walks into the room with a duffle bag over her shoulder. "You girls always said you wanted to spend your eighteenth birthday at Disneyland!" She grins at me expectantly, waiting for me to scream, or . . . I don't know, jump up and down. Poppy rushes out of the room to finish packing.

"When we were five."

Her smile falters. "Aren't you excited?"

"I have homework and stuff . . . I can't go right now." I have a pounding headache, and all I want to do is go to bed.

I'm not in the mood to spend six hours in the car with Mom and Poppy droning on incessantly about the reality show, which is all they talk about these days.

"You only get one eighteenth birthday."

"I know." *And I just spent mine desperately untangling the mess you created*, I add mentally. Her eyebrows scrunch in confusion. She has no idea. And I'm tired of all the secrets.

"Can we talk? It's important."

"Sure. We'll have plenty of time to talk in the car."

I grit my teeth. Doesn't she even care where I've been? Where I spent my real birthday? "You're not listening. I'm *not* going."

Poppy bounds down the stairs two at a time. "Then we're going without you." She brushes past me out of the house and slams the front door behind her. I feel like I've been slapped. Like my whole life is crumbling. I've been rejected my birth mother, and now by Poppy.

"Mom?"

"Please come? I promised her."

I slowly shake my head. If Poppy's so eager to leave me behind, I'm not going to force myself on *her* birthday celebration.

Mom kisses the top of my head and follows Poppy out that door.

And I'm alone.

Chapter 26

Later that week, Jackson and Cami come over for Thanksgiving dinner. Which is a relief, honestly. Mom, Poppy and I have been tiptoeing awkwardly around each other since they got back from Disneyland. Once Mom chose Poppy over me, I abandoned the idea that we could actually talk about what happened. All Mom cares about is cranking out content and pretending our lives are shiny and happy. Plus, she's busier than ever in discussions with STARR Network, and Poppy's making up for lost time by filming new hair tutorials every day. I've been avoiding everyone (Rafael included) by lying low in the school library and leaving my uncharged cell phone in my room. I just don't have the energy to deal with the constant deluge of comments and texts and emails and likes.

"How's the college search going, Claire?" Poppy raises her eyebrows at me over a steaming bowl of mashed potatoes. Nothing says Thanksgiving like passive-aggressive hostility, right?

"I thought you girls had decided on ASU and the reality show," Cami says.

"One of us has," I say through a bite of turkey.

"Claire still needs convincing," Mom says, as if it's as simple a matter as changing my mind about what shoes to wear with my outfit.

"I think Jackson was looking forward to being a guest star." Cami winks at me, and I wonder if she still thinks there's a chance we will get together. Someone has to tell her the truth. Unfortunately, no one at this table is going to do it. Jackson never outwardly encourages her suggestions, but he never denies them either.

"I still don't understand what you're thinking."

Obviously.

"This is a once in a lifetime opportunity."

One can only hope.

Mom moves the floral centerpiece a fraction of an inch to the left and takes another picture.

"Oh relax, Ashley. You deserve a day off. Everything looks beautiful."

"Just one more. Claire, scoot closer to Jackson and smile." Mom lifts the camera to her eye and waits for me to cooperate. I take another bite of turkey and pretend not to notice. "Lean in, Claire." She sounds impatient, but I don't move. The table falls silent.

"No offense, Jackson," I glance at him with a look of apology, "but I'm not going to pose for a picture with you."

He shrugs, unfazed.

"What are you talking about, Claire Bear?" Mom's cheery voice is strained.

I turn to Jackson. "Did you know that people think we're dating?"

His eyes dart from Mom to me.

"That's a yes."

"Oh Claire Bear," Mom laughs. "It doesn't matter what people *on the internet* think."

"It matters to me! I don't want people assuming things about me based on what they've read, and Jackson probably doesn't either."

"It's not that big of a deal," Jackson says through a mouthful of potatoes. "If someone asks, I tell them the truth."

"See, Claire? You shouldn't care what strangers think about you. People who know you in real life will know the truth." She's still standing with her camera in her hands, a smile plastered to her face.

"Not everyone." I slink down in my seat.

Still smiling, Mom picks up the untouched bowl of cranberry sauce and hands it to me. "Don't make a scene."

I slump further into my seat. "At least then you'd have something to write about," I mumble. Out of the corner of my eye, Jackson stifles a laugh.

Mom breathes into her hands and rubs them together to warm them up. I pull my sweater tight around my shoulders, cursing myself for not wearing a thicker jacket.

"You know the drill." Mom pulls three copies of the same list out of her purse. She hands me a piece of paper with several items highlighted in orange. These are the things I'm responsible for picking up while Poppy holds our place in the checkout line. When it comes to Black Friday shopping, Mom leaves nothing to chance. There is no line too long, no store too crowded, no discount too small for her meticulous planning.

We had to wake up at 3:00 a.m. for this, and the only reason I'm here is because I need a distraction from thinking about my birth mom, and about Rafael. Poppy was hoping we'd film a Black Friday vlog but took one look at my unbrushed hair and bare face and slipped the camera back in her bag. Too bad I didn't learn that trick several years ago.

Poppy glances at me sideways as we're swept into a current of bodies and jostling elbows. "Cheer up. Think of today as retail therapy. It'll help you forget your boy problems."

I flex my fingers in an attempt to warm them. "I don't have boy problems."

"Riiiiiight. That's why you lied to me about dating Jackson and then blamed Mom for the fact that people think you two are a couple." She shakes her head and ditches me to make a sprint for the checkout line snaking its way through the store.

We spend the morning with a "divide and conquer" mentality, but my heart's not in it. I grumble my way through crowds and discounts, looking forward to getting home for a much-needed nap and some leftover pie. Eventually Mom and Poppy abandon me in a shoe store at an outdoor mall, probably because I won't stop complaining about how a stranger in stilettos just stomped on my foot.

I don't have a list in this store, so I just wander up and down the aisles. A pair of cognac-colored booties catches my eye. Eighty percent off. By this time, I'm too tired and hungry to fully appreciate the discount, but I grab them anyway.

"Don't even think about it," a woman growls and yanks the booties from my hands. She's about Mom's age with bleached blonde hair and way too much makeup. "These are mine!"

I look around for help, but we're alone between two towering racks of women's shoes, size seven. "I was holding those."

"I saw them first," she says, as if that matters. She pushes past me, sits on a small bench at the end of the aisle, and pulls off her stilettos. They're the same ones responsible for my bruised foot, and something snaps in my brain.

"Don't touch me."

"What?"

"I said, don't touch me."

She wrinkles her nose in disgust, but I stand my ground. What happened with the girl in Superior was not a fluke. I'm done being afraid of people. I'm done letting strangers tell me what to do or how to feel. And *no one* gets to touch me without my permission.

"I'm not touching you." She yanks on the first bootie.

"You pushed me when you walked past."

She ignores me and zips up the second bootie.

"Please apologize."

She stands and looks at them in front of the mirror.

"Apologize now."

An anxious-looking employee about my age walks into the aisle. "Is there a problem?" His voice squeaks. He's two inches shorter than me and looks terrified to be here.

"Yes," the woman says. "She's yelling at me because she wants these shoes."

My blood is pounding in my ears when the employee turns to me. "I . . . I'm sorry, ma'am. If you can't be civil, I'm going to have to ask you to leave."

I'm dumbstruck. *Is this a joke?* And then the woman smirks in the mirror, and I find my words again.

"Are you kidding me? She stole the boots from my hands! And then she pushed me! You should kick *her* out!" I gesture wildly toward the front door and accidentally smack my hand into a display. "Ow!" I yell, pulling my hand back in and dragging a plastic shoe stand with me. Shoes come cascading down around me, knocking me to the floor in the process. In a fraction of a second, I'm sitting on my butt in a pile of ankle boots with a throbbing hand and no dignity.

Despite this, the woman is the one who is screaming. "She's trying to attack me!"

The small employee panics as security rounds the corner.

As the pudgy guard takes in the scene, the woman launches into a story about how I viciously attacked her. Meanwhile, I'm still drowning in a pile of boots. No one offers to help me up, which is fine. I'm too tired to stand anyway.

"Is this true?" The security guard turns to the employee for more information.

"Don't tell me you're going to believe this kid over me?" the woman demands, gesturing to me.

I don't love the emphasis she puts on the word *kid*, as if I'm untrustworthy just because I'm a teenager. The employee refuses to meet my eyes. That's when I know what he's going to say before he says it.

Thirty seconds later, I'm escorted out of the store and asked to never return.

I throw myself onto a bench next to the toddler play place and lie down. The air is crisp and cool this morning, and around me, children squeal happily, and people laugh and talk as they walk from store to store, collecting their purchases. I wish I could join them, but I don't know how. Everything in my life is so tangled up, and I have no idea how to fix any of it. What I need is a big pair of scissors that I could use to cut through all the mess until something makes sense again.

"There you are, Claire! Have you seen your sister?" Mom walks out of a perfume store with a pink shopping bag swinging from her wrist. "Come in for a picture!" She holds her hand out to help me up from the bench, and that's when I grab my metaphorical scissors.

"No." To my surprise I sound incredibly calm. Calm, but sure of this decision that has been years in the making.

Mom sighs. "Not today, Claire. I'm tired. Just get in here."

This is the moment. Everything inside of me is screaming that I have to do this now. If I don't, I might never get another opportunity. I've imagined this moment a million times, but I never expected it to take place in front of twenty wild toddlers crawling on top of giant plastic ladybugs.

"I'm done with your Instagram, and Twin Tuesday, and the YouTube channel."

Mom raises her eyebrow. "What does that mean?"

"That means no more vlogs. No photo shoots. And most importantly, no reality show. I'm *out*."

Mom smiles nervously and glances around. There are dozens of parents surrounding the play place, and several of them are pretending not to listen to us. She walks closer to me and hushes her voice. "I know you're upset about Jackson—"

"This isn't about Jackson! But since we're on the subject, I don't understand why you're *still* pretending we're together!"

"At this point, we're characters more than anything. You, Poppy, even me! The readers love the Jackson storyline. I know you're upset, but don't quit the blog simply because of a misunderstanding with a boy."

"This isn't about a boy!" My voice rises, and several faces turn in our direction. "This is about the fact that you've lied to me every day of my life. I found your journal. I know everything."

The color drains from her face.

A familiar shriek pierces the air. Poppy marches toward us with her phone in her hand and a livid expression on her face.

"What the hell did you do?"

Incoming Email

From: yournightmare@gmail.com
To: poppyandclaire@dixondaily.com
Subject: Video

I'm gonna make this real simple. If you sign the STARR
Network contract, I'll release this video and send everyone
after your precious boyfriend and your crazy mom.

And that will just be the beginning.

Chapter 27

I open the attachment on Poppy's phone and play the video of Rafael and I arguing.

Loudly.

It's not pretty.

"This isn't anything." My voice wobbles, betraying my lack of confidence. I hand the phone back to Poppy. "I'm not the first girl to get in a fight with her . . . whatever he is."

"Then why is someone using it to blackmail me?" She spits the words at me furiously.

"The better question is, who's blackmailing you?" Mom takes the phone. The lines on her forehead deepen as she watches the video.

"Probably the same people whose been harassing us for a year."

"Get a grip! It's *not* Emily and Erica!"

"You met Brittany?" Mom asks quietly.

"Who's Brittany?"

I nod and tears swell in the corners of Mom's eyes.

"Are you okay?" she asks.

I nod again.

"What's going on? Who is Brittany?" Poppy looks back and forth, waiting for an answer.

"She's my birth mother."

Poppy's jaw drops open.

I look back at Mom. "Why didn't you tell me about her?"

"I always planned to, and then she did . . . what she did, and I wanted to protect you from that awful truth." Mom looks around at the busy shopping square. "We have a lot to talk about, but we shouldn't do it here."

The words spill out as soon as we're on the road. I sit in the backseat as Poppy drives and piece together the story for them. Poppy knows some of it, Mom knows other parts, but both of them turn around with shocked expressions when I describe the scene in the café. By the time I'm finished, we're sitting in our garage. It seems like no one knows what to say.

"Is this a scandal? Will it scare off STARR?" Poppy asks. *And thus, we resume our normal programming.* Her eyes dart toward me. "If Claire decides to do it."

"I have to make several calls, starting with my lawyer. Claire, we'll talk more later, but for now, are you okay?" I nod as she reaches back and squeezes my hand. Seconds later, she's out of the car, fingers already dialing.

"Are you mad?" I ask, even though it's probably the dumbest thing I could say at this particular moment.

Poppy's answer surprises me. "Yeah. And also sad. About you. About us, not being sisters, I mean. And about the fact that you didn't think I would want to be there for you when you met your birth mom."

"I thought you said you didn't care?"

She shakes her head. "You should know me better than that. Did you honestly believe me?"

Did I believe her when she said she didn't care? Or did I just convince myself it was the truth, because it meant I could do what I wanted? I'm not sure I'm ready to answer these questions, so I ignore them. "Why'd you lie?"

She sighs as she crawls out of her seat and into the back with me. "I was scared of losing you. It's obvious you hate all the online stuff we do. I've known it for years. But you've always gone along with it because it's the family business. When you told me that you were adopted, I knew you had finally found the excuse you needed to quit the vlog and move away for school. And selfishly, I was afraid of losing out on the show."

"You could have told me that," I say, but I understand better than anyone how hard it can be to say important things to the people you love.

"I didn't want you to stay out of guilt or obligation. Besides, you've never been one to do what people tell you to." She smiles and rolls her eyes.

"Why do you want to do the show so badly? What's all this for? And don't say *influence*."

"The day you were almost taken was the worst day of my life. I've never felt so powerless. To this day, every time you wake up screaming from a bad dream, or mentally shut down around strangers, all I want is the power to help you. I decided a long time ago I had to take any opportunity for power, so that one day, we'd be so rich and so important that you wouldn't feel scared anymore. All this internet stuff is the only way I knew how to help."

My heart swells. In her own, Poppy-ish way, she was trying to help me. Because that's what we've always done for each other. But stress and fear tricked my brain into thinking she was the enemy. "I'm sorry I've been a terrible sister."

"Just don't forget you *are* my sister, no matter what some stupid DNA test says." She reaches out for a hug.

For the first time, I realize it's true. It doesn't matter if we're biologically related or not. We'll *always* be Poppy and Claire.

She's quiet for a minute and then asks, "Do you remember the last thing Dad ever said to us?"

Right after the accident I used to think about this all the time. Eventually, I gave up hope of ever finding out. "No. Do you?"

"Nope. Mom doesn't remember either."

"She told you that?" I'm shocked. Mom never talks about the accident or the weeks that followed. Maybe that's why the whole thing is a giant blank in my memory.

"I read it on the blog," she says. "It kills her that she can't remember the last words he said to her or the last time he kissed her or what she made for their last dinner together. That's why she still does the Twin Tuesday thing. She doesn't want to forget anything else."

The guilt that has been threatening to suffocate me all morning lands squarely in my chest. I sometimes forget that I didn't just lose my dad. Mom lost her husband. For years, I've judged Mom for what she does. For the fact that outfit photos are "trivial." I've never given her enough credit for building an entire brand on her own while being a single parent. If I lost Poppy or Mom, I would fall apart. But the blog would be there with its lifetime of pictures and stories to glue me back together.

Poppy's phone beeps. "It's another email."

I roll my eyes. "They're getting desperate."

She opens the email and her face drains of color. "Not this time."

I pry the phone out of her fingers and see pictures from the Halloween party I didn't attend. Poppy's in her sexy strawberry costume, and judging by the beer in her hand and the spaced-out smile plastered on her face, she's completely wasted. As the pictures go on, she gets sloppier, and her skirt rides higher. In the last one, it's yanked to her hips as she straddles some guy, in the midst of a make-out session.

Her hands shake as she accepts her phone back. "I'm going to lose them both." Tears spill out of her eyes, pouring down her cheeks. Her nose turns red and snotty as she sobs. "I'm going to lose the show and Brayden."

Seeing her like this, my body floods with anger and adrenaline. It's my turn to protect my sister.

"Not if I have anything to say about it." I jump out of the car and march toward the house. "I refuse to let Emily and Erica do this to you after you've defended them for so long."

"It's *not* Emily and Erica," Poppy shouts as she follows me down the hall, but I'm too busy to argue with her. I burst through the door into Mom's office. She looks up in surprise and holds her hand over her phone, blocking out the noise.

"Where's the STARR contract?" I demand. She points to the corner of her desk.

"What are you doing?" Poppy is in the room now.

I pick up the contract, flip to the back page, and sign my name. "I'm not letting anyone cyberbully me or my sister for another second." I drop the contract in front of Mom. "Tell Stella we're in."

Chapter 28

Poppy blocks the front door, refusing to let me drive to Emily's. Or Erica's. I don't care which once I see first, because they're both going down.

"Listen to me. I'm *promising* you, as your sister, it wasn't them." Her voice is full of conviction. She believes what she's saying, at the very least.

I give up with a sigh and retreat to my room, with every intention of confronting them as soon as Poppy lets me out of her sight.

I spend the rest of the day scrolling through the Twin Tuesday posts on the blog. What surprises me most is how, in the beginning, they were about my whole family, including my dad. Apparently, he made breakfast for us every Sunday morning, and I loved his blueberry pancakes. He watched nature documentaries, taught a kickboxing class on the weekends, and always wore wacky, mismatched socks. There's so much about him I don't know. I can't believe so many of the answers were here the whole time.

As I read the stories, I wonder what my dad thought about the blog. Did he care that Mom poured so much of his life onto the screen? In the early days, not everything she wrote contained a fashion-affiliate link. She wrote about arguments and money troubles and bad days. It feels like a completely different blog than the one she writes now. Her audience was smaller and her posts contained so much more life.

I read about the trip to California when my dad got lost and drove one hundred and fifty miles out of their way. By the time they arrived in San Diego, they were tired and hungry and furious with each other. If Mom had written that story about me, I would've been embarrassed about getting the directions wrong and wasting hours of our time. I would've said that it was "not her story to tell." But what does that even mean? Poppy was right when she said that all our stories are mixed together. Mom was in that car with my dad. It was his story, but it was also hers.

I'm her daughter. She's the one who read me books and put Band-Aids on my knees and drove me to swim practice every single day. She didn't just observe our life . . . she lived it. My story is her story. It's impossible to separate the two. So where is the line between what is okay to share with the world and what isn't? *Is* there a line? Should there be? People have been telling stories since the beginning of time. Cave paintings on walls. Oral renditions of the *Odyssey*. Aesop's fables. The Bible. Shakespeare. It's all stories. This blog isn't Shakespeare but a collection of stories passed down from mother to daughters. What's so wrong with that? Maybe the reality show won't be so terrible, and I'll find a way to tell my own story.

I click on another post.

My Claire Bear,

Poppy is sleeping soundly in her crib. You're sleeping soundly in my arms. It's always been this way. She sleeps better on her own. You sleep better with me. My arms were sore the first six months of your life. The shadows under my eyes resembled bruises. I'd never been so tired. But I'd never been so happy.

Your dad always offers to take the night shift. "I'll get her. You sleep," he says. But I never take him up on it because I'm selfish. I love this time we have together when the house is quiet and it's just the two of us. Sometimes you look up at me with a grin on your face and stick your fingers in my mouth. You tangle them in my hair. You pull on my cheeks. I look forward to these stolen moments every single day.

I love having twins. Seeing you and your sister play together makes my heart burst. But this time we have in the middle of the night is just for you and me.

I love you, Claire Bear. I'm so glad you're mine.

Happy birthday,

Love,

Your Mom

I look at the time stamp. November 22. 11:59 pm.
My first birthday.
She didn't forget.

I didn't realize my browser was open to BITES in the background until a chat from Serge pops up on my screen.

---

signofthetimes

🧕 ?

---

girlcode

I found her. Thanks for the help.

---

signofthetimes

🐦 💩 👧 ? 😂

I think he's asking me how I'm doing since the viral video at New York Fashion Week. I shake my head, amazed by how much has happened since then. At the time, that video felt like the end of the world. Now, I actually don't care about it at all. Not the comments or emails or any of it. None of those people, the ones who love me and the ones who hate me, have any idea what my life is actually like. It's not necessarily bad or good. It's just a fact.

Mom was right about one thing. Internet strangers don't deserve to control my happiness.

girlcode

I'm over it.

signofthetimes

😂

girlcode

Yeah, I know. My life is one hilarious embarrassment after another.

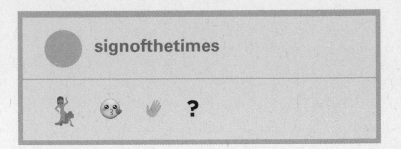

signofthetimes

The Jackson high five.

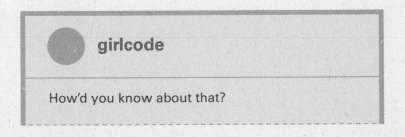

girlcode

That one still stings.

My fingers freeze over the keyboard as realization hits.

girlcode

How'd you know about that?

Damn it. Damn it, damn it, damn it.

"POPPY!"

Chapter 29

I trip over my own feet in my rush to get downstairs. "I know who's been harassing us."

Mom and Poppy look up from their spot on the couch. Poppy's eyes are rimmed in red and her cheeks are streaked in makeup.

"It's *not* Emily—"

"I know. Listen. It's Nora from BITES."

Poppy's mouth opens in surprise. "Nora? Why?"

"I have a guess, but I don't know for sure." I sit next to them and take Mom's computer off her lap. "Can I borrow this?"

"Where did she get that video of you and the pictures of me?"

"I don't know that either," I say as Poppy rolls her eyes. "I'm going to find out, but first, I need your help, Mom." I fill her in on my plan, and she agrees. She types a long text message into her phone, but before she hits "send," she gives me a nod.

I send Nora a video chat request. She answers, revealing a dimly lit hotel room. She leans back against the bed's plush headboard. "What's up?"

"I'm a little bit curious why you did it, but mostly I'm wondering *how* you did it?"

"My money is on jealousy." Poppy leans in front of the camera and waves.

"Mine too. Nora's always been jealous of the fact that we get to live in a normal town and go to a normal high school. Is that it?"

Her face hardens. "You got me. I'm jealous of your basic, boring life." There's no mistaking the sarcasm in her voice, but I know we're getting to her.

"Ooh, I get it. You're jealous that STARR Network doesn't want to give you a show. You jet set around the world every day of your life, and we're still more interesting than you, even in sleepy Gilbert, Arizona."

She doesn't respond, a clear sign that I've hit a nerve. Nora's anonymous comments started right around the time our vlog got big, implying she wasn't jealous of us before that. We've figured out why she blackmailed us, now I want to know how she did it.

"We'll start with the video of me in Superior. I'm assuming it was posted on an anti-Claire message board?" More silence. This is easier than I'd thought. "What I can't figure out is how you got the pictures of Poppy at the Halloween party, unless you're in contact with people at our school." Nora leans forward to disconnect the call. "Wait! You don't want to do that!"

"Actually, I do. I have some pictures to email to a friend of mine. She's a reporter at *MyStyle* magazine. I think you know her." Nora flashes a self-satisfied smirk and crosses her arms over her chest, daring me to contradict her.

"Go for it," Poppy says with a shrug. "STARR Network has already seen them, and so has Brayden." She practiced this line a few times before we called Nora so it would sound convincing.

"I don't believe you." Her eyes dart between Poppy and me.

Mom takes the computer from my lap. "Hi, Nora! Long time no see. You've grown up into such a *lovely* young lady. I still keep in touch with your mother though. Did you know that? In fact, I'm about to send her a text right this very minute." She holds her phone in front of the camera so Nora can read the detailed explanation of everywhere Nora hides her weed while they're traveling.

Nora's eyes widen in alarm. "You can't. They'll kill me."

"I can and I will, unless you destroy those files of my daughters."

We watch as Nora deletes the files from her computer. She might have backups somewhere else, but I'm not worried. The threat of a convent is enough to keep her in line. If she thinks our life is boring, she wouldn't last a week living with nuns.

I smile at Nora, genuinely pleased with the results of this conversation. "You're an idiot if you thought I was going to let you blackmail my sister. And one more thing, don't let me see you around BITES ever again."

I disconnect the call, feeling triumphant. "Too cheesy?" I look at my family, expecting them to look relieved. Instead, Mom is on the verge of tears and Poppy looks downright miserable.

"What's wrong? We did it! Everything is fine now."

"I'm sorry, Claire," Mom says, blinking her eyes to keep the tears at bay.

"For what?"

"For telling you to have thicker skin when Nora was bullying you. For not telling you about Brittany. For the way you found out about her. For the fact that you've been scared of strangers for the last nine years and I didn't realize it." She takes a shaky breath.

"My lawyer's going to contact Brittany and remind her about the conditions of her parole. If she ever comes near you again, she'll go back to jail."

"That's okay," I say, and Mom and Poppy each raise an eyebrow. "I mean, I'm grateful, but I'm not as scared as I used to be." Brittany has a lot of anger, but I still think somewhere deep down, she cares about me. Maybe someday that feeling will manifest in a healthier way.

"Did she say anything about your biological father?"

"Not much. But I'm fine. I have a dad. He made the world's best blueberry pancakes."

Mom wipes another tear from her eye before she continues. "Things were difficult for her." She's choosing her words carefully, still trying to protect me. "There was no way she could take care of a baby. She loved you enough to understand that you deserved a better life, so she left you with me. Part of the reason why I've put so much of myself into the blog is because it brought us together."

I wonder if it's hard for her to talk about the woman who tried to kidnap Poppy and me. I wonder if it's hard for Poppy to hear. Her life was almost ruined because of me. She meets my eyes and gives me a quick smile, assuring me that she doesn't hold it against me. A weight I didn't know I was carrying lifts from my shoulders.

Mom takes a deep breath. "It's time to shut down the blog."

"What?" Poppy and I ask in unison.

"Are you serious?" Poppy looks shocked.

Mom nods. "I've been holding on to it for way too long. I'll shut it down and run all the fashion business from my Instagram account, but I won't ask you to be in any of the pictures, Claire. You deserve your privacy."

Poppy stands up suddenly and leaves the room. When she comes back, she's holding my STARR Network contract in her hands. "Thank you for doing this for me. Now it's my turn to do something for you." She tears the contract in half once, then twice.

"What about your dream?"

"I'll get a new one. Or I'll become famous enough that they'll want me on my own. Either way, I can't let you compromise your happiness on my behalf. Not anymore." She pulls me in for a hug, just as I'm wondering how I got so damn lucky to be in this family.

"There's one more thing," Mom says, interrupting our happy moment. "No reality show means no exclusive interview for Lena. She'll probably run the article about the kidnapping."

"Is there any way around it?" Poppy asks.

"I'll let you know if I think of anything," Mom says.

Chapter 30

Poppy's reading a book in the backyard with her feet in the pool. She's grounded for her drunken revelry at the Halloween party and has been out here a lot since then, reading or filming or talking to Brayden on the phone. Not just talking, but confessing. Turns out, he's had some "indiscretions" of his own, so they called it even and decided to wait and see what happens when he flies here to visit during Christmas break.

I slip my feet in next to hers. The icy temperature bites my skin, and I immediately pull them back out. "I need help."

"With what?" She doesn't take her eyes off her book.

"Rafael."

She dog-ears her page and sets the book down next to the pool. "It's about time. What's going on with you two?"

"Nothing," I say truthfully. It's now been a week since Rafael and I have spoken to each other. I desperately want to talk to him, but I don't know how to start. "I'm sorry," sounds so lame. "Forget it," won't solve anything. "I like you," is an impossible sentence. When it comes to Rafael, I'm at a loss for words.

"You have to suck it up and apologize."

"I know." I spent the entire day brainstorming ways I could get my message across without my mouth getting in the way, and I finally have an idea. "That's where you come in."

"What do you need me to do?" Poppy asks, because sometimes she really is a people pleaser. Especially if those "people" are her sister, and especially if the topic is a boy.

"Help me plan a meet up with our local fans?"

She raises her hands in mock heavenly praise. "I thought you'd never ask!"

"Don't get too excited. This is a onetime deal." I try a toe in the pool again, but nope. Still cold.

"I have a favor to ask, too. Now that we know Nora was behind the cyberbullying, you should apologize to Emily and Erica."

"No way! Nora obviously got her information from them. No one else knew about Jackson and the high five."

Poppy winces. "Olivia did. She was the one who sent Nora those pictures of me. They met on some message board, apparently."

Olivia's words ring in my head. *At least I'm the same bitch online as I am in real life.* I can't say she didn't warn me.

But now I'm filled with even more guilt. I've spent the last year blaming two of my old friends for something they didn't do. "Wait, so you told Olivia about the high five?"

Poppy shakes her head. "That was all Jackson."

I laugh, both stunned and not. I agonized over that high five for months, while Jackson was blabbing about it behind my back.

"What do we do about Olivia?" Poppy asks.

I shrug. High school will be over before long, and then I'll never have to think about her again. It's not worth the emotional burden of icing her out like I did with Emily and Erica. "I don't care. But honestly, I *knew* I hated her for a reason. I felt it."

Poppy opens her book and nudges me playfully in the side. "Don't pretend like you felt anything other than good, old-fashioned jealousy."

It's the Sunday of Thanksgiving break, and autumn has finally arrived in Arizona. Poppy and I are in a crowded park surrounded by people smiling and waving at us while their booties crunch over fallen leaves. We're wearing matching sweaters and scarves. It's not really cold enough to justify the scarves, but sometimes it's okay to make sacrifices for fashion, especially when other people are making sacrifices for me.

Over the years, Poppy and Mom have scheduled meet ups with fans, and I have always flat-out refused to attend. Today's event was my idea, but when Poppy offered to come with me, I was relieved. Thanks to an Insta-invite, our fans are at the park this afternoon to chat with us and take pictures.

There are at least a hundred people here so far, and I don't recognize a single face. I smile at the three teenage girls in the front of the line and try to ignore the knot in my stomach. I was convinced that my encounters with the girl in Superior and the lady at the shoe store had cured me of my stranger phobia, but now I'm not so sure.

"I think I need to be angry." I take a sip from my water bottle as Poppy checks her lip gloss in a compact mirror.

"Do you want me to punch you in the face?"

"No, but thanks for offering."

"Anytime." She snaps her compact shut with a wicked smile.

"So how does this work?"

"Just be nice. Smile. Ask them something about themselves. Say 'thanks for coming' and pose for a picture."

I take a deep breath and nod. "I think I can do that."

"Oh, and don't forget these." She picks up a stack of posters from the ground and hands them to me.

My legs tremble as I walk toward the long line that snakes through the park. "I can't believe there are so many people," I say under my breath as Poppy waves to the crowd.

"People love you. It's not a crime." We reach the line and I drop the posters by my feet.

The girls at the front squeal in high-pitched unison. "I can't believe it's really you!" The smallest one launches herself forward and hugs me without warning.

I stagger back a few steps but manage to put my arms around her and return the hug. "What's your name?"

"Sandy. Thank you so much for doing this. I just love you and Poppy!" She clutches her phone in her hands, and I have a feeling I know what she wants.

"No problem! Want to take a picture?"

"Yes, please!" She holds her phone out and snaps a picture of us with our arms around each other.

"I'll tag you in it so you can see it," she says as she studies her screen.

"Great. Thanks!"

She turns to leave and the toe of her shoes kicks the corner of my posters, reminding me why I'm here. "Wait! Can we take one more?"

She grins. "Of course!"

I pick up the poster on the top of the pile. "Will you do me a favor and hold this sign for me?" She reads it and furrows her brow, obviously confused.

"It's for a boy," I explain.

"A cute one?"

I nod and she giggles. I hold out my phone and snap a picture while she displays the sign. Then I smile at the next person in line and get ready to do it all again.

My heart thuds in my chest as I approach the porch. Two large, red-and-green Christmas poinsettias flank the door. My palms are sweaty despite the chill in the air. I wipe them on the legs of my jeans and wrap my scarf tighter around my neck. My sandpaper tongue prevents me from swallowing.

I have no idea what I'm going to say. I hoped something funny and brilliant would come to me on the drive here but it didn't. I'm on my own. It's fine. Who needs to be funny and brilliant when you can be sweaty and tongue-tied?

I finally knock and Rafael's dad answers the door. They have the same brown eyes, the same unruly hair. The only difference is that Dr. Luna is graying at the temples.

"May I help you?" He looks confused. Probably because I'm staring at his salt-and-pepper hair.

"Is Rafael here?"

"I don't think so. Hang on." He turns his head. "Rafael?" he bellows up the stairs. We wait in silence. No response. "He must have gone out."

"Where?" I blurt without thinking. As if Rafael isn't allowed to have a life I don't know about. His dad raises his eyebrows with an amused expression.

"I'm not positive. A girl called him a little while ago."

"A girl?"

"Olive, maybe?"

My heart drops through my stomach and lands on the floor. I waited too long and now he's with Olivia. She's a bully and a blackmailer, but he doesn't know that. I bet she doesn't lie to him or yell at him or drag him through her ridiculous family drama. I doubt she *has* ridiculous family drama. She probably doesn't talk when he's trying to kiss her. The thought sears a hole in my chest.

"Is everything alright?" Dr. Luna looks uncomfortable. "Do you want me to call him?"

"No. That's okay. Sorry to interrupt your evening." I back away from the door, tripping over my feet in the process. But just as he's about to shut the door, I change my mind. "Can you give him this for me?" I hold out the envelope of pictures that I just had printed at the drugstore.

It's all very old-fashioned, holding actual printed photos in my hand. He nods, takes the envelope, and closes the door.

When I'm on the road again, I roll down my windows and drive north. The cool air rushes over my arms as I drive. It feels amazing, but my thin Arizona blood isn't used to the cold, so I turn on the heat to balance it out.

Windows down. Heat on. Rafael would laugh at me. I know it's ridiculous, but the contrast makes my skin hum. Thinking about Rafael makes me think about Olivia, which gives my stomach the same feeling I got the year I ate a dozen sour Warheads on a Halloween dare from Poppy.

I turn on the radio. An upbeat, jingly Christmas song is on the radio. Now that Thanksgiving is over, my favorite radio station will play nonstop Christmas music until December 26. The festive music makes me want to change the station, but I turn it up instead and let the catchy melody and the jingle bells work their way into my brain.

As I drive, I realize with fresh pain that this whole mess is my fault. If only I'd talked to my mom when I found the journal, or told Poppy the truth about Jackson and me. If I'd told Rafael how I felt about him, maybe he'd be with me right now instead of Olivia. We all text and blog and email so often that we feel connected, but we were never really communicating honestly with each other. And now it's too late. It's out of my hands. I can't control what pictures other people post of me online or what Lena writes in her article, and I can't control Rafael and Olivia. But I do control my own actions, and I acknowledge the fact that I screwed up.

I can also acknowledge the fact that I'm a little bit in love with Rafael, and it sucks that he's not here with me. Tonight, that's my story.

I park my car, hop the fence, sneak through the backyard, and am up on top of the mountain in no time. I wait for the familiar sigh of relief that usually accompanies this moment but it doesn't come. I don't feel the stress lift off my shoulders. For once, it doesn't feel good to be alone at the top of the world.

It just feels lonely.

I don't know how much time has passed when I hear a car come to a stop and the crunch of gravel below me. My heart picks up its pace. I look around but there's nowhere to go and no time to get there. Is it the homeowners? Did they call the police? I don't know who I'd rather see. Police have guns, but then again, so do lots of civilians. I make the decision to stand out in the open so no one thinks I'm a wild animal or a criminal. I guess I *am* a criminal, given the fact that I'm trespassing on private property, but at least they'll know I'm not a violent one.

I hold my breath as a figure uses his arms to hoist himself over the rocky ledge. He stands up and looks at me as if I'm a pool of water in the middle of the Sahara. Medicine for a dying man. A flame in the midst of darkness.

He looks at me as if I'm the only thing that matters in the world.

Now that I know I'm not in danger, I expect my heart to slow down. It doesn't. It picks up pace as Rafael and I stare at each other. I can feel it beating violently against my chest, straining to get to Rafael.

"How'd you find me?" It's not witty or brilliant, but it's a start.

"My dad gave me the pictures." He pulls the envelope out of his back pocket and holds it up.

"But how'd you know I'd be *here?*"

"I didn't." He puts the envelope back in his pocket and walks toward me. Now is the time. Now is when I say everything I should have said last week. Last month. The first time he sat across from me at lunch. But before I say that, I need to know one more thing.

"Your dad said you were with Olivia."

He stops short and groans, running his fingers through his hair. The familiarity of the gesture makes my bones ache. "He's trying to take an interest in my life. Olivia called this afternoon, and we talked for a few minutes. He must have assumed we went out but we didn't. I was at the park, shooting hoops."

I'm so relieved, I tip my head back and send my laughter into the sky. Rafael crosses his arms over his chest, waiting for an explanation.

"You're not with Olivia." I shrug.

"You're not with Jackson." He closes the gap between us. After the briefest moment of hesitation, he reaches his hand out to me and brushes my hair away from my face. I close my eyes as he runs his thumb down my jaw, from my ear to my chin and back again. The pressure is as soft as the wind, but it lights my skin on fire. It's magical. His touch puts a spell on me that freezes me to the spot. Steals my words. Fogs my brain. I couldn't move or speak if I wanted to. Why would I want to? I could stay like this forever.

He moves his head back and I open my eyes. "It's funny, isn't it?"

The fog clears enough for me to speak. "What's that?" I stare into his dark eyes and realize I can't stay like this forever. I want to move, to pull his body against mine. The need to touch him is a compulsion I can't ignore any longer. I run my hands down his arms. He cocks an eyebrow as a slow smile spreads across his face.

"We have all these stupid devices that are supposed to keep us connected. I didn't want a phone, but now that I have one I sleep with it on my pillow, waiting to hear from you. Your entire life is chronicled online. It should be so simple. We're both available to talk or chat or text twenty-four seven. But we've been kept apart by these stupid misunderstandings that could have been avoided if I'd been braver. All I had to do was open my mouth and tell you the truth."

"It's my fault," I say. Rafael looks like he's going to respond, but I don't give him the chance. "I'm sorry about our fight. I know you were just trying to keep me safe."

He takes my hand in his and rubs a small circle on my palm. I feel my concentration slipping again and fight to regain it. "I'm sorry too. I should've known you're more than capable of protecting yourself. And you've already apologized more than enough times." He takes out the envelope and opens it as proof. He pulls out the stack of pictures that I took at the meet up. Each one is me standing next to a person I don't know, with one or both of us holding up a homemade sign.

Claire is sorry.
Please forgive me!
Rafael was right.
Let's be friends?

"You didn't need to do this."

"I wanted to. I was afraid that, if I tried to say it in person, I'd screw it up."

He looks down at the top picture and smiles to himself before putting them back in the envelope, which he returns to his pocket. "Our last conversation got all messed up, and that's on both of us. But it doesn't matter, because I've been falling in love with you since the moment I first saw you. The second you told me you weren't with Jackson, I should have done the thing I've wanted to do since our first conversation." He slides his fingers through my hair and rests his hand on my neck. A shiver runs down my body. He leans in until our lips are almost touching. I close my eyes and wait for him to close the final distance between us.

"Is your phone with you?" The scent of spearmint clouds my senses. My head spins and it takes me a few seconds to process his question. When I do, I lean back.

"It's in the car. Why?"

He grins. "I tried to kiss you once before, and your phone got in the way, if I remember correctly."

"And I tried to kiss you once before, and what happened? You felt guilty because you thought I had a boyfriend?" The feeling of embarrassment that burned through me the night we went through the haunted house is not one I'll soon forget.

"Bingo." He touches me on the nose and then takes both of my hands in his. "But if you're sure your phone isn't going to interrupt us . . ." He leans in again and presses his lips against mine.

Explosions erupt in my head, in my chest, in my stomach. An ache runs through my body, all the way to my finger-tips. His lips are soft but firm against mine, and it's better than I ever imagined a first kiss could be.

He pulls back slightly. "I hope that was okay." His lips brush against mine as he speaks. A cold wind blows around us, but his breath is hot and sweet. I tilt my head forward in response, and this time, I really kiss him. His hands slide out of mine and rest on my hips. I loop my arms around his neck and pull his body into mine. A soft moan escapes his lips, and I know I'll never be the same again.

"I've been falling in love with you since our court-ordered eye contact," I whisper.

His lips smile beneath mine, and I can't help but match the gesture. "I'll send Ms. Grant a thank-you note," he whispers in my ear before moving his lips down to my neck.

"When we first met, I used to worry about all the other girls," I confess. We're lying on a picnic blanket from the trunk of my car. Above us, the dark sky sparkles.

"What other girls?" he asks. I'm folded into the crook of his body, and he scoots me closer.

"The ones from around the world that you charmed with your questions and answers and your hair. Priya and Gloria and Ada."

The corners of his mouth turn up in amusement. "You named my fake girlfriends?"

"You'd better believe it."

He plays with a lock of my hair, brushing it lightly against my neck. "What changed?"

"Even if you had a new girlfriend every year—"

"It was *not* like that," he cuts me off.

"But even if it *was*, it doesn't matter because you always make me feel like I'm the only person in the room. At first, I thought it was because you didn't have a phone to distract you. But then you got one, and you still treated me like I'm special, like I'm not just one half of The Dixon Twins. You make me feel seen, and I love that about you." A breeze blows around us, and Rafael rubs his hand up and down my arm.

"You're giving me way too much credit." He props himself up on his elbow. "The reason I see you is because you demand attention. You're smart and beautiful and thoughtful and stubborn and impatient—"

"I thought these were compliments!" I accuse with a laugh.

"They are. Every single one of them. They make you shine. If I did anything right, it's only because I was trying to get you to dump your boyfriend and chose me instead."

"When you put it that way, you don't come off so great," I tease.

"I regret nothing." He kisses my cheek, then the corner of my mouth. I'm about to turn and sink into the kiss when I remember something else I wanted to ask.

"You said earlier that your dad is trying to take an interest in your life?"

"We had a good talk. This year is the first Thanksgiving he's been home in ages. He even dug around the boxes in our garage until he found an old memory book." His eyes are closed, his face smooth and relaxed. A smile plays at the corner of his lips. He looks happier than I've ever seen him.

"That's amazing!"

Rafael opens one eye and looks at me. "It's not much. A few pictures. Important dates. My first words."

"But he kept it," I point out. "He's lived all over the world, packed and unpacked boxes over and over again, and he kept it."

He closes his eyes again. "Thanks for telling me to say something. You were right."

"You were right, too, you know, about talking to my mom." I prop myself up on my elbow and fill him in on the whole story.

"You don't sound happy," he says when I've finished.

"Should I be?"

"Sure. Your mom and Poppy have forgiven you. The blog is ending. You're not doing the reality show. What more could you ask for?"

On the surface, it must seem like I'm getting everything I ever wanted. I'm definitely relieved that the online rat race is finally over. No more scrambling for likes and shares and comments and pageviews. I can finally relax. I don't have to wear makeup or sponsored clothes if I don't want to. I don't have to smile if I'm not happy. But it's all coming at the expense of my family. In the course of one evening, my mom lost her blog, and Poppy lost her reality show.

And then there's Lena and the *MyStyle* story, which gives me the sour Warhead feeling in my stomach every time I think about it. It'd be one thing if she was going to tell my story, but she's going to tell *her* version of my story, in which Mom will come off looking like fame-obsessed at best, and like a negligent or selfish mother at worst. That may be the truth as Lena sees it, but it's not my truth.

That's when I realize why I still feel uneasy. "It's not her story to tell."

"Your mom's?"

"Lena's. For so long, I said it wasn't Mom's story, but I was wrong. It *is* her story. She's living it. It's her life. But I still got mad and I blamed her for writing about me. So what did I do? I turned around and gave my story to someone else. Someone who has not lived it at all. Someone who will use it to tear apart my family."

"What are you going to do?" Rafael asks.

"What *can* I do? She's not going to listen to me."

Rafael takes my hand and tangles our fingers together. "Maybe not, but other people will."

Chapter 31

"Don't do it yet!" I run through the front door and into the kitchen, thankful to see my mom at the table with her laptop. "Is the blog gone?"

"I'm archiving it right now. Are you okay?"

"I'm fine. I'm great, actually. But I need the blog. I want to write a post." I have so much energy built up inside me that I'm bouncing up and down on the balls of my feet.

"Whoa. Slow down. What are you talking about?"

"I need to write one last post."

"About what?"

"I need to tell my story before Lena tells it for me. Is that okay?" I ask, suddenly worried that she won't want me to.

She smiles and looks like she might start crying again. I hope she doesn't. There have been more than enough tears in our house lately.

"It's more than okay. I'm really proud of you." She pushes the laptop in front of an empty chair and I sit down. I click "new post" and watch the cursor blink in the top corner. Suddenly, my mind feels as blank as the screen.

"What do I write? How do I start?" I can't believe Mom has done this thousands of times.

"Just start typing. The words will come." She stands up and kisses me on the head.

"Don't you want to stay and help?"

She shakes her head. "This is something you have to do on your own. You'll figure it out."

I stare at the blank screen for five minutes. Check my email. Get a drink of water. Make myself a leftover turkey sandwich. Take off my shoes. Type a sentence and delete it. Lather, rinse, repeat.

After several minutes of complete paralysis, I watch Rafael's "Happy Birthday" video again to relax. The pressure of this post is too much. I can't help but imagine the thousands of people who will read this in the morning. Except for schoolwork and the stuff on BITES, I've never written anything that was meant to be read by real, live, actual people. Coding is always kept behind the scenes. *Except when it's not*, I realize, as pumpkins fall from the sky.

I log into Scratch and spend the next few hours animating my story. When I finally finish, there are no floating birthday cakes, but it's ridiculous. It's also one hundred percent *me*. It's the way I want to tell my story in the place I want to tell my story. I post it to my YouTube channel and hope for the best.

And even though I'm so tired my eyes are burning, I log into Because They Said So and scroll through the never-ending game of one-up. I'm not going to miss the blog, but I will miss this.

Because, honestly, I need a break from everything. Poppy is not the only addict in the family. Only instead of being addicted to the internet, I've been completely obsessed with what other people are saying about me. I need to figure out what it's like to live away from all of that. I type out my farewell and then send a direct message to SIGNOFTHETIMES.

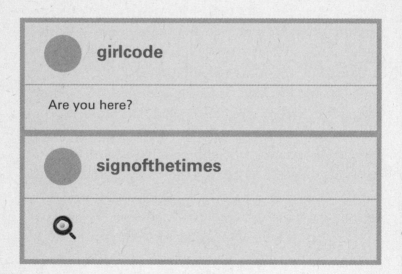

girlcode

Are you here?

signofthetimes

🔍

I look at the clock and figure out that it's already morning in France. He must be eating breakfast.

girlcode

I'm off the hook. No more internet for me.

signofthetimes

🍀 🎰

girlcode

I think we all are luckier than we realize.

girlcode

I'm not going to be around for a while, so I'm going to leave the site in your hands, okay? Don't let anything bad happen to my baby.

signofthetimes

🙇

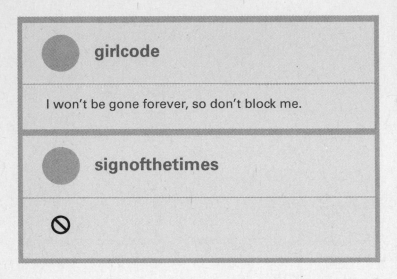

I smile as I log off. Maybe it's the fact that it's after midnight, or maybe I'm getting sentimental, but I think I actually understood that entire conversation.

"You brat!" Poppy bursts into my room and jolts me awake. I sit up and look at her, wondering what I've done wrong now. But she's grinning. "You convince Mom to stop posting pictures of me online and then you go and take all the attention for yourself." She smiles and shoves me to the side of my bed so she can sit next to me.

"Look at these comments." She holds up her phone and scrolls through the comment section of my video. "'You're so brave!' 'You're amazing!' 'Post more videos like this!'" She smiles and hands me the phone. "They love you."

"That's not why I did it."

"Trust me, I know. That's why you're better than the rest of us. You never cared about keeping up with the Joneses . . . or the Kardashians." She stands up. "Better get ready for school. I still have to look camera-ready, even if Mom is abandoning the blog." She winks as she leaves my room.

School is weird, but everyone is nice. Almost everyone, anyway. Olivia conveniently skipped out on lunch and our usual meeting at the drinking fountain. Lots of people tell me they're sorry about the kidnapping thing. Some people tell me I'm brave. One girl invites me to a PTSD club on campus. I probably needed it last year, or even last month. And maybe I'll go someday. But right now, I'm feeling better than I have in years.

I don't know if I'll ever get used to the attention, but I'm not as nervous when people want to talk to me. I feel strong and in control instead of vulnerable and overexposed.

Lena's editor calls Mom while we're at school and tells her that she has decided to cancel the story. Apparently, the magazine isn't interested in publishing an exposé that doesn't actually expose anything. Especially when that exposé casts a negative light on one of the internet's favorite families.

True to her word, Mom makes the blog private, so only our family can see it. I'm grateful for that, so I can learn more about my dad.

Rafael comes over after school to work on homework. As soon as my mom leaves for a photo shoot, however, he pulls me on to the couch and kisses me.

"Get a room," Poppy says as she passes by the couch. I laugh because I can practically hear her rolling her eyes.

Rafael and I go up to my room where we definitely, positively, will eventually work on homework. He sits next to me on my bed and nuzzles his face in my neck. I've never felt so happy.

Our final project for College Prep is to narrow our college choices down to the top three and make a pro-and-con list for each, complete with tuition costs, scholarship opportunities, and information about room and board. We've been working quietly for several minutes when Rafael looks over my shoulder.

"U of A, huh?" he asks.

"It's close. But not too close. And it has a great computer science program."

"It's a good school." He angles his paper so I can see that U of A is at the top of the list.

"Are you serious?"

"They have a great medical school. Plus, my dad says he's going to stay in Arizona for a while. I could come home on the weekends. Like you said. Close, but not too close. Can't argue with that."

"So you're sticking with the med school plan?"

"I have four years to change my mind. Nothing is carved in stone yet." He smiles. "There's still plenty of time for us to write our story."

My stomach flips in excitement at his choice of words as he nudges me with his foot. "Our story?"

"You heard me. We'll go to Tucson together. Maybe even start a vlog of our adventures."

I roll my eyes and flop backwards on my bed. He collapses next to me. "We'll call it 'Rafael and Claire Take Tucson.'" He winks and I laugh and shake my head.

"'Rafael and Claire: Freshman Year.' 'Rafael and Claire: Living off Cheez-Its and Vending Machine Burritos.'"

"Catchy. But no."

"Fine. I get it. You want top billing. You're the famous one, after all. How about, 'Claire and Rafael Tell a Story?'" He grins and fixes me with a stare that makes me wonder if he's still thinking about colleges or if his mind has drifted elsewhere.

"That would never happen in a million years—," I say, but he tangles his hands in my hair and cuts me off with a kiss, pinning my body under his. A flutter starts in my chest and snakes its way down my body. I thought first kisses were supposed to be the best, but every kiss with Rafael has gotten progressively better than the one before it.

When he pulls away, I hold up my phone to snap a picture of us together. "Mind if I post this?" I ask, thinking about Rafael's ridiculous plan to start our own vlog. It's certainly not the worst idea I've ever heard.

"Seriously?"

"Why not? You, Rafael Luna, are total boyfriend goals."

He levels me with a gaze that makes my cheeks flush. "I'll show you boyfriend goals."

I smile and hug my phone to my chest, changing my mind. This is one moment I want to keep entirely to myself.

Acknowledgments

The idea for this book came to me in a flash of inspiration one Sunday morning. The next day, I hung up my "Mommy Blogger" hat and focused all my energy on telling Claire's story. I'm still in awe that what started as "what if?" is now a published book, and I have so many people to thank for helping me achieve my lifelong dream of becoming a published author.

To my literary agent, Kristy Hunter, you were the first person willing to take a chance on this story, and for that, I cannot thank you enough. Your passion, excitement, hard work, and endlessly encouraging emails guided me through those hard times when it felt like this book would never see the light of day. I could not have made it this far without you!

A big thank you to my publisher, Dayna Anderson, and to Kayla Church, for your combined enthusiasm in acquiring my book. Thank you, Jenny Miller, for pushing me to make my characters stronger and more nuanced. To my copy editor Elizabeth Mazer, thank you for double-checking every comma and hyphen, and for researching the difference between Boo! At the Zoo and Howl-O-Ween. And to the entire Amberjack team, including my editor Cassandra Farrin and the head of publicity and marketing Joel

Bartron, many thanks for all your hard work on this book and helping it find its way into the hands of readers.

To Brenda Drake, you are a fairy godmother of publishing dreams. Thank you for letting me be the Pitch Wars underdog! I'll forever be grateful! Heather Cashman, thank you for reading this book so many times, for making me a stronger writer, and for celebrating my publishing highs and letting me vent during the lows. Without the two of you and your mentorship, this book would not exist today.

Mom and Dad, thank you for giving me a childhood full of books and learning and magic and lakes and love. I'm the luckiest to have you both. To Sandy Durkin, my sister, my friend, and my first beta reader. Thank you for believing in this book even when it was full of plot holes, and for the countless hours gossiping about bloggers as if we know them in real life. To my brothers, William and Michael and Tommy, I love you. My boys are so lucky to have you as uncles. To my Grandma Carolyn, you always knew that all I ever wanted for Christmases and birthdays was a book. Thank you for filling my shelves.

To the McDowells, thank you for welcoming me into the family, for teaching me how to play 10-to-1, and for being excited to read my book. Sorry I made you wait so long!

Krystal Klei, remember senior year of high school, when I wanted to be an author and you wanted to be a meteorologist? Can you believe we actually accomplished our dreams? Thanks for being my oldest friend and for always believing in me. I'm so proud of you!

ACKNOWLEDGMENTS

To the entire 2016 Pitch Wars Facebook Group, thank you for celebrating and commiserating, for the encouragement in the face of rejection, and for always being there for me when I need a partner for writing sprints. And many thanks to Jennifer, Amaris, and Jeanette for reading my first chapter and providing insightful feedback right when I needed it most.

To everyone in the AZ YA/MG Writer's Group, I still can't believe I know so many cool, talented authors. Thanks for letting me hang out with you!

Owen, Graham, and Emmett. My boys. Being your mom is the best, hardest, most rewarding thing I've ever done. You make me stronger, braver, sleepier (so sleepy!) and most of all, happier. I love you!

And, finally, Scott. Your support means the most. You always said "When your book is published." Always when, never if. I love you for that, and for the thousands of other ways you've loved me and encouraged me and held me up during our last eight years together. Someday we'll get that boat.

About the Author

Born in the mountains and raised in the desert, author Kara McDowell spent her childhood swimming, boating, and making up stories in her head. As the middle of five children, she entertained her family on long road trips by reading short mystery stories out loud and forcing everyone to guess the conclusion. After graduating from Arizona State University with a BA in English Literature, Kara worked as a freelance writer. Now she writes young adult novels from her home in Arizona, where she lives with her husband and three young sons.

Just for Clicks is Kara's debut novel.